Praise for the works o

The Missing Piece

…What I enjoy most about Kat Jackson's writing is she doesn't feel the need to follow the formula. Her characters are just as unconventional as their creator. Her writing is intelligent, and her characters show tremendous growth as the novel progresses. Jackson is a unique voice in the sapphic community and one who seems to improve with every book.

-Laura G., *NetGalley*

Another good read by Kat Jackson! She's becoming one of my favourite authors and I certainly look forward to future releases. I love her writing style, her enjoyable characters that always have that chemistry needed from the onset and her great storylines that capture you from the start.

-Jo R., *NetGalley*

Golden Hour

Kat Jackson has written another excellent book! If you've not already, check some of her other books out. *Golden Hour* is no exception, I love her writing style and her books have "drawn" me in.

-Jo R., *NetGalley*

Rapidly becoming one of my favourite lesbian authors, she writes intelligent books that explore more than just a romance.

-Claire E., *NetGalley*

I am coming to find that I really love books by Kat Jackson, she manages to pull me in on an emotional level and I enjoyed the pairing between Lina and Regan very much. The way Lina's PTSD was handled and described gave the book more depth than the average romance novel and when it's done in the way Jackson does it, it's very much lifting the book to a next level. *Golden Hour* can be read as a standalone, yet Lina was first introduced in an earlier book (*Across the Hall*) and that couple has a role in this one as Lina's best friends. Highly recommended!

-Dominique V., *NetGalley*

The Roads Left Behind Us

5 star, 5 star, 5 star...did I like this story...yes! The writing is beautifully filled with so much emotion and intelligent dialogue, I was sad when it ended. The environment is academia which makes the content of many conversations slightly elevated over other romance novels. Yet very understandable and warm. The characters are real, interesting, and distinct. I liked all of them. I highly recommend this story.

-Cheryl S., *NetGalley*

That was some marvelous writing; the vocabulary alone was spellbinding. The two MCs and every single supporting character are so well fleshed out that you feel as if you stepped into a room full of your friends and are catching up on all the gossip. The "will they, won't they" makes quite a pull at your heartstrings, but the end result makes the shipwreck all the more survivable. Their love story is charming, it's refreshing, it's as stormy as it is placid, and you will find yourself smiling hard at the MCs' antics throughout. A play at the Student/Professor fantasy, but you'll find these two are on equal footing in the PhD program where a delicious age-gap and big, beautiful brains war to find shelter.

-Alice G., NetGalley

Across the Hall

I loved Kat Jackson's first book, *Begin Again*, and I've been not-very-patiently awaiting the release of her second. I was not in any way disappointed! If you're looking for a layered tale of wonderfully flawed people, look no further. What enchanted me so much about *Begin Again*, and what runs through *Across the Hall* is one of the things that makes humans so interesting is that we are not perfect.

Mallory and Caitlin are complex characters with great depth, who I alternately wanted to hug and shake. Their stories are carefully crafted, and I am so thrilled to hear that Lina is getting her own book!

-Orlando J., NetGalley

Kat Jackson's *Begin Again* was an incredible debut and she became my favorite new author of 2020. Needless to say I was really looking forward to this sophomore effort. It didn't disappoint.

It's a workplace romance featuring two mains with a lot of baggage to bring to a fledging relationship. This story is really told in third person from Caitlin's POV, so we don't really know what's going on in Mallory's head. I really enjoyed following the ups and downs of the relationship and it was hard to tell where it was going. I started reading and next thing I knew, I was finished. That's what I love about a book.

-Karen R., NetGalley

Begin Again

Begin Again is one of the most beautiful, heartrending, and thought-provoking books I've read. Kat Jackson manages the rare feat of making a lesfic novel that toys with infidelity meaningful and elegant. While this all might sound a bit grim, it does have plenty of lighthearted moments too.

-Orlando J., *NetGalley*

Begin Again is one of the most thought-provoking, honest, emotional and heartrending books I've ever read. How the author managed to get the real, raw emotions (that I could believe and feel) down on paper and into words is amazing. If you read the blurb you will know, sort of what this story is about. But it's much more than that. As other reviewers have stated, it's not a comfy read but was totally riveting. I read it in a day, I just couldn't put it down. Definitely one of the best books I've read and if I could give it more stars I would for sure! Superbly written. Totally recommend.

-Anja S., *NetGalley*

In Bloom

KAT JACKSON

Other Bella Books by Kat Jackson

Begin Again
Across the Hall
The Roads Left Behind Us
Golden Hour
The Missing Piece

About the Author

Kat Jackson is a collector of feelings, words, and typewriters. She's an educator living in Pennsylvania, where she enjoys all four seasons in the span of a single week. Kat's been consumed with words and language for essentially her whole life, and continues to spend entirely too much time overthinking anything that's ever been said to her (this is a joke, kind of, but not completely). Running is her #1 coping mechanism followed closely by sitting in the sun with a good book and/or losing herself in a true crime podcast.

In Bloom

KAT JACKSON

BELLA
BOOKS

2023

Bella Books, Inc.
P.O. Box 10543
Tallahassee, FL 32302

Printed in the United States of America on acid-free paper.

First Edition - 2023

Editor: Alissa McGowan
Cover Designer: Heather Honeywell

ISBN: 978-1-64247-499-2

PUBLISHER'S NOTE

Acknowledgments

First and foremost, thank you to everyone at Bella for providing the space and opportunity for writers like me to bring their dream stories to life. I'm grateful and still a little stunned that I get to do this.

Alissa: It kills me to delete my words; however, I'll never admit the number of times I hit "accept" then shook my head, saying, "She's right, let it go." I so appreciate your patience with tightening up my wild verbosity, and please know I'm always looking out for your lols. You, me, and commas: a story for the ages.

The woman at the funeral home whom I called on a random afternoon: Thank you for answering my weird questions. I hope I didn't sound *too* interested in death.

And now, for the long list:

LSG: I didn't realize it when I started writing this book, but you were exactly who I needed to give me real-time reader feedback. Thank you, endlessly, for getting it, but also for getting me (because we all know I'm challenging. But fun! Sometimes). I promise I'll never let you back into another tree. Probably, anyway. Love you.

Hot Stacey: I love you weirdos, and I'm so grateful for the shenanigans, laughter, and support. You're the best writing community a gal could ever have.

DS: Many thanks for being willing to beta-read for me, even though it turns out once I get in the groove, I forget to share documents with you. Will I be better at this next time? Only time will tell...

LL: You deserve an award for listening to parts of this story for as long as you did. That's all I'll say about that. (Also, thank you.)

KV: I mean, where do I start? Your support while I took on this writing journey was exactly what I needed to keep going. Thank you for helping me set realistic goals, encouraging me to take breaks, and holding me accountable along the way. Also, boob cupcakes. Also also, your friendship. Also also also, can't wait for you to read it.

My family: I'm so glad we're weird and therefore come with strange and amusing experiences that turn into excellent sub-sub-plots in my books.

Rachel & Becky: Sunday, Jan. 29, 2023, 3:12 p.m.: "AT SOME POINT…" Please see Chapter 24. All my love & gratitude & Gatoritas.

Blaze: Forgiveness is a funny thing, and so is love.

Dedication

"If I'm not the one for you, why have we been through what we have been through?"
Adele, "Water Under the Bridge"

"What about all the broken happy ever afters?"
Pink, "What About Us"

CHAPTER ONE

Late afternoon sunlight shifted across the pale-green walls in gentle waves. The scent of lavender hung like a perforated cloud, wisps of peppermint sneaking through with every lazy spin of the ceiling fan. A trickle of late winter air, the kind that wants to warm to the oncoming spring but is still tipped with a frost that won't let go, wound itself around the room, sweeping into corners and swirling idle dust motes into flurries.

Nicole Callahan stood facing the closet doors. Despite the peaceful current dominating the bedroom, her internal tornado was as powerful as ever, yanking her senses one direction, then the next. She'd love nothing more than to take a deep inhale of that spa-like air, let it consume her until she drifted into a serene nap. Hell, she'd even let the window stay cracked even though she ran cold.

Her eyes, betraying her as always, darted over to the bed. The sheets were in total disarray, a cool contrast to the perfectly made bed she'd encountered upon walking into the bedroom. No, she wouldn't become an icicle if she cocooned herself in that luxurious down comforter. She was familiar enough with that particular bed to know that regardless of how much February air whipped through the room, she'd be perfectly comfortable and warm. Too comfortable, maybe—yet never quite the right kind of comfortable.

Nicole focused her eyes on her shirt, resuming the task of buttoning up. It shouldn't take that much concentration, but for some ridiculous reason, Nicole inevitably misbuttoned her flannels every damn time. She'd tried watching herself in the mirror, not watching at all, buttoning one and then letting her hands do the rest of the work while her eyes and brain went somewhere else—it all led to the same lopsided result. The only solution was to stare at her fingers as they fumbled their way down the line, one by one, the entire time.

The sound of a fitted sheet being yanked from its corner made Nicole jump the slightest bit. She inhaled deeply, willing the lavender and peppermint to do their soothing and energizing work. ("Soothe the brain enough to energize the will to live," she'd joked once, and received an unamused eye roll in response; no one got her admittedly dark humor anymore.) She held the therapeutic air in her lungs, and on the exhale, pushed out a "Thanks."

A snorted laugh bounced back to her. "You can thank me via Venmo."

Shame rimmed with embarrassment flooded her as she turned to face the other woman in the room. "Excuse me? Since when is that a thing? I'm not—I'm not some kind of *whore*."

Another laugh rang through the quiet room, this one less snorted and more amused. Brynn crossed the space between them and stood in front of her.

"Technically, if you're paying me, that makes me the whore." Brynn's deep-brown eyes glittered. Nicole couldn't help but stare at her smile, which was amused and bright as ever. It was easier than looking her in the eyes at moments like this. "But I was referring to lunch yesterday. You never paid me."

"Oh," Nicole breathed, shaking her head. She took a step backward. "Right. Sorry, I'll do that." She glanced down, realizing she hadn't put on her pants yet. "When I find my phone."

"Poor comedic timing?"

"The worst, Brynn, seriously. Please don't do an open mic night anytime soon." Nicole cracked a smile, not caring that it was as lopsided as her misbuttoned shirts. Awkward moment averted. She knew Brynn—she knew what they were doing—and she should have known that was a joke. That day, though, nothing felt funny. She swatted Brynn's shoulder before grabbing her pants from the floor. "But I guess it was kind of funny, considering."

"See, I knew you'd get it. You could put your clothes on the chair, you know."

"You say that every time," Nicole murmured, pulling her jeans up and zipping them.

"And you never listen." Brynn laughed again, this one light and carefree.

Nicole sat on the aforementioned chair to put on her socks and shoes. She'd promised herself she wouldn't get used to this, wouldn't get complacent or expectant—and definitely wouldn't get feelings—but after three months of sex-on-demand, she'd come to accept Brynn as part of her life. A needed part of her life. And, if she was being honest, a helpful part. A part she relied on.

"You might want to splash some water on your face before you go," Brynn said casually as she finished stripping the bed.

Even though Brynn's back was to her, Nicole nodded politely. Once she was confident the laces of her shoes were tied in such a way that they definitely would not untie themselves, she wordlessly left the bedroom and made her way down the hall to the bathroom. She could never bring herself to use the en suite; it felt too personal. Too real. Too intimate.

Nicole closed the bathroom door behind her. Avoiding her reflection in the too-large mirror, she glanced down to make sure her buttons were snug in their assigned holes. Her fingers drifted down the line slowly, prolonging the moment to avoid facing the music.

Or, more accurately, facing herself. In the mirror.

During the first few weeks, she'd gasped every time. By now, she was accustomed to the angry red blotches scattered across her cheeks. She was used to the paleness hovering beneath the colored spots. Her lips, colorless and bruised all at once.

But she could not get used to the swollen eyes that stared back at her, stripped of their usual lively cornflower blue color. It was like someone came in and suctioned out every bit of life from her eyes, leaving them an icy pale blue, a shade alarmingly close to white. No shield remained to hide the emptiness.

If there was a word that went beyond "empty," that's what Nicole felt. Plundered, perhaps. Devoid.

Like her dad once said: "Someone stole your flowers, leaving you an empty vase with legs." Hank Callahan wasn't the most philosophical guy, but the day he dropped that on her, she'd stared mutely at her phone for a full two minutes while her dad switched topics and rambled on about the new golf course in his town.

"Vase, *vaz*," Nicole said to her reflection. One corner of her mouth lifted while the other seemed to drag down. *Don't think about that now.*

The splash of cold water on her face snapped Nicole's attention away from the enticing edge of a memory. She focused on scrubbing her face, letting the cold numb her.

A few minutes later, she paused outside the bathroom door, listening carefully to deduce Brynn's location in the house. Running water followed by the snapping sounds of a dog's ears shaking back and forth cued her to the kitchen, and she walked in that direction.

Brynn was waiting, holding out a glass of water. Nicole took it gratefully, draining it before handing the glass back. Bronx, Brynn's goofy black Lab-pit bull mix, looked back and forth between them, probably wondering who was going to take him for a walk.

"That was a big one," Brynn remarked. Her voice was casual, as always, giving Nicole the space to engage or run away.

"Anniversary." It was one word, eleven letters, five simple syllables, but heavy and strewn with meaning.

"Ooh. Today?"

Nicole shook her head. "Tomorrow."

Brynn reached over and patted Nicole's shoulder. Fifteen minutes ago, she was deep inside of Nicole, her teeth scraping Nicole's hips as she nudged her into a powerful, limb-tingling orgasm. And now, the extent of their intimacy was a friendly pat on the shoulder—something a near stranger would do. Nicole fought back a giggle.

"What are your plans for tomorrow?"

With a shrug, Nicole picked up her keys from the kitchen counter. She still wanted to giggle. "I haven't figured that out yet. I'm sure I'll be okay."

"Okay," Brynn echoed, raising her eyebrows. She crossed her arms over her chest. "Well, try to keep yourself busy."

"Sage advice." Nicole grinned, tempering the mood back to light, where she preferred it.

"That's not why you come here," Brynn said, teasing. With Bronx trotting at her side, she walked Nicole to the door, opened it for her, and leveled her with a serious look. "I hope tomorrow is really okay for you."

"Thanks." Nicole hesitated, and couldn't help herself. "And thanks."

Brynn rolled her eyes and shook her head, but the movements were both tinged with amusement. "Stop thanking me. We're both benefiting from this…arrangement."

With a nod, Nicole left. There was really nothing more to say—there never was, and she meant that in the kindest way possible.

Once back in her apartment, Nicole headed straight for her bathroom and stripped. She turned the water on as hot as she could stand it and slid the glass door closed behind her.

Time lost meaning as she stood under the stream of steaming water. She glided her hands over her skin, reclaiming her body. Brynn never left any marks, an agreement they'd made after their first encounter left Nicole with pleasurable but ugly bruises on her inner thighs.

Nicole waited under the heady stream for more tears to come, but her eyes remained dry. She was surprised; this part of the ritual usually coaxed out any remaining tears. Brynn's words filtered through her mind: "That was a big one." Nicole sighed, resting her forehead against the cool, pristine white tile. Apparently so big that it had completely wrung her out.

As she toweled off, she dared another look in the mirror. Some of the swelling in her eyes had departed, allowing whispers of bright blue to ease back into her irises. They still looked vacant, though. Sad. Glossy, in a strangely pretty way. But sad.

Deciding it was pointless to get dressed, Nicole made her way to her bedroom and crawled under the blanket. Lying on her side, she hugged her knees to her chest. She waited for the pressure in her chest to dissipate, knowing it wouldn't. Maybe someday, but not today. Grief had a way of digging its claws into the most tender parts of a person's body, latching on and holding tight, and it had a grip on Nicole that felt everlasting.

Something internal, quiet and annoying as always, compelled her to poke an arm out of her blanket nest long enough to grab her phone from the bedside table. In the shadows beneath the blanket, Nicole scrolled until she reached the app she swore she'd never download, never use, never even entertain. It was Brynn's fault, actually: they'd had a little too much wine one night a couple weeks ago, and after Nicole cried about being alone forever, she'd gone to the bathroom, leaving her unlocked phone next to Brynn. When she returned, Brynn had a devilish smile on her face. It wasn't until the next afternoon that Nicole found the app on her phone, the sole icon in a folder titled "Someday You'll Want This."

She'd cried again, then, realizing it was true and Brynn was right.

With a huff, Nicole shoved her phone back out of her sacred blanket nest. Someday, probably, but someday wasn't today.

CHAPTER TWO

"Oh, hell no. No. Absolutely fucking not."

The workroom went silent, voices and clippers and shears dropping to zero. The only sound, aside from Avery Pullman's bare feet slapping the concrete floor with fiery authority, was the ever-present hum of the coolers.

The only thing stopping Avery from getting to the phone as fast as she would have liked was the errant thorn she stepped directly on. She squealed, letting loose a litany of language that would surely cause elderly ladies to clutch their handkerchiefs in horror, and hopped the rest of the way to her office, where she threw herself into her chair and grabbed the phone.

"Hi, this is Avery, how can I help you?" Her voice, just moments ago fueled with ire, was sticky sweet.

Jay, the part-time receptionist Avery hired just a month ago, hovered in the doorway. She glared at him, and he gave a frightened smile in reply.

"Yes, Avery, this is Clara Longwood. I'm calling on behalf of my daughter, Genevieve."

"Oh, of course, Genevieve!" Avery grimaced as she frantically flipped through the stuffed binder on her desk. "I hope everything is going well with the wedding planning."

"That's why I'm calling." Clara cleared her throat. "There's been a bit of a...change of plans."

Avery's throat constricted. No, no, no. This wedding was over the top, every bit of it that Avery had been privy to—and that was quite a bit, because Clara loved nothing more than to brag about her daughter and her absolute catch of a fiancé. They could not afford to lose this job.

"Oh dear," Avery managed, the uncharacteristic phrase scratching against what she really wanted to say. She ignored Jay's giggle from the doorway. "I—"

"Unfortunately, the wedding has been called off. I'll see that you receive the remaining balance of the deposit, but as per the clause in the contract, that will be the final payment."

"Mrs. Longwood," Avery scrambled to say, "I'm sure we can—"

"Thank you, Avery. Goodbye."

The resounding click echoed in Avery's brain as she slowly reached out to hang up the phone. She bit her lower lip and gripped the edge of her desk with both hands.

"I tried to tell you," Jay said quietly.

"Mmm, no." Avery shook her head. "Do not speak."

"But—"

"I said," Avery said evenly, still staring at her desk. "Do. Not. Speak."

She looked up at the sound of a strange, muffled yell, and a grin broke across her face, disrupting the rage burning inside her. Zuri had wrapped her hands around Jay's mouth and was dragging him down the hallway.

"Shit." Avery dropped her forehead to her desk, banging it lightly several times before coming to rest. The Longwood-Sherman wedding was—*was*—going to be the most lucrative event of the winter season. Sure, there were other things going on and being planned for, but Avery had been banking, quite literally, on that single wedding.

A throb in her right foot drew her attention away from her moment of self-pity. She bent her leg for a clear view of her foot and yes, there it was: a ripe rose thorn stuck defiantly in the center of her arch. With a deep breath, Avery gripped it and yanked, freeing her foot of the offending intruder. She pulled open a drawer and found a Trolls Band-Aid, slapping it on without doing the smart thing and cleaning the cut first. Ignoring the pain, and the fact that she should just wear shoes like a normal person in a place of business, Avery stood up and strode back to the workroom.

Zuri was alone, spreading stems of vibrant pink heather across one of the stainless-steel counters. Her long braids were twisted on top of her head in a wrap, except for two that were swinging gently against her face. She hummed a tune Avery couldn't place.

"Thanks," Avery said as she crossed—okay, limped across— the room to grab the arrangement she was fine-tuning.

"Give him time," was all Zuri said.

Zuri and Veronica, both part-time arrangers, had been with Avery from the start. They knew how to handle her, how to maneuver around her, and how to calm her down. More importantly, they knew how to make themselves invisible when something went unexpectedly wrong, and Zuri in particular knew how to help Avery move past something she was stuck on.

It wasn't Jay's fault that he hadn't learned her yet. Zuri was right; she needed to give him time.

And maybe not bite his head off in the meantime.

"Longwood-Sherman is a no-go." Avery thrust her hands into a bowl of cold water.

"Shiiiiit. Cold feet?"

"I didn't get details." Sighing, she wound a strand of ivy around a long sunflower stem. "But probably."

"Women."

Avery laughed despite herself. Zuri, she of few words, always said the right thing.

Later, after her three employees had left to begin the next part of their days, Avery plopped into one of the sapphire-blue armchairs in the display area of her shop. As always, an overwhelming sense of pride enveloped her.

The Twisted Tulip was a pipe dream, one Avery had continually pushed aside as she made her way through college. It lingered in her mind even after she graduated with a degree in art history. To this day, she still couldn't explain that particular path; it may have had something to do with a particular professor who caught her eye during her undeclared freshman year, but Avery would never admit that. Anyway, she used her degree to enter the workforce, again pushing her dream aside. Several years of working in a museum nearly bored her to death, until the day an absolutely horrific flower arrangement arrived for her boss.

Avery gaped at it for hours as it stood, bold in its ugliness, on the front desk. She walked past it, glared at it, willed someone to remove it. Finally, she couldn't stand it any longer and whisked the arrangement off to a dusty storage room. She didn't have as much to work with as she would have liked, but she was quite proud of the improved result. Her boss, of course, was none the wiser, but Avery couldn't shake the feeling she had when her fingers were tangled in stems and petals.

It took years and research and pleading for loans, but the last six years of incredibly hard work had been absolutely worth it. The Twisted Tulip was thriving, having just undergone a delicious interior remodel that made the display and meeting area sparkle. The walls were a muted soft pink, so pale they appeared white, but pink enough to glow a warmth that enhanced the flowers. Avery stuck with the original concrete floors but had them repainted a gray that had tiny silver sparkles in it. The new furniture was muted with bold accents—the sapphire armchairs, for example—and modern with a touch of classy. She'd even splurged for a small refreshment area, which was already proving its worth with customers who spent a little more time, then a little more money, while consulting for arrangements. The overall result was everything Avery had hoped for.

And now she'd lost the biggest event of the season.

Not wanting to slip back into a maudlin puddle, Avery pushed herself out of the comfortable chair and locked the front door. She twisted her hair into a haphazard bun atop her head as she walked back to the workroom to knock out one more arrangement, an easy anniversary bouquet, before she headed home.

Just as her bare feet crossed the threshold into the sterile workroom, a frantic knocking stopped her in her tracks. Her pulse quickened and she felt for her cell phone in her pocket. Balsam Lake, Pennsylvania, the town that housed both her home and her shop, was reasonably safe, but Avery knew all too well the dangers that faced a woman alone.

She peered around the corner instead of walking directly into the path of light leading to the front door. The knocking began again, this time coupled with a woman's voice calling out, "Avery? Are you still here?"

The voice sounded vaguely familiar, and Avery was pretty sure it wasn't a trap, so she walked into the light. The knocking stopped immediately.

"Genevieve?" Avery said aloud, though she was certain the woman couldn't hear her. "What the fuck?"

"Hi!" Genevieve waved. "Can I come in?" she yelled, gesturing to the door.

Avery pasted a grin on her face, mumbling under her breath as she walked forward. "Did you fucking come to apologize in person for the massive loss of money you're causing me by— Genevieve, hi! I wasn't expecting you! So great to see you!" Avery held the door open and Genevieve hurried inside.

"Wow, it got really cold out there." She shivered dramatically.

Avery gave her a once-over. She was cute. And young, probably no more than twenty-four. Like her mother, Genevieve was very put together, wearing preppy clothing that looked tailored to her body. Her shoulder-length blond hair was in perfect place and she was smiling radiantly, showing no signs of having recently called off a very expensive wedding.

"My mom told me she already spoke to you," Genevieve said, not waiting for an invitation as she dropped into one of the armchairs. "But I wanted to talk to you in person."

Avery waited, worried she'd start cursing again.

"I'm so sorry. I wanted to be the one to call, but you know how my mom is."

Avery forced a smile. "Sure do. So you came by to apologize?" If Zuri were there, she'd thrust an elbow into Avery's side, silently reminding her to be more polite.

"I did. But I also still want the flowers."

Avery cocked her head to the side, certain she'd misheard. "You what now?"

Genevieve grinned, her face lighting up with an intensity that would warm an entire room of, well, wedding guests. "For my party. Not a wedding, obviously, because that's definitely not happening. But I want to celebrate!"

"I'm not sure I'm following you," Avery said, trying to reconcile Genevieve's words with her mother's clipped lack of an explanation.

Genevieve leaned forward, her gloved hands (an expensive looking leather, Avery couldn't help but notice) pressing against her knees. Her eyes were downright sparkling, a happiness spreading over her face that was contagious—or it would be, if Avery didn't have armor protecting her from such things.

"I'm gay, Avery! That's why I can't marry Jason. He's fine," she added with a roll of her eyes, "but I finally realized the algorithm kept taking me to Lesbian TikTok because I kept liking videos on Lesbian TikTok."

Avery pressed her hand against her head. What in the actual fuck was this person talking about?

"It's like, I thought maybe I was just bi? Or just liked girls that kind of look like guys?" Genevieve laughed. "Nope! I like lesbians because I'm a lesbian. Anyway, my mom absolutely freaked out when I told her the wedding was off. But I figure, why waste the food and flowers and everything? I deserve a damn celebration for figuring out what I really want."

"This…Okay. I need a minute."

"Oh, I know it's a lot, trust me. But I'm so happy I figured it out before I actually got married, you know?"

Avery nodded slowly. "That is a very good thing."

"I knew you'd understand." Genevieve shot up straighter in her chair. "Oh, God, wait, I'm not hitting on you. I mean, you're super hot but you're not my type. Sorry." She winced. "I'm obviously new at this."

Avery waved her hand to clear the air between them. "You're way too young for me anyway."

Genevieve burst into joyful laughter and Avery, despite herself, joined in.

"So you'll do it? I'll pay you, of course."

"Just to be clear, you want everything we'd planned for?"

"Yes. This party is going to be incredible."

"You deserve it," Avery said, surprised by the sincerity in her voice.

Genevieve's eyes sparkled with tears, but she was smiling a full-wattage smile, so Avery was fairly certain she wouldn't have to deal with a near-stranger's emotional outpouring.

"Thank you, Avery. Oh! Will you come to my party?"

"Oh—I—I don't usually stay. After setting up the flowers, I mean." She felt her cheeks heat up.

"Okay, well, think about it. I'm planning on inviting every lesbian I know." Genevieve wiggled her eyebrows, then laughed. "Turns out I know a lot of them."

Being in a room full of lesbians was the absolute last thing on Avery's list of desired activities, but she smiled and nodded anyway, not wanting her dark storm cloud of romantic pessimism to rain over this sweet, hopeful gayby.

"I'm so glad you stopped by," Avery said as she stood. She didn't like the way her stomach was twisting and she needed Genevieve to leave. Now.

"Me too. I'll be in touch!" With a gleeful wave, Genevieve bounded out of the store, leaving Avery alone again.

Just as the door closed, her phone vibrated in her pocket. The double vibration, signaling a text from one specific person. Avery shut her eyes and steeled herself, hoping that, for once, she had the strength to not engage.

CHAPTER THREE

Nicole paused by the floor-to-ceiling windows of her loft, letting the sun warm her as she sipped her London Fog latte. February was doing its maddening dance of spring-fakeouts. The daily forecast was fifty-five and sunny, which felt downright balmy compared to last week's ice storm. But Nicole wasn't fooled; she knew not to trust Pennsylvania's whimsical winters. No doubt tomorrow would bring flurries or sleet. She would, however, enjoy the sun while it was here.

She set her mug on a side table and, like a cat, arched her back and breathed deeply while stretching. Feeling little pops and crunchy rustles, she made a mental note to schedule a massage. It had been too long, and as a Taurus, Nicole took self-care and treating herself very seriously.

Stretch completed, she shook out her limbs before curling up in the cream-colored, oversized armchair that sat right in front of the windows. The chair was one of her reckless purchases, definitely not necessary when considering the amount of furniture that had moved with her from her house to this apartment, but *she* needed it. She needed an independent buy, a piece of furniture without memories stuck to it like stubborn Velcro.

She glanced around the airy room. It hadn't been easy, leaving her comfortable fixer-upper, which had been very fixed-up, to move into this space. In comparison, the loft was stark. Sure, the original brick on two of the walls gave off warm vibes, and the honey-colored wide-plank hardwood floors kept the area from being sterile. But the non-brick walls were white. Flat, boring white. It had been a full year since she moved in and she still hadn't decorated. The space rang silent of personality, something most people would be surprised to see in Nicole's home. Then again, no one had seen it.

"Okay," she said to the empty room, giving it a firm nod. "We're doing okay."

Leaning forward, she pulled her laptop closer. She had a meeting in five minutes and one thing she'd learned in this new side hustle was that her clients were always, without fail, early.

Sure enough, when Nicole opened the online meeting room, the Bankhursts were already in the waiting room. She smiled, feeling a sense of purpose and calm settle over her. That, or it was the sun warming her shoulders. Either way, she felt good, and she grabbed on to the feeling, winding it around her like a soft blanket.

Before letting her clients into the room, Nicole glanced over the notes from their first meeting. The one time she didn't do that, she mistook one client for another, and in this business— well, it wasn't a good look.

"Here we go," she murmured, pressing the button to begin the meeting.

Their faces filled the screen. The Bankhurst family, or what was left of it: mother, Julie, and twin siblings, Colleen and Colton. Nicole felt a little prick in her heart. She'd forgotten, somehow, how young this family was. The twins couldn't be more than thirty, and Julie, though recent events had understandably taken a physical toll, didn't look a day over fifty.

"Hi, everyone, good morning," Nicole said, smiling and looking at each member of the family. "Thanks so much for meeting with me."

"Hello, Nicole." Julie smiled but it was watery, flecked with a sadness Nicole recognized all too well.

"Before we begin, I want to make sure the arrangements are correct. The viewing is this Thursday evening, and the funeral is Friday morning, correct?"

The twins nodded. Julie clutched a tissue to her mouth.

"I know this may seem like a strange question, but—how are you all feeling about that?"

There was silence for a moment, like always. Nicole had learned quickly that while this question was unexpected, it was usually strangely appreciated, as though no one else had taken the time to ask a family how they felt about the timeline of death to funeral.

"It feels fast," Colton said, clearing his throat after speaking. "I mean, this all happened so fast, but...I don't know. The finality of it feels too soon."

Nicole nodded, waiting to see if Julie or Colleen wanted to add anything.

"I don't like it." Yup, there it was: the anger. Nicole nodded again, encouraging Colleen to continue. "It's our dad. His entire life, just gone." She snapped her fingers. "And we have to turn around and put him in the ground like he's a fucking plant or something."

That's new, Nicole mused, fighting a smile. Over the past year, she'd heard some really strange analogies about death and burials, but never a reference to gardening.

"Colleen," Julie said firmly. "Your father is not a plant. He *hated* yard work, and it would really piss him off to hear you compare him to something he'd eventually have to weed."

The twins turned to look at their mother, a move choreographed to the millisecond, and burst out laughing. Nicole sat back in her chair, letting the family dissolve into slightly hysterical amusement. This was the moment she looked for: the release. Families dealing with recent deaths, especially those that were sudden, needed to let themselves feel all the feelings, not just the anguish and despair. Nicole had worked with families who sat concretely in the negative feelings, and their meetings never resulted in a heartfelt product. These families, though? The ones that could let the light in, even if it was the tiniest streak from a dull bulb? There was hope there. There was life.

And there was laughter, a willingness, a need to remember the good in the midst of the devastation.

Once the Bankhursts had composed themselves somewhat, Nicole leaned back in. "So I'm thinking we can use this gardening angle."

Hours later, her fingers and eyes ached. She wasn't sure how long she'd been sitting in her chair, but she had three drafts to send to the Bankhursts, which she did before shutting her laptop and standing up.

The sun was still out, meaning she had time to get in a mind-clearing walk before the second half of her workday—the one that actually paid the bills.

Downtown Balsam Lake was quiet as she strolled down Main Street, no real destination in mind. She never thought she'd like living in the city; though, arguably, Balsam Lake's downtown consisted of a handful of blocks of restaurants, cafés, and small shops before ebbing into suburbia. It wasn't exactly a bustling city. It was quiet, usually, and when it wasn't, the noise didn't penetrate the third-floor walls of her loft. People-watching from her windows, though? A+ entertainment during the summer.

As Nicole walked, she registered the buzzing of her phone. It was probably Brynn, or maybe her dad. Both could wait. She needed this time to herself to empty her brain and usher in clean, clear thoughts so she could pack away the Bankhursts for the time being.

Eulogy writing wasn't something Nicole had set out to do. Honestly, it was a strange side hustle, and she knew it. Everyone assumed that the best people to write eulogies were those who were close to the deceased: family members, friends, even coworkers. But the truth was, sometimes those people needed a little help. And Nicole, having always had a way with words, was more than happy to oblige.

She saw herself as more of a liaison, or an assistant. In her year of writing eulogies, not one single client had used her draft word for word. There were slight changes, additions and subtractions. Tweaking to make the voice sound right. Sometimes there was even an ad-lib in the moment of delivery, and that always thrilled her. But what she offered was, for some, irreplaceable. She gave the families distance from the death while looping them back into everything they loved about the deceased. She led them through memories, funny stories, heartbreaking moments, the simplest events that left lasting impressions. It was more than a eulogy; it was a step toward healing.

That step, Nicole knew intimately, wasn't the easiest to take. It was far easier to trip over it, repeatedly, than to actually lift your foot and step over the threshold into healing.

On second thought, Nicole pulled her phone out of her pocket and looked to see who had been offering a distraction.

"What? How? No."

She stopped in her tracks, staring down the offending dating app notification on her lock screen. The desire to delete it tangoed with the curiosity of opening it. Nicole shifted her weight from foot to foot, waiting for the familiar anxiety to spread through her torso. Her expectation was met with numbness, which surely had to be an improvement.

Still, she swiped the notification to clear it, and pressed instead on the missed call from her dad.

"There's my baby girl." Hank Callahan's voice boomed over the phone. He was never a man of quiet nature, something Nicole hadn't inherited.

"Hey, Dad. How's your day?"

"Oh, the usual. I met the young men for coffee this morning, then spent some time in my workshop. I think I've finally decided on a new project."

Nicole smiled widely. Her father's reference to "the young men," who were actually his former coworkers who hadn't retired yet but were right around his age, never ceased to amuse her. "What's the project?"

"A spinning spice rack!"

"Wow. That sounds truly thrilling."

"You say that now, but wait till you see it. She's gonna be a beaut, Nicole." The familiar sound of Hank scratching his beard floated into her ear. "What are you up to? Enjoying the sunshine?"

"You know it." Nicole stopped and looked around. It was a beautiful day, even if the temperature was starting to drop. "I needed a break between jobs."

"And how many grave speeches did you write today?"

She grinned. Her dad kept pushing her to make her work official and name her business Grave Speeches, but Nicole liked the autonomy of freelancing. "Three. I feel best about the first one, always do. But we'll see what the family thinks."

"I'm sure they'll love them all. They always do, kiddo."

Hank was Nicole's biggest fan; he had barely blinked when she announced her side hustle. He had, however, demanded that she begin drafting *his* eulogy because he wanted to hear it before he could, well, no longer hear it.

She hadn't started that one yet.

"So what, now you're gonna head back home, write some ad copy, forget to have dinner, and fall asleep on the sofa?"

Nicole laughed. "Am I that predictable?"

"Nic…"

"Dad…" she teased.

"I worry about you, honey. I know things got real tough for you, and—"

"And I'm doing fine. Really. I am." Hank was right when he predicted Nicole's evening: she had several hours' worth of ad copy to write, and if she let him go in his desired conversational direction, she'd never be able to write anything of worth.

"I want you to be doing great. Not just fine." More beard scratching. "How did you treat yourself today?"

A wave of warmth rushed through her. They used to joke about that, the way Nicole always made a point to treat herself. But over the past two years, when she'd stopped announcing her "treat yo' self" moments, he'd started reminding her. It was how he showed love, and if she was being honest, Nicole would admit she hadn't resumed telling him so that he would remind her. Plus, a little extra treat never hurt.

"I stretched a lot. Oh, and I had a London Fog latte."

"You can do better than that." His voice was gruff.

"I..." Nicole stopped and peered at the storefront ahead. "I'm going to buy myself flowers," she announced.

"That's my girl. Send me a picture when you get home."

"I will. Love you, Dad."

"Love you more, baby girl."

Nicole slid her phone back into her pocket and continued looking at the wood and steel sign. The store was at the end of Main Street, and for some reason, though it didn't look brand new, she didn't remember ever noticing it before.

"Probably because you've been staring at the ground when you walk," she chastised herself. She then stepped forward and opened the door to The Twisted Tulip.

CHAPTER FOUR

The scent of homemade marinara tickled Avery's nose as she leaned over the kitchen counter. Her phone sat before her and she scrolled, only half-paying attention to the various profiles.

"If you're not going to bother swiping right on anyone, why swipe at all?"

Avery looked up so she could glare at Gavin, who sent a cheeky grin in response before turning back to the stove.

"I'm just looking," she said stubbornly.

"Right, right. For what, exactly? Because I'm pretty sure I overheard you on the phone last night, and—"

"Stop right there, soldier. That situation is over."

Gavin looked over his shoulder. "And yet the phone keeps ringing."

Avery made a menacing face as she stared down her phone, which was, in fact, ringing. With a call from the very person who was *not* supposed to be calling anymore.

"Why don't you just block her?"

She let out a dramatic groan as she collapsed onto a stool at the island. "I can't, Gavin. I've tried. The longest I went was five minutes. *Five minutes.* That's all I could manage."

"You're torturing yourself."

"No shit." She stared at the time display on her lock screen, wondering how long she could go without calling Shannon back.

Her phone disappeared before she could start a timer. Gavin slipped it into the back pocket of his jeans and returned to the stove.

"That's not necessary."

"Apparently it is. If you need something to distract yourself, make a salad. Dinner will be ready in five minutes."

Knowing it was useless to complain, Avery pushed off the stool and dug in the refrigerator for the salad makings. She didn't remember buying any of this. Kale? Sprouts? She held out the offending items and waited for Gavin to acknowledge her, but he was far too involved in his famous sauce.

It had been almost two years of friendly cohabitation, and Avery was still getting used to not being by herself. Granted, she'd lived on her own for ten years prior to Gavin moving in, so the adjustment period was understandable. There were certainly perks to having her closest friend since college live with her, and the obvious top entry of the list was the fact that he loved to cook. He was also very, very good at it. So much so that Avery often prodded him to make a career change, give up his boring accountant job and go to culinary school—or even better, skip that bullshit and open a restaurant. He calmly shot her down every time. "Retirement," he'd say with a shrug. "If it's meant to happen, it'll happen then." So he continued juggling numbers all day, ingredients each night. If Avery was extra nice—a feat, most days—sometimes he even made her lunch.

"Yum!" An excited squeal followed the proclamation, prompting Avery to look over her shoulder.

With one hand clutching a worn stuffed platypus and the other firmly planted on her hip, Thea stood, one foot on the tile of the kitchen floor and the other toeing the hardwood of the great room. Her dark-brown pigtails, streaked with auburn, sat askew on her head. She had a smear of peanut butter on her chin, leftover from her post-preschool snack, but there was no mistaking the hunger in her eyes. At her side, like always, was Houston, Avery's formerly loyal golden retriever.

"I love sketti," Thea said excitedly, walking all the way into the kitchen. Houston followed, sniffing the air as though she, too, loved spaghetti. As Thea's faithful subject, she probably did.

"Well that's good, because dinner is about to be served." Avery tossed a cucumber slice at the four-year-old.

Thea caught and promptly dropped the vegetable on the ground, never losing her grip on her stuffed animal. "No thank you." She trotted over to the table and sat down. Houston looked at her, then at the cucumber, then at Avery. A second later, the cucumber slice disappeared.

Avery stared at Thea, her mouth gaping.

Behind her, Gavin snorted. "At least she's polite."

"Don't you want your child to eat a well-rounded meal?" Avery chucked a kale leaf in Gavin's direction, but it fell lifelessly to the floor. She knew Houston would scarf that up as well.

Gavin walked past her and put the pasta and sauce on the table. "There's veggies in the sauce, Avery."

She held up her hands in mock defeat. Thea's nutritional intake was none of her business, and it also wasn't something she needed to worry about. Gavin was an excellent father: caring, even-tempered, attentive. Avery, a sort of bonus mom since Thea's bio mom bailed before she was even a year old, provided the fun.

The makeshift family of three sat down at the kitchen table and dug into dinner. Houston sat patiently next to Avery, though she watched every move Thea made. Thea, between giant bites of noodles, regaled the duo with tales of her scintillating day at preschool. It seemed there was a heated battle over who got to go down the slide first, as well as a mysteriously exploding juice box that caused one child to have to change his shirt. Tears had ensued, naturally, as the original shirt was his favorite and the back-up shirt could not measure up.

Throughout the meal, Thea offered forkfuls of pasta to Penelope, her platypus companion who sat in the chair next to her. Each time, Thea turned to Gavin and Avery and said, quite seriously, "She's not hungry. Too much salad."

Meanwhile, Avery choked down the kale salad, making a mental note to do the next round of grocery shopping. There was nothing wrong with iceberg lettuce, yet Gavin spoke of it with intense disdain and refused to buy it.

After the dishes had been done and Thea was busy playing with Play-Doh, Avery held out her hand.

"Phone, please."

"You sure?"

"Gavin, come on. I need to check in with Zuri."

He handed her the phone and sat down with Thea, grabbing the container of yellow Play-Doh. "To see if Shannon stopped in the store the one night you decided to go home early?"

"Not funny." Avery looked through her notifications, nodding when she saw Zuri's text letting her know she'd had a few walk-ins before closing up.

"I just want you to be happy, you know."

Avery's throat tightened. It wasn't the first time Gavin had said this, and both knew it wouldn't be the last. In fact, if Avery had a dollar for each time he'd said those exact words to her over the last seven years, she'd have a nice little cash cow.

"Me too," she mumbled. "Anyway. I'm gonna go up."

Gavin narrowed his eyes at her. "It's not even seven."

"I'm not—" Avery cut herself off. She didn't actually know what she was going to do, but she didn't want to lie to Gavin. He was her constant, the one friend who at least semi-understood what she was trying to untangle herself from. "I'm going to read."

"I'll be up for a while after I put this baby angel to bed," he said pointedly.

"No bed." Thea shook her head, pigtails bouncing. "Play-Doh." Houston sniffed loudly from her spot on the floor next to Thea's chair.

"Bed after Play-Doh," Gavin said gently. "Can you make me a platypus with your pink Play-Doh?"

Thea's entire face lit up at the suggestion, bed already forgotten. "One pla-pus coming your way!"

It was a little painful, leaving the very cute moment between father and daughter, but Avery was starting to itch. She whistled for Houston, who somewhat begrudgingly left her chosen child and followed Avery up the stairs and into the silent safety of her bedroom at the end of the hall. Houston curled up in her bed, though they both knew she would leave as soon as she heard Thea coming upstairs.

Door shut, lights off, Avery sat down on the edge of her bed. Her phone felt like a bomb in her hands.

She had two choices: call Shannon back, or flat-out ignore her. Texting to say *Sorry I missed your call* would only encourage Shannon to call *her* back. Right now, the ball was firmly in Avery's court. That's where it should be at all times, but the fucking thing kept getting caught in the net, or hidden behind Shannon's back, or shooting itself so far off the court no one could find it.

After seven years of trying to keep that ball constantly in motion, of habitually smacking it back across the court when she'd be better off sitting on it, Avery was tired. Worse than that, she was scared to let go, terrified to face the fact that she had been alone the entire time and would continue to be alone if she remained on this path.

This wasn't what she'd thought would happen. She was still having a difficult time admitting the truth of the situation, that she'd been giving and giving and giving all she had and getting nearly nothing in return. Avery loved Shannon. She always had, and she imagined some part of her always would. And most of the time, she believed Shannon loved her, even though she had an absolutely abominable way of showing it. Worse—because, yes, there was lots of "worse" in that pseudo-relationship—it seemed that Shannon *couldn't* show it. She could say she loved Avery, and oh, she'd said many things over the years, all of which stuck in Avery's brain like they were covered in Gorilla Glue. There was an entire section of her brain that was devoted to Shannon and it was dense, filled with gluey weeds that spread and clumped and darkened any sliver of reason.

Worse—told you so—Avery's heart refused to let go. It was as though her heart was determined to prove them all wrong, to continue loving this woman who simply could not, and would not, choose her.

And Shannon... Shannon didn't want to let go either. As Gavin had said, why would she? Avery was filling a need for her. Avery was constant, always available. She had given Shannon unlimited access to her for so, so long, and neither woman knew how to find the access point and flip the switch to close the door.

Avery sighed into her dark room. After cracking the door so Houston could make her inevitable exit, she placed her phone on the bedside table and half-heartedly willed it not to make any vibration whatsoever for the rest of the night. She wanted to have the strength to ignore Shannon. But the temptation, the desire to engage, had been built up so strong over the years. It wasn't as easy as snapping her fingers and cutting the invisible string, but she was trying.

By the time Houston slunk out of the room to go supervise Thea's bedtime rituals, Avery was nose-deep in a psychological thriller, thoughts far away from the status of her heart.

CHAPTER FIVE

Nicole would never admit it to anyone other than the funeral directors she small-talked with during viewings, but she found funerals very peaceful. They started off quiet, underscored with a murmured flurry of activity to ensure everything was in its rightful place. Once the family began trickling in, the peaceful vibe shifted into something with hurt, rounded edges, but still, usually by the time they reached the viewing or funeral, the family had also reached a point of acceptance. Later, as a wild array of guests streamed in and out, handshakes and hugs and tears littering the room, there still remained an undercurrent of serenity.

The raucous funerals were fun, too, the ones more aptly called celebrations of life. Nicole loved the families who picked upbeat music, though she still wondered about that one family who had "Happy" by Pharrell Williams on repeat during the funeral of a ninety-some-year-old mother, grandmother, and great-grandmother. Who, exactly, was happy? And...why? A chin scratcher, for sure, but the family had loved Nicole's humorous additions to their eulogy drafts, sealing their status on her Favorite Clients list.

A loud exhale brought Nicole out of her memories. Will Conway, the director of Conway Funeral Home, had come to stand next to her as she surveyed the room, waiting for the Bankhursts to arrive.

"This is a tough one," he said, voice low and friendly. "He was too young."

Nicole made a noncommittal noise in response. She liked Will, truly, but she had learned over the years that death didn't care about age. When it decided a person was ready, that was it. There was no bargaining, no "it's too soon; he has so much time left." Age was simply irrelevant to the passage of life.

Before Will could engage Nicole in conversation, their attention turned to the doors that had just opened, ushering the Bankhurst family in along with a gust of chilly air.

Each of them was remarkably tan for the end of February, the golden hue of their skin illuminating their matching blond hair and blue eyes. While they wore black, it wasn't oppressive; each family member also wore something that set off the otherwise boring and predictable funeral attire. Julie had a bright pink scarf printed with what appeared to be tiny lemons wrapped loosely around her neck, and Colton was wearing a white-and-green-striped tie. Nicole remembered then how Colton had gone on for more than five minutes about how he'd grown up watching the Philadelphia Eagles with his dad. They'd never missed a game together.

As Will walked over to greet the family, Nicole took a moment to look at Colleen. She was truly striking. Her long blond hair was done in a fishtail braid that hung over her shoulder. Nicole was sure she was wearing makeup, but her overall appearance was so natural, so untouched. Colleen wore a simple, black, long-sleeved sweater dress, and while Nicole was acutely aware of the fact that she had no place admiring a woman's body at a time like this, she couldn't help but appreciate the athletic but feminine lines hugged intimately by the dress. A large silver and turquoise belt looped around her waist, a souvenir Nicole knew had come from a trip to New Mexico with her father when she'd graduated from college.

Mortification spread through her when Nicole realized Colleen was not only watching her but also making her way over. It figured that the first woman she'd found attractive in two years was the daughter of a man she'd had to write a eulogy for. Nothing like someone being so far off-limits that there wasn't—

"Hi," Colleen said, voice surprisingly bright. "Thanks for being here."

"Oh, of course. It comes with the gig." Nicole's cheeks heated. "And I'm also happy to be here. For your family," she added, stumbling over her words.

To her relief, Colleen gave a short laugh. "I know it's part of your job. It's just, I don't know…nice, I guess, to have a friend here." Colleen creased her eyebrows. "Not that we're friends? Because we met under these weird circumstances? And we really don't know each other at all, but you wrote my dad's eulogy so I feel like you know me? Sort of? And I should just shut up?" With each up-ticked statement, Colleen's blush deepened, and Nicole's amusement grew.

"Totally normal feelings," Nicole reassured her. "It's a forced closeness that forms through death."

Colleen took a step back and studied her. "For so few words, that was oddly deep."

Nicole shrugged. "Comes with the territory."

"Say more."

A mixture of pride and confidence wound its way through her, forcing her to stand up a bit straighter. "We don't know each other, or at least, you don't know me. But because you and your family shared loving and funny memories and experiences with me, it probably feels like I've been in your life for longer than I have. And because we met under difficult and emotional circumstances, there's this unexpected bond between us that feels more prominent than it actually is."

Colleen was quiet, still studying her. "That's not the first time you've given that speech."

Nicole coughed out a laugh. "Hardly."

"You're good, you know. At this." Colleen spread her hands out. "Why are you so good at this?"

There it was, one of Nicole's Top Five Most Hated Questions. Luckily, she'd been asked it often enough to have a stock answer locked and loaded.

"I'm good with people," she said easily, giving no indication of the sadness that was sloshing like anguished waves in her stomach. Practice. So much practice.

"And death?"

Nicole registered the joking tone but couldn't play along like she normally would. She lifted her right shoulder a nearly imperceptible amount. "Yeah, actually. Turns out I am good at death."

Colleen's mouth opened and closed several times. Before she could form words, her mother called for her and she walked off to rejoin her family, sending one parting look over her shoulder.

Another little bullet dodged, Nicole thought, moving to another area of the room. She always considered being honest, giving more information that might help her clients to understand why she'd become so good at death, but there was something sacred about her truth.

"Nicole." Julie walked toward her, holding out a piece of paper Nicole assumed was the eulogy. "Can we go over this one more time? I want to make sure we've included everything."

"Of course, I'd be happy to." As Nicole sat down with Julie, she snuck a look at Colleen, only to find her staring back, a curious look scrawled across her face.

Nicole fought a smile as she took the paper from Julie. She may have been a little dead inside, but she was pretty certain she still understood the meaning behind that look.

* * *

"So you're telling me you almost got hit on at a funeral." Across the table, Brynn held her iced tea in shock as she gaped at Nicole.

"Seems so."

"Those are words I never expected to hear you say."

Nicole laughed as she picked up a tater tot and dipped it in ranch dressing. "Honestly, they're words I never wanted to say. But the funeral is over, and I'll probably never see her again."

"You could, though."

"But I don't want to."

Brynn set her glass back on the table. "Nic…"

"Uh uh, no. I don't need another lecture about the impermanence of our arrangement."

"That's not exactly where I was going. I was going to point out how this is the first time you've mentioned anything about another woman. That, my friend, is what we call *significant*." She smiled, exposing the little gap between her front teeth. "And at some point, yes, you will need to move on from this."

"Moving on from this implies that I'm attached to it." Nicole raised her eyebrows, ready for a jocular spar.

"As a friend, I'd hope you're attached."

Nicole waved her fork in the air between them. "Yes, on that end, you're stuck with me. The other part…I can give that up whenever."

Brynn's laugh, full and earnest, sounded like it had started in her toes. Nicole narrowed her eyes, hoping to look menacing. It was no use; they both knew any kind of emotion—good, bad, happy, angry—was off the table between them.

It had been Brynn's idea. Or at least that's what Nicole remembered. The truth was that the beginning was blurry, quiet, and fueled on both sides by two different shades of grief. Nicole hadn't even met Brynn before the funeral, though she'd heard countless stories about her over the years, so she felt, in a sense, that she knew her. And when Brynn walked into the room that horrible day, when they made eye contact and Nicole watched Brynn sidestep several people who tried to get her attention as she strode straight to Nicole, she knew: This was the person who would understand.

"So you're Nicole," Brynn had said, stopping just inches away.

"You must be Brynn."

She gestured toward her outfit. "Did the uniform give me away?"

Nicole mustered a smile. "No. Ginny told me that if the day ever came, you'd be here, and I'd know you the moment you walked in."

She watched Brynn's confident expression falter. It was morbid, Nicole knew, to speak of her wife's death that way: "if the day ever came." But the fine print underscoring the event detailed the truth: all three of them had, in fact, known that that exact day, in that exact form, would come. They just hadn't known when.

From that moment, Brynn hadn't left Nicole's side. Her presence gave Nicole just enough space to greet other mourners, to share tears and memories. And when the funeral finally ended, when Nicole was just starting to realize she would be going home to face an empty house for an undetermined number of years, Brynn was there. Steady, firm, and kind.

She was still there two years later when Nicole, teetering between anger and denial, was scream-crying about being "ruined" and "never going to be able to touch another woman without thinking about *her*." It was so casual, the way Brynn suggested they test out that theory together. So casual and emotionless that after gawking at her for several seconds, Nicole had grabbed Brynn and kissed her.

The magic of it, Nicole thought now, was that almost a year had passed and their friendship had grown, but there remained no strings on their no-strings-attached sexual relationship. Brynn, for her part, eventually disclosed to Nicole that sex was more mechanical than feelings-related for her. She wasn't sure what that meant, if it was permanent or situational, and wasn't ready to put a label on it, or herself. So a true romantic relationship wasn't something Brynn could offer, nor something she wanted to participate in—which worked out perfectly for their situation.

And Nicole... As it turned out, she could touch another woman without thinking about her dead wife. It had taken some time and a lot of tears, but without the literal sexual healing journey she'd embarked on with Brynn, she was fairly certain she would have collapsed into sobs the first time she was intimate with another woman after her wife.

Something neither woman ever brought up was the reality that had they known each other while Nicole was married to Ginny, this would have never happened. It only worked because they had been virtual strangers despite each knowing the other existed and living just twenty minutes from each other. Brynn had served in the Army with Ginny and was, as Ginny always said, "a trigger to my triggers." She couldn't see Brynn but kept in loose touch with her, hence Brynn knowing of the marriage but never meeting Nicole.

It still bothered Nicole sometimes, imagining her wife knowing she was occasionally having healing sex with her battle buddy. But on some weird level, she felt better about that than imagining her wife knowing she was dating someone new, someone Ginny had never met.

Nicole shook her head, trying to step out of those well-worn thoughts.

"Is that a no, you don't want dessert?"

"That's not what it was. You know I want that lemon pie."

Brynn gestured to Nicole's phone. "You can have pie if you spend five minutes on that dating app."

"Are you trying to get rid of me?" Nicole tried to make herself look horrified by the suggestion.

"Yes," Brynn said bluntly, sending Nicole into a fit of laughter. "Now open the app."

Still giggling, Nicole unlocked her phone and swiped to the dreaded dating app. No notifications, just as she liked it. She handed her phone to Brynn, who shook her head. She scooted her chair closer and leaned in, gesturing to the phone.

"We're going to look together. And before we leave here, you're going to swipe right on at least two people."

Panic clenched Nicole's throat. "No," she said immediately.

"Oh, yes. Now start swiping but don't go all fast and wild. I need to see what these women are posting. We need worthy contenders."

Knowing there was no use fighting Brynn, and also knowing the likelihood of her swipers not swiping back, Nicole began the search. She also noted the time. No way in hell would she spend more than five minutes scrolling this dumpster fire.

"Her," Brynn said, pushing Nicole's ready-to-swipe finger away. "She has good energy."

"She's…existing in a picture on my phone. She has no energy."

"Look at her smile. That's authentic. All the women before her had fake-ass smiles." Brynn huffed, sitting back and crossing her arms over her chest. "No wonder I don't bother with this shit. Just swipe right and trust me, Nic."

"Fine," she murmured. This woman was attractive and had a job. She also did yoga, hence the energy Nicole assumed Brynn was "feeling." Nicole kind of hated yoga, but she could look past that…provided this woman didn't want her to do Sun Salutations at five in the morning.

She and Brynn continued scrolling. Fortunately, they saw eye to eye on most of the women. They did argue about swiping on someone named Tara, who looked alarmingly like Ginny. That was a bit too close to home for Nicole's sake.

"There." Brynn leaned forward. "Her. Wait, she looks familiar."

"Did you date her?"

"No, and you need to stop thinking I've dated every woman in this town." She leaned closer to the phone. "I swear I've seen her somewhere."

Nicole glanced at the photo again, taking in the woman's wide, greenish-brown eyes that sat above a slightly crooked nose and a smile that quirked up on the right side of her face. It wasn't a full smile, and Nicole felt a little crazy for thinking so, but there was something in the woman's eyes that felt familiar. She snorted, realizing she was starting to sound like Brynn, feeling things from looking at a picture.

"You're staring," Brynn said lightly, nudging her. "Just swipe on her. No harm."

She waited a few seconds, not bothering to read the rest of the profile but trying to capture a sense of what was reflected in the woman's eyes. Then, with a sigh that nearly quaked the ground beneath their feet, Nicole swiped right.

CHAPTER SIX

Avery was in her zone. Elbow deep in stems and leaves, flecks of dirt clinging to her impossibly short fingernails, bare feet tapping along to the steady beat of the lo-fi electronic music pumping through the workroom. The room was pleasantly warm, not stifling as it sometimes got in the afternoon when the sun lowered to a particularly aggressive angle. She had a streak of blood drying on her forearm, injury forgotten seconds after the thorn had done its damage. The bouquet in front of her was taking shape exactly as she'd imagined it would—a rare feat for her sometimes scattered creative brain, but an accomplishment that never ceased to thrill her.

As she plucked another sprig of anthurium from the bunch lying on the stainless-steel counter, she heard the distant sound of Jay greeting customers in the front of the store. Avery smiled. Nothing boosted business like the end of winter, when people were crawling out of their skin in search of warmer weather. A bursting, colorful flower arrangement was the perfect antidote to the lingering winter blues, and The Twisted Tulip was more than happy to help.

"Nice," Zuri said as she walked behind Avery, arms filled with ivory roses.

"Thanks." Avery turned slightly to watch Zuri dump the roses onto her workspace. "Are those for Monday's funeral?"

"Yep."

Avery crossed one bare foot over the other and leaned against the counter. "I always think it's weird when people choose roses for funerals."

"Ivory is classic."

"I guess." Avery bent closer to examine the stems of the Queen Anne's lace. She didn't love how one looked a little brown at the tip, so into the trash it went.

As she rooted around in the cooler, her mind focused on her flower-finding task, she thought she heard Zuri say something. Considering Zuri didn't say much, she assumed it was her imagination and didn't say anything as she returned to her workstation, fresh Queen Anne's lace in hand.

"I can't believe you're not asking a thousand questions."

Avery looked over at Zuri, whose dark-brown eyes were focused on lining up the ivory roses on the counter. "About what?"

Zuri sighed heavily. It was true she didn't say much, but when she *did* say something and it fell on deaf ears, she made sure the irresponsible listener knew they'd screwed up. "Someone came in for pink peonies the other day."

A smile instantly warmed Avery's face. Pink peonies weren't some rare, bougie flower, but they were Avery's favorite and always had been. She made a point to stock multiple shades of pink peonies, mostly for her own aesthetic enjoyment, but occasionally for a random buyer too. She knew entirely too much about peonies, and both Zuri and Veronica had informed her that she shared an embarrassing amount of information when people selected them for arrangements. This, a missed opportunity to chatter another person's ear off about peonies, was a sad moment for Avery.

"Oh yeah? Which pink did this person select?"

"The palest of the pale."

Avery stopped what she was doing and stared at Zuri. "Seriously?" She shot a look over to the cooler and noticed the stock of her favorite shade was down to just two flowers. She mentally kicked herself, remembering there was a delay in the delivery schedule.

"She was cute," Zuri added, a devilish smile lifting the edges of her lips.

"She?" Avery shook her head. She didn't care if the buyer was a she, or if the she in question was cute. Not one bit.

But it was nice to know someone else out there loved her favorite shade of peonies.

"Probably buying them for her mother," Avery added.

"No, she said she was buying them for herself."

Avery's heartbeat did a funny little trip. She nearly punched herself in the chest, right there in front of Zuri, to ensure that never happened again.

"Very nice," she said, closing the conversation and turning her attention back to the arrangement in front of her.

The two women worked in silence, each caught up in perfecting the art they were creating. Avery loved many things about Zuri: her work ethic, her quietly dark sense of humor that always seemed to come out of nowhere, her surprisingly boisterous laugh that was contagious and made it impossible for anyone to remain in a bad mood. But what she loved most was that Zuri understood silence. She treasured it as much as Avery did, and never filled the air between them with words that didn't hold importance.

So, the fact that Zuri even mentioned this random peony-purchaser made Avery's mood darken. She'd thought Zuri understood her better, and that she wasn't trying to force Avery into moving on like everyone else in her damn life—

The down-tempo music abruptly crescendoed into the hard pounds of classic rock. Metallica, in particular, which could only signal one thing.

"Right on time," Avery muttered, wiping her hands on her overalls. Zuri said nothing, just nodded as Avery left the workroom.

There stood a police officer, her back to Avery. She was telling an animated story, speaking loudly to be heard over "Whiskey in the Jar." Veronica and Jay, both traitors now as far as Avery was concerned, were leaning on the counter, watching the officer with rapt attention.

Fallon adjusted her belt, making Avery stifle a laugh. Her sister had been blessed with a lean, narrow-hipped body, making it difficult to keep her duty belt where she wanted it. She had back pain from it, too, the cost of years of service and having at least twenty extra pounds looped around her hips for eight hours a day, more if she worked overtime or a roster job.

While Fallon was distracted by her story, Avery snuck behind the counter and turned down the music.

Fallon spun and glared at her. "Can't you let me live?"

"Not in my shop." Avery gestured to Veronica and Jay. "Is Cops and Kids story time over? These two have work to do."

"But this is our favorite part of the day!" Veronica exclaimed. "She was just getting to the good part."

"The part where she has to run after some teenager who just stole fifty dollars' worth of vape pods and then she trips over a crack in the cement and face-plants?"

"And the young lad runs free as my pride bleeds out onto the sidewalk," Fallon said, her voice despondent as she hung her head. Her tight blond bun didn't move an inch; it never did, even when she was off duty.

With some grumbling, Veronica got the hint and went back to the workroom. Jay busied himself with straightening up things that didn't need to be straightened.

"Busy day, Sergeant Knight?"

"Always." Fallon leaned against the white oak counter-height desk. She winced and reached down to adjust her belt again. "How's business?"

Avery looked over at the display cooler, immediately seeing empty spots that she was certain Veronica was in the process of filling. Sure enough, the bucket that had held six of the palest pink peonies was empty. Again, the pang in her heart. This time Avery did slap her chest.

"The fuck is wrong with you?"

She shook her head. "Nothing. Hiccups. Business is good."

"Ohhh," Fallon said, settling her ocean-blue eyes on Avery. Yes, she had the perfect blue eyes to go with the perfect blond hair. That, however, is where the All-American Girl comparison stopped. Fallon cursed more than anyone Avery had ever met, which was probably why Avery herself had a resplendently foul mouth. She was also a total gym buff but had cracked the code on keeping her body toned and frighteningly strong without looking jacked with muscles. Despite having an incredible body, Fallon hated showing it off. Avery sometimes wondered if she was coming up against the clash between the impression her looks gave and the reality of her profession. Whatever the case, Fallon was hot, and she was a really good cop. She couldn't escape either of her realities.

"I know this Avery," Fallon continued. "How many times have you talked to Shannon this week?" She tapped her chin. "Her platoon is on middles, so I'm guessing every day."

Avery scoffed, batting Fallon's hand as she reached out to punch Avery in the shoulder. Yet another miserable piece of the Shannon puzzle was the fact that she and Fallon were cops in the same police department. "Shut the fuck up."

"Give me your phone."

"God! What is it with you and Gavin? I can handle this." When Fallon didn't immediately shoot back a retort, Avery narrowed her eyes. "You talked to him."

"Of course I talked to him, asshole." She had a point; Gavin and Fallon were nearly as close as Gavin and Avery. So close, in fact, that Avery sometimes plotted ways to get them to fall in love. She'd yet to be successful, but she was not deterred.

"Okay. Listen. You two need to stay out of my bullshit," Avery hissed, suddenly very aware of Jay lingering in the background. He was doing a lovely job of dusting the dustless nooks and crannies of the reception area, but he had perfectly good ears.

"End your bullshit and we'll stay out of it permanently." Looking very proud of herself, Fallon swept her hand over the edge of the desk. "Anyway, listen to the shitshow I dealt with this morning."

Avery fell into the familiar cadence of another one of Fallon's work stories. They were always engaging, but in that moment, Avery couldn't bring herself to concentrate.

Fallon wasn't wrong. Her current mood had everything to do with the fact that she'd spoken with Shannon, her ex who wasn't even really her ex, three times in the last two days. They were friends, after all. At least that's what Shannon said. They'd been friends for two years, then became more, but even when they were "more," they were still…friends. And now they weren't "more" anymore, hadn't been for a while, but they still said, "I love you." Because they were friends. Shannon also liked to say that they'd never be "just friends" because of how they loved each other.

Oh, the things Shannon said. Avery rubbed the side of her head as the ever-present mental tornado of the last seven years of her life picked up speed.

"I know you're not listening," Fallon said.

Avery took her phone out of her pocket to pull up her calendar. No sense in arguing the truth, so she changed the subject. "The parents want to do dinner next week. You're working middles then, right?"

"Yeah. I'm off Thursday."

"Fine for me." Avery sent a quick text in their family chat. Predictably, Fallon rolled her eyes when her phone buzzed. She hated group texts with a passion. Avery, along with her mother and Fallon's dad, found it the easiest way for the four of them to communicate.

Before Avery put her phone away, she slid down her notifications and felt her eyebrows crease. Thankfully, Fallon was back to her original work story now that Jay had abandoned his pointless dusting and Veronica had come back out to fill in the display cooler.

In other words, Avery had a small window of opportunity to check out the notification from the stupid dating app she was on, not even knowing *why* she was on it. A window of opportunity without Fallon hovering over her, swiping right on every woman who appeared on Avery's screen (she'd done it once, she'd undoubtedly love the chance to do it again).

The app burst happily onto the screen and Avery's throat tightened. She knew she wasn't emotionally open to finding someone—she was fairly certain there wasn't that *someone* out there for her, anyway—but she couldn't stop herself from making a profile once every six months or so, then deleting it in agony and defeat after a few weeks (and one time, after two days). She scrolled once a week, more if she was in a particularly bad place with Shannon, her non-girlfriend who stubbornly held court in Avery's brain as her girlfriend. It was rare that someone caught her eye on the apps, probably because her vision remained centered on someone she couldn't have.

But there was a part of her, a whispering, gentle part filled with air Avery couldn't breathe, that wanted to be open to the idea of someone other than Shannon.

The profile of the woman who had liked her was sparse. Avery appreciated that, knowing hers was similarly empty. She was a Taurus. Avery could work with that. She lived in the same town. Oof. Not what she'd expected, but also how had she never seen this woman before? Avery scanned the photos, sliding past three of stunning sunsets that looked like they'd been taken over the lake that was a couple miles from The Twisted Tulip.

The fourth photo, however, was definitely not of a lake. Or a sunset. Avery took a step back. She wanted to put her phone down and walk away. She wanted to never open this godforsaken app ever again.

But all she could do was stare.

The woman in the picture—chasingsunsets, no real name provided—was stunning. Her black hair was pulled back into a loose bun that sat at the nape of her neck, and her face was turned away from the camera, showing more of her profile than her whole face. Her jaw was strong and feminine, her nose perfectly straight. Thick eyebrows, gently arched, sat above blue eyes that were shocking in their vibrancy. Avery didn't want to stop looking at them.

There were no more pictures, leaving her feeling strangely bereft. She continued to stare at the profile. Surely something would jump out at her that was an instant red flag. There had to be something horribly, morally, devastatingly wrong with this woman. Maybe she was a criminal; she could ask Fallon—nope, then Fallon would know about the dating app, and that would simply not do. Okay…chasingsunsets was probably a serial dater with commitment issues, *or* she had a girlfriend already, hence the three sunset pictures before the singular personal photo that didn't completely expose her, and, oh! The screen name—aha! No real name—it had to be a catfish!

Smug in her staunch belief that she'd uncovered the truth, Avery flicked her finger over her phone screen. She then gasped out loud as animated confetti sprinkled over the screen, the words "YOU'VE BEEN MATCHED!" bright green in the background.

"Aves?"

"Nope!" Avery clicked the button to turn her screen dark. "No, I'm good."

She finally looked up to see Fallon, Veronica, and Jay all staring at her with odd expressions on their faces. Not a bone in Avery's body wanted to engage with any of them; the fear of having to explain what she'd just done—*accidentally*—loomed as she mumbled excuses and hightailed it back to the relative safety of the workroom.

Zuri barely looked up as Avery stormed in, dropped onto a stool, and pressed her palms against her forehead. Minutes ticked by and her phone remained silent, allowing Avery to breathe normally and slowly regain her footing.

There was no way the catfish would message her. Not a chance. Avery nodded, pushed her phone back into the front pocket of her overalls—certainly not because she could better feel the vibration against her chest than she could against her thigh—and got back to work.

CHAPTER SEVEN

"Explain it to me again. And talk slowly, like I'm a small child who wasn't paying attention the first six times."

Nicole rolled her eyes even though Brynn was on the other end of the phone and couldn't see her. "I honestly don't think you were paying attention when I explained it to you."

"Oh, I was. I'm just struggling to put the pieces together in a way that makes sense."

"You and me both," Nicole admitted, curling her legs under her. She looked out the windows, wishing winter would end already. The sky hovered with the threat of snow: thick, white-gray, and impenetrable. She wondered idly how planes flew through such dense clouds.

"Seriously," Brynn said. "Walk me through it again."

With a sigh, Nicole obliged. "You sat with me and encouraged me to swipe right on two people. I did."

"And that was Friday afternoon," Brynn clarified.

"Yes. You need those kinds of specifics?"

"Yeah, Nic, I do. Keep going."

She shook her head, feeling strands of hair escaping her loose bun. She wasn't sure which one of them was more perplexed by this turn of events, and rehashing the time stamps only seemed to make it more confusing. "I happened to look at the app Friday night before I went to bed. That's when I discovered that one of the women had, uh, matched with me."

"Got it. And then?"

"I could make you a PowerPoint. That way you can study it and find the holes on your own, and I can—"

"Keep going, Nicole."

The phrase, and the tone that came along with it, sent an eerie tingle down Nicole's arms. She tried not to think about how Brynn sometimes reminded her of Ginny but there were certain things Brynn said—this being one of them, often stated when Nicole was going sideways in a conversation that should be linear—that took her right back to her marriage, to her wife who had left her too soon. Cognitively, Nicole knew this was one of the invisible strings that kept her linked to Brynn. She liked those bursts of memory, even if they hurt in places she hadn't known hurt could exist.

Pushing that away, Nicole plowed forward. "I sent her a message."

"Yeah, okay, this is where I'm getting stuck. *You* initiated?"

"I did. Why not, right?"

Brynn was silent for a moment but Nicole could hear the muffled sound of Bronx play-growling. "This is why I have to keep repeating this story," she said, adopting a snotty tone. "You're distracted by your dog."

"I can play tug-of-war with him while I try to let go of my shock that after all your resistance, you actually messaged someone on a dating app."

"I'm turning a new leaf." She hoped her voice sounded more confident than she felt. "Isn't that what spring is for? Out with the old, in with the new?"

Brynn snort-laughed. "Um, that's the new year. I think you're thinking of March. It comes in like a lion, goes out like a lamb."

"Okay, well, that doesn't work." She fell silent, turning her stare once again to the stark skies hanging outside her wall of windows.

"Nic, it's okay if you're not ready." She hated the gentleness in Brynn's voice. "You don't have to do this. I mean, there's no harm in meeting someone casually—"

"And that's all I'm doing." The assurance was as much for Brynn as it was for herself. "Anyway, to wrap up," she said, getting up and walking into the kitchen, "I messaged her Friday night, she responded Saturday afternoon, I replied on Sunday morning, and on Sunday night she suggested we meet up today."

"As in Tuesday."

"Yes. A mere four days from the moment we matched. And literally the non-sexiest day for a date." She cringed. It wasn't even a date; they were just meeting to see if there was any kind of spark, any reason to continue communicating. Nicole had appreciated the cut and dry nature of their exchanges, even if she was surprised to be met with the same unemotional engagement she was giving. It felt strangely black and white in a world that was dominated by shades of gray. She got the sense neither of them had any room for gray in their lives, so if nothing else, maybe they could be friends.

Brynn cleared her throat. "Share your location with me."

Nicole took a sip of water, setting the glass gently on the concrete counter. The tingles were back. That was such a Ginny move, a protective maneuver that probably felt controlling to some people. It was status quo for Nicole, though, and it comforted her to know Brynn was looking out for her. And, you know, making sure she didn't end up kidnapped or dead in a ditch, the victim of a random woman (was she even a woman? It was impossible to know!) on a dating app.

"I will. Am I nuts?"

"Nah." More muffled growling from Bronx. "I'm proud of you. This is a big step, and you did it without me badgering you."

"She's pretty," Nicole blurted, immediately pressing her hand against her flushed cheek. "At least I think she is? She only has that one picture. And she looks nothing like Ginny, which is good, right? I mean, it would be super weird if I was only meeting up with women who—"

"Relax. You're allowed to think another woman is attractive. Even women who look nothing like your dead wife."

Nicole sputtered out a laugh that turned into a full-fledged bout of hysterical giggles. When she composed herself, she mumbled, "What's wrong with me?"

"There's nothing wrong with you. It's grief, Nic. You're allowed to feel whatever your body tells you to feel."

"Just don't sit in it," Nicole said quietly, repeating the words her therapist—whom she should probably schedule an appointment with—had said to her countless times as she waded through the stickiest parts of learning to live with her wife's death.

"Exactly. Okay, go get ready. And don't forget to share your location."

"Doing it now." Nicole set her phone on the counter, put Brynn on speaker, and completed the task. "See me? In my kitchen?"

"Got it. And, Nic? Have fun. You're allowed."

"I know," she said softly, more to herself than to Brynn, before saying goodbye.

* * *

Nicole paused at the door of Looper's, the quasi-dive bar that was a convenient two-minute walk from her apartment. It wasn't her first choice for meeting someone, but she liked the idea of being somewhere comfortable, somewhere familiar. Plus, Looper's had excellent fried pickles, and that alone would make the night worth it.

She glanced down at her outfit, hoping it was giving the right mix of "I'm not trying too hard but I do want to look cute." Black jeans with casual rips at the knees hugged her legs. She'd gone for her standard black Doc Martens, completing a very monochromatic look on her lower half. It had taken extreme bargaining with herself to toss aside the black sweater she'd wanted to wear. Instead, she had thrown on a plain black T-shirt and a heather-gray hoodie, plus a black puffer vest. Was it too casual? Maybe, but Looper's wasn't known for its classy clientele. At the very least, Nicole was comfortable. That was all she cared about at the present moment.

With a deep breath, she pushed open the door and slipped inside. Noise assaulted her immediately, reminding her of the impracticality of deep conversations in this environment. Just as well. She was here to meet, make small talk, and get back home.

It was a great plan, one that tilted dramatically to the side when Nicole made eye contact with those bright greenish-brown eyes from all the way across the room. She noticed that they lit up when they settled on her, but behind the brightness was a veil of something much darker, something Nicole recognized superficially. She nodded slightly, received one in return, and made her way across the bar.

"Chasingsunsets, I presume?"

Nicole halted next to the chair she'd been about to slide into. "Oh, God. I never told you my real name."

The other woman—AP on the app, though Nicole suspected that definitely was not her name—laughed, but it sounded tight, almost forced. "I'm just as guilty." She reached up to adjust her messy bun of wavy hair the color of sundried tomatoes. A weird comparison, maybe, but Nicole didn't have other words for the shade of this woman's hair. She noticed, too, the smattering of dark freckles across that crooked nose. She'd somehow missed the freckles on the app, but they were unbelievably cute in person. Nicole gripped the back of the chair, suddenly realizing she was still standing. She had a funny feeling that this woman would not like her freckles referred to as "cute."

"I'm Avery," the woman said, leaning forward slightly, then immediately pushed herself back into the chair as though her body had made a move she didn't approve of. "Wanna sit down?" She smiled but it didn't reach her eyes. "Or at least tell me your name?"

CHAPTER EIGHT

"Nicole," the woman said, still clutching the back of the chair. She looked like she wasn't sure if she wanted to run away or sit down.

Avery waited, not sure if *she* wanted Nicole to sit down or run away.

She was far more beautiful than that single profile picture had implied. Shorter, too, maybe 5'4"? Avery, standing a little over 5'8", tended to assume everyone was around her height, which didn't make any sense, but she'd grown up with tall people, so it wasn't entirely her fault.

The other thing the profile picture hadn't shown was the way Nicole's body seemed to be made of nothing but gentle, feminine curves. Avery had no business drooling over this woman's body—really, when had she become such a dude—but, wow. Just wow. The sweatshirt she wore was a little baggy, but it didn't hide what Avery suspected was—

Stop. She cleared her throat and eyed the chair pointedly. Nicole should sit down. They could at least fumble through small talk for five minutes before one of them bolted.

After another moment's hesitation, Nicole pulled off her puffer vest and hung it on the back of her chair. She sat down, finally, and turned her cornflower blue eyes directly on Avery.

"Hi," she said, a small smile tugging at her lips. "It's nice to meet you."

"You too," Avery managed. Her body was shifting into full-on fight or flight, and she knew it would be really poor form to go into attack mode on this stranger. Too, it would be shitty for her to sprint out of the bar. Frankly, she didn't know what to do, so she sat, silent.

"Have you been here before?" Avery marveled at Nicole's ability to just *talk*. She even looked comfortable, or at least she'd stopped looking like she was thinking about hightailing it back the direction she'd just come.

"A few times, yeah." Avery picked at the edge of the sticky plastic menu. "I like their wings."

"Me too. Wanna get some apps and share?"

"Okay. Sure."

Nicole nodded slowly. Avery knew she wasn't being fair, or even kind. She felt like her insides were spooled tightly around a ticking bomb. Maybe a drink would help.

"Do you have a wing flavor preference?"

The question—innocuous, silly somehow—unspooled Avery a bit. She dropped her shoulders as much as her muscles allowed. "Lemon pepper."

Nicole wrinkled her nose. "Okay, so we won't be sharing wings."

"What's your preference?"

"Sweet and sweaty." She was still looking at the menu, but a genuine smile lit up her face. "I'd eat that sauce on a lot of things." Her smile disappeared, replaced by a furious blush spreading over her smooth, pinkish-pale complexion. "Sorry, that came out wrong."

It hadn't, though, or at least that part of Avery's brain wasn't activated and hadn't even acknowledged the double entendre until Nicole graciously pointed it out.

"I like that sauce," Avery said, surprised to find herself wanting to please Nicole, or at least lessen her discomfort. She was used to having that feeling for people she knew and loved, not for some random woman she'd just met after exchanging no more than six messages on a dating app she didn't even want to be on. "Or we could each get wings. So we can both have what we want," she added, stumbling over her words.

"Six and six?" When Avery nodded, Nicole continued, "Thoughts on fried pickles?"

"Love them."

"Good." Nicole put the menu down and looked back at Avery. Her expression was calm, subdued almost. She gave no hints as to what she was thinking or feeling, and Avery shifted uncomfortably in her chair. She wasn't sure what kind of sign she was looking for, but an emotionless stare wasn't it.

Nicole cleared her throat. "So…Should we get the annoying small talk out of the way?"

Avery nodded. That seemed like safe territory. "Yeah, okay."

"Are you from here?"

Another nod. "I grew up in the suburbs, still live there. You?"

"Not originally, no. I grew up in Ohio, then I went to college in Philadelphia and stayed there until—uh, until I moved here." Avery noticed the hiccup in the explanation, filing it away to examine later. "I've lived here for almost ten years."

"It's a pretty nice place to live."

"Yeah, I really like it." Before she could continue, the waiter arrived, and Nicole gave him their food order. Avery asked for a Tröegs Nugget Nectar, and after a moment, Nicole asked for the same.

"So you like good beer," Avery said appreciatively. She'd never admit it to anyone other than maybe Fallon, *if* she ever told Fallon she was even on this meet-up-date-thing, but that had totally been a test. And Nicole had passed.

"I don't drink much, but yeah. I prefer the good stuff." With that, Nicole seemed to draw into herself, leaving Avery scrambling for the next topic.

"What did you go to college for?" Not her greatest attempt, but it would have to do.

"Communications," Nicole said easily, as though she'd been expecting this boring subject to surface. "I write copy for a marketing firm. I get to work from home, make my own schedule." She shrugged, the corner of her mouth lifting. "I like it. What about you?"

"Oh, I have a degree in art history. I don't really use it, though." She reconsidered. "Maybe I do. Not how you'd expect, I guess."

"So what do you do?" Nicole pressed.

"I'm a florist. I own a shop down the street." Avery heard the pride in her own voice, and for a moment, she felt herself open, but tentatively and in the cloak of darkness, like a night-blooming cereus.

"Oh, The Twisted Tulip?" Nicole was smiling now, a genuine smile that revealed a dimple in her right cheek. "I just discovered that place."

"Yeah, that's me."

Their beers arrived in front of them, supplying a fortuitous break for both women. They sipped and fell back into silence. The smile that had graced Nicole's face gently slid away along with their lackluster conversation.

You're blowing it, Avery thought, then began peeling at the label on her bottle of Nugget Nectar. It didn't matter if she blew it; she didn't even want to be here, meeting someone. Not really, anyway.

On cue, her phone vibrated in the pocket of her hoodie. Her pulse shot up with a mixture of anger and disbelief. She'd purposely put her phone on do not disturb, and she'd taken Shannon off her Favorites list weeks ago, which meant the only way her call (still programmed with an identifiable vibration for reasons Avery could not explain) was coming through was if she'd called, got sent to voice mail, and immediately called a second time.

Avery wanted to throw up. She also wanted to dunk her phone into a vat of Nugget Nectar, but that would be a waste of excellent beer.

Fuck her, she thought, leaning forward in her seat. Nicole looked up, surprised, Avery's abrupt shift in posture pulling her out of wherever she'd disappeared to in her own head.

"Don't you think it's weird that we haven't met before now?"

"I—yeah, I guess so?"

The buzz of her phone had doused her night-blooming cereus with harsh desert daylight, prompting the petals to shutter together again. Avery took a steadying breath. She could do this, even if she'd lost the nighttime shadows of protection.

"Balsam Lake isn't that big." She pointed around Looper's as though to prove her point, which failed spectacularly, considering the amount of people in the bar. "And, you know, the gay scene is even smaller."

"Right." Nicole's voice was quieter than it had been, but she was watching Avery intently. "It seems like everyone knows each other in our community."

"Exactly!" A horrible thought dovetailed through Avery's brain. "Especially in our age range." She remembered that much from Nicole's profile—just two years separated them, Avery's thirty-nine years coming in just under Nicole's forty-one.

"And yet we've never met."

Avery nodded enthusiastically. She plucked a fried pickle from the basket as soon as the waiter set it down. Caught between wanting to continue her little path of verbal destruction and wanting to shut herself up, she stuffed the pickle into her mouth and was flooded with immediate regret.

"Oh, fuck," she gasped, reaching for her beer. "They're hot."

Nicole gestured to the basket. "The steam didn't give that away?"

Nicole's tone and expression were amused, teasing, but Avery couldn't bring herself to appreciate the humor.

She swallowed hard, knowing she should keep her mouth shut and appreciate the fact that she'd just made a bit of an ass out of herself and Nicole's response was, well, perfect. She didn't belittle Avery. She didn't make fun of her. She teased her, appropriately. It was a nice change. But it was a change Avery's brain could not compute.

That damn pre-pickle thought rose again. "We've probably dated some of the same people," she said. "I guess that would make the whole 'we've never met' thing make sense."

"I doubt that." Nicole's voice was light, holding no indication of her thoughts or exes.

"It seems likely, given the circumstances," Avery pushed. She touched the tip of her tongue to the roof of her mouth. She'd burnt the fucker. Great.

"I see your point, but I'm pretty certain we don't share any exes."

Vague. That was it, the burr that was sticking stubbornly in Avery's thought process. Nicole was being irritatingly vague. She crossed her arms over her chest. She wanted Nicole to say whatever it was she wasn't saying. The vagueness was needling all her sensitive spots, hitting too close to everything she'd been through with Shannon. She weighed her options as she thought back to Nicole's bare-bones dating profile. She could cross catfish off the list; Nicole was definitely the woman in the photo. And she didn't give cheater vibes. There was something weighing on her shoulders, Avery could see that much, but she couldn't place it. And then it hit her.

"So you're divorced?"

Nicole, who'd been leaning over the table to dunk a pickle into the chipotle ranch dip, hurriedly sat ramrod straight in her chair. Her eyes flickered with something Avery couldn't place. "W–what?"

"You have to be." Avery shrugged, trying to look casual even though she felt everything but. "It's the only thing that makes sense."

She looked up long enough to catch a glimpse of Nicole's face. She was starkly pale, the life having gone out of her eyes along with her complexion. Another thought occurred to Avery, one that made more sense given Nicole's reaction, but to her surprise, Nicole spoke before she could share her new theory.

"How does that make sense?"

Avery shrugged again. "You probably got married before you moved here, so we couldn't share exes." She loved this part of her rationale: the moment the thought of Shannon and Nicole having dated or even knowing each other hit her mind, she'd been scrambling to find a way to destroy it. Her divorce theory worked beautifully. "Maybe it was recent," she continued, sauntering straight down the devil's path to her next angle. "A lot of women in our age range are separated. You know, testing out the dating pool while they're still technically married." Some part of her registered that she sounded like an absolute asshole, but she was on a roll and the hill was steep. "It's fucked-up, and it hurts people. If you're still married, you're still attached to someone else. It's shitty to put yourself on a dating app and not be upfront about that." When she swallowed a sip of beer that was meant to be refreshing, it felt like she was swallowing glass. Or, you know, a sharp sliver of her own fucked-up truth.

Across the table, Nicole had morphed into a marble statue. *Bingo*, Avery thought, but she took no satisfaction from exposing Nicole's secret. Somehow, she felt worse.

Despite the noise surrounding them—clinking silverware, thuds of glassware on tabletops, snippets of conversation looping through a steady backdrop of nineties grunge music— Avery felt like she and Nicole had slipped into a hushed bubble. She was acutely aware of the way Nicole still had not moved. Had she even blinked during Avery's diatribe? Her eyes had lost almost all their color; the vivacious cornflower blue had leaked out, leaving glacier-blue irises in its place. Avery had never seen anything like it, and she was unsettled by the change.

No. She felt upset by the change. Because she and her stupid fucking mouth fueled by her stupid fucking heart had caused it.

Before she could battle past her bullshit and say something, anything, to bring the life back to Nicole's eyes, Nicole pushed back her chair and stood up. She dug into her pocket and laid two twenties on the table. As she pulled on her vest, she glanced at Avery before saying, "I think I need to go."

She was gone before Avery could even register the fact that she didn't want her to leave.

CHAPTER NINE

"I've been seeing too much of you lately."

Nicole turned away from the window and came face-to-face with Will Conway. "What can I say? Business is booming."

He snorted then immediately cleared his throat. "One of these days I'll convince you to work for me. I need your dark humor around here all the time."

"What kind of job would you possibly give me, Will? I'm a writer, not a mortician."

"Some families want us to create memorial items, like pamphlets and stuff. You'd be great at that. Oh!" he said, perking up. "You could run our social media. The Facebook page gets a lot of traffic, and we just got on TikTok."

Nicole widened her eyes. "A funeral home with multiple social media accounts? Your grandfather must be rolling over in his grave."

Will laughed, nodding between chuckles. He had taken over the family business while his grandfather was still alive, and everyone in town knew Bob Conway was a man of tradition and simplicity. Even Nicole, who was a relative newbie in town despite having been there for nearly ten years, knew of the legendary Bob Conway. He wouldn't so much as touch a computer, let alone a cell phone. Under Will's guidance and leadership, Conway Funeral Home had scurried into modern life, complete with a social media following...which Nicole still couldn't wrap her head around.

"The offer stands," Will said, rubbing his hands together. "I'm not looking forward to this one," he added, his voice low even though they were alone in the room. Well, aside from the deceased lying in the casket, that is.

Nicole shook her head in agreement. "I don't know why this family hired me. I gave them tons of feedback and suggestions, but it all fell on deaf ears. They were dead set on their ideas."

"Pun intended?"

"Always." Footsteps and a rather loud expletive echoed into the room from the hallway. Nicole looked over her shoulder to see an armful of bright yellow flowers peeking around the corner. "Looks like your flowers are finally here."

"Great. Right on time."

Nicole watched Will hustle over to the extremely oversized arrangement. She wasn't surprised; the Ploughman family oozed over-the-top energy in everything they did. The matriarch, Betty, had died in her sleep. She was three months shy of turning 100, and that—a silly number, as far as Nicole was concerned—was all the family could focus on. She had tried to suggest other aspects of Betty's life for the eulogies. She was a star majorette in high school; she had been attached to her horse, Alpha, from the time he was a foal until he died after thirty-three unbelievable years; she met her husband, Sturgis, in kindergarten and only ever had eyes for him (even though he was rumored to have had more than eyes for several other women over the years, resulting in at least one half-sibling that everyone knew about but never talked about; Nicole was secretly hoping the mysterious half-sibling would show up at the funeral just to stir things up). And Betty had never worked a day in her life. Nicole was awed by that, both impressed and a little disappointed. Betty had, however, raised seven children without complaint. All seven, five girls and two boys, were prim and proper, married with multiple children (Betty had *twenty-five* grandchildren, a number that made Christmas sound like a prime time for bankruptcy). Nicole had spent the last week searching for cracks in the façade of any of them and had come up empty-handed.

She wasn't convinced there weren't any skeletons lurking in those closets, though.

Will left the room, presumably to go wait for the family to arrive. Meanwhile, the obnoxious yellow flower arrangement was lowered onto the bottom half of the open casket. For as big and bright as it was, Nicole had to admit it wasn't ugly. There was a classiness to it that Betty surely would have approved of. Still, it was enormous.

A knot of unruly dark-red hair hovered behind the flower arrangement. Nicole's breath stuck in her throat. *No way.* Yes, she now knew Avery owned The Twisted Tulip, but she'd never seen her at a funeral before. Haldeman's, the centuries-old (an exaggeration, but everything about the place screamed "ancient") flower shop on the other side of town was the go-to for funeral flowers. It seemed to be an unspoken rule in the funeral community.

But no, there Avery was, stepping out from behind the casket. Nicole watched as she purposely avoided looking at the upper half of the casket, where Betty was lying peacefully in a blush-pink dress.

Avery, in overalls that held flecks of leaves and dirt, looked entirely out of place in the ornate room. Nicole couldn't help but smile at the image before her, even if the memory of their awkward and uncomfortable meet-up from three days ago was still very present in her mind. As obnoxious and rude as Avery had been, she was still very attractive.

Attractive and a little broken. After dissecting their interaction several times, that was the conclusion Nicole had drawn. Definitely a little broken.

"Son of a bitch," Avery muttered to herself. She held her finger to her mouth.

"Need some help?" Nicole hadn't gotten the full sentence out before Avery jumped at least a foot in the air and gasped, clutching her chest with her non-bleeding hand.

"What the fuck!"

Nicole bit back a smile. It was a cardinal rule of funeral homes: always, *always* scope your surroundings. The dead didn't talk, but if you thought you were alone in a room and heard a voice, it was jarring, to say the least.

"You didn't see me?"

Avery took a step back and as her hip brushed the side of the casket, she jumped again, but forward this time, away from Betty. "Obviously not!"

It was killing Nicole not to mess with her, but she kept her mouth shut and allowed Avery to get her bearings. It was obvious Avery wasn't "down with death," as Nicole joked darkly about herself.

When Avery took a few steps away from the casket and turned her full attention on Nicole, it was clear she'd regained her footing, but there was still a slight tremble in her hands. She'd have to play nice after all.

"What are you doing here?"

Nicole coughed out a laugh. She hadn't expected Avery to be so direct, thinking she'd take a softer, somewhat apologetic approach after their disastrous encounter earlier that week. Clearly, she didn't know Avery, but now she was curious about what was behind her firm, boarded-up exterior.

"Working," Nicole said.

Avery's beautiful eyes narrowed. "I thought you worked for a marketing firm."

Interesting. Nicole figured Avery had written her off, so it was a surprise to hear she remembered that inane detail. "I do. I also…help out here."

"In a funeral home." She shivered.

"Yes. In a funeral home." Nicole wavered, unsure of how Avery would take the news of her side job. "I'm down with death," she settled on.

Avery stared, confusion scrawled across her face. At least it was confusion and not disgust. Nicole fought back a laugh. She *could* be honest here, and just *tell* Avery what she did. But part of her was still pissed about the way Avery had come at her about divorce and separation and emotional attachment without giving Nicole a soft, understanding place to speak the truth of her romantic past. And so, she rescinded her earlier decision to play nice.

"I like how peaceful it is here," she continued, spreading her arms wide. "Quiet. No one really bothers you because, well"—she leaned forward—"they can't. Plus, I like to help put the fun back in funeral."

"You're twisted."

Nicole did laugh at that. "For as often as I'm dealing with the dead, I have to be. Speaking of," she said, eyeing Avery. "How is this the first time we've run into each other like this?"

If Avery was taken aback by the abrupt shift and direct question, she didn't show it. In fact, she didn't move at all. "Changing of the guard," was all she said.

"Vague," Nicole countered, feeling a flicker of irritation.

Avery mumbled something as she crossed her arms. She looked around the room before settling her gaze back on Nicole, seeming to decide something. "Most of Haldeman's clientele is…well, dying off." She grimaced. "Plus, the Ploughmans are family friends." She angled her head to the side, reconsidering. "Not exactly. My stepdad is friends with James."

James, the youngest of Betty's seven children, and also the male child who deftly avoided being named Sturgis Ploughman IV, an honor bestowed to his older brother (who had three daughters, ending the trend). It was an interesting connection, one that made Nicole wonder about Avery's family…and whether or not they would be attending the funeral.

Avery went on. "Funerals aren't really my thing, but I'm not going to turn down business." She pointed to the overabundance of yellow on the casket. "Especially when a family goes this over the top."

At least they agreed on that. Before Nicole could get a word in, Avery walked toward the doorway.

"I have more to bring in." She paused, turned to look back. "It was nice to see you."

Something in Avery's expression unlatched a locked door in Nicole's chest. There was a wound there, Nicole could clearly see now. All that brashness and bravado Avery had exuded when they'd met at Looper's was a wall, a thick measure of defense. She was shocked she hadn't noticed it then. Now, it was all she could see.

She realized Avery was hesitating, that her "nice to see you" was more likely an apology than a truth. Nicole nodded, not trusting her words, not wanting to say the same unless it was *her* truth—and currently, she had no idea if it was nice to see Avery again.

Avery seemed to take the hint, or maybe she just switched gears back into work mode. When she left, heading back to her truck for more ostentatious flower arrangements, Nicole slunk out of the room to hide in the bathroom and stayed there until she was certain all the flowers had been delivered and placed and the flower arranger was gone.

Over the top didn't scrape the surface of describing Betty Ploughman's funeral. The room was bursting with flowers and a soundtrack that hadn't repeated a single song in two hours. Everyone wore dazzling outfits, some fit for mourning, others that looked entirely out of place but were defended by proclaiming Betty's proclivity for "the finer things in life." This far in, and people were still arriving with condolences and stories. Granted, one hundred years of life had to touch a lot of other lives, but Nicole was growing weary of watching the performance before her. She wanted to leave, but the eulogies hadn't been given yet, and she'd promised she'd stay until they were over.

Only one of the Ploughman children—Angela, the middle child—had taken Nicole's suggestions into consideration, and she was the only reason Nicole was willing to stay. Angela was the most down-to-earth of the brood, and visually, she stuck out. Nicole squinted. Actually, now that she thought about it, Angela looked almost nothing like the rest of her siblings. DNA was wild, sure, but the Ploughman children all had Sturgis's prominent nose and heavy eyelids. All except for Angela, who was said to be a carbon copy of a younger Betty.

Unless… Nicole grinned, wondering if good old Betty had some secrets of her own.

She scanned the room again, telling herself that she definitely was not looking for anyone who resembled Avery. Even if her stepdad had shown up to support his buddy James Ploughman, Avery wouldn't have recognized him because, duh, they didn't share DNA. But maybe Avery's mom had come along. Surely she'd bear a resemblance to her daughter. It didn't matter— she'd probably never see Avery again, so what was the point of trying to track down her mother in a packed funeral home?

That was the snag, though. Nicole knew, fully and strongly, that she would see Avery again. She just *knew*.

"Hi." It was whispered, kind of, from Nicole's right. She couldn't place the voice until she turned and came face-to-face with Colleen Bankhurst.

"Um, hi?" Nicole scrunched her face in confusion. "What… hi?"

Colleen smiled widely. "I thought I might find you here. Weird, I know."

"An understatement." Nicole peered at her, still confused. "Are you here looking for me?"

"Yes and no." Colleen nodded toward the hubbub in front of them. "I came with my mom. She grew up with the Ploughman kids."

"Small town," Nicole remarked. It wasn't, at least not by most small-town standards, but funerals made it feel like everyone knew everyone else in Balsam Lake.

"Feels too small sometimes. Anyway, since I found you…" Colleen straightened, seeming to bolster her confidence. "I have to go to this party next weekend. Any chance you'd go with me?"

It was a first: being asked out at a funeral home, while a funeral was in progress. Nicole couldn't wait to tell Brynn.

"So?"

Nicole studied Colleen, who was undeniably pretty, wondering if there was an attraction between them—wondering, fleetingly, if she could have sex with her without having an emotional response. It would be a step in the right direction, even if it ended up just being a hookup. That wasn't normally Nicole's thing; she was an emotional-attachment kind of gal, but she wasn't ready to go *there* with anyone.

Seeing as the sexual benefits of her friendship with Brynn had recently ended, silently and mutually, this Colleen situation might be a good way to ease back into the dating world. Nicole wasn't sure how she would feel being with someone else, but she felt healed enough to let go of her reliance on Brynn. Some healing, it turned out, she had to take care of herself.

"Nicole?" Colleen prompted.

"Sorry, yeah," Nicole said. "Yes. A party sounds great."

"Yeah? Cool. I'll text you the details." She grinned, her face lighting up with devious delight. "After I get your number from my mother, that is."

Nicole laughed, then remembered where she was and cut it off as quickly as she could. "Sounds good."

Colleen waved and disappeared into the grieving crowd.

A flicker of dark red drew Nicole's attention to the side of the room, but instead of Avery's attention-grabbing hair, she set eyes on a scarf wrapped around an octogenarian's neck. Nicole shook her head. She was pretty certain Colleen wasn't going to be the next great love of her life, if such a thing existed. Avery was currently the only other contender, but after their failed first date, putting her in the running for that spot seemed like an idea that would only bring more pain.

And more pain was something Nicole could live without.

CHAPTER TEN

It had been a day. Seeing Nicole at the funeral home had twisted Avery's insides in a peculiar way. She hadn't had time to analyze it because once she got back to The Twisted Tulip, she'd been faced with a lily emergency that had taken up the rest of her workday. By the time she'd gotten home, she was worn out, frustrated, and feeling strangely raw.

She sat on the back deck, wishing it was about ten degrees warmer. At least the sun was still clinging to the sky, giving the backyard a cool glow. Houston darted between the trees, chasing something only she could see. It was muddy back there, and Avery knew she'd have to spend part of the evening giving her a bath, a chore they both loathed.

Her phone, resting on the railing, began to vibrate. Avery shut her eyes before picking it up and saying hello.

"Hey," came the response. "What are you doing?"

"Sitting out back. You?"

"I'm on my way home from work."

"Roster job?"

"Yeah, basketball playoffs. The Hurricanes won."

"Nice." Avery scuffed her shoe against the worn wood. "Good game?"

"It was all right."

There had to be a reason Shannon had called, but Avery wasn't about to press her on it. Their communication had increased recently, long, winding conversations that reminded Avery of when they'd first met. Shannon had started making her little comments again, the breadcrumb statements about "what if" and "how would it be" and "do you ever think about." She'd even sent a few pictures of the two of them together in happier (read: actual committed relationship) times. Avery, falling for it but not as hard as she usually did, had done her part in accepting a FaceTime call that had turned…risqué. She'd even reverted back to old habits, and, after being playfully prompted, texted Shannon an artfully posed picture that left little to the imagination.

And just as quickly as the tempo increased, it had fallen flat once again—so flat that communication had ceased entirely for two days last weekend. Avery was used to the pattern, but it still shot poison darts into her stomach. She assumed (no, she *knew*) what the silence meant, but Shannon refused to give her straight answers, so Avery usually talked herself out of it and picked up, slowly, where they'd left off.

Which led them right into this conversation, a weak attempt by both parties to get back to normalcy. Whatever normal looked like that week, anyway.

"I'm gonna stop by."

There it was. It was never a question with Shannon. She just announced her intentions, and Avery could do little to refuse them because the truth was, she wanted to see Shannon.

"Okay, come around back."

They hung up, and Avery waited, rolling her thoughts around the pit in her stomach. Drive-bys were Shannon's thing and always had been, ever since they officially broke up after being together for three months and began a seven-year stretch of "are we, aren't we" friendship that was at times incredibly intimate and at times silent and distant. It was a situationship to the nth degree, and Avery was so entangled in it that she had a hard time seeing past it.

But things had begun to shift over the past year or so. Not enough for Avery to cut the tie completely, but enough for her to at least begin to move on.

It was just that every time she thought she'd found her footing to walk past Shannon, she appeared and stood directly in the path, daring Avery to get around her.

"Hey," Shannon said now, coming around the side of the house.

Avery looked at her, taking in the person she loved so deeply but had been so repeatedly, deeply hurt by. Shannon's dark-brown hair was slicked back into an unmovable bun. She was still in uniform, giving her that untouchable air that was both sexy and frustrating. Her vest made it very difficult to hug her, and sometimes all Avery wanted was to hold her without a barrier.

That was the catch, though. Shannon was surrounded by barriers that Avery had tried to make her way through, for years, only to be repeatedly bounced back to a reality she simply did not want to accept.

"Hi. You must have been close. Wanna sit?"

"No, I'm good." Shannon looked out at the yard. Houston ignored her arrival, as she generally did, continuing her zoomies through the trees. "How was your day?"

"Frustrating," Avery admitted. She gave Shannon the CliffsNotes version of her day, avoiding all things Nicole. She didn't have to leave Nicole out. On paper, Shannon and Avery were both clear on the fact that they were not in a relationship. In their hearts and heads, however, it was a different story depending on the day—and depending on each of them. Avery knew Shannon loved her and cared about her; Avery felt the same, and they were both quite aware of their chemistry. But she also knew Shannon couldn't be with her. It was torture, and added to the torment was the simple fact that neither of them was honest about anything else happening in their romantic lives. It was a silent void between them, one that would send out a ripple of final destruction if either dared to admit their truths.

"Hopefully tomorrow's a better day." Shannon leaned against the railing of the deck. "Are you going to refinish the deck this summer?"

"Yeah, it's on my list." Avery stood and brushed off the back of her jeans. "That and more landscaping."

"Yeah, me too." Despite living less than two miles from each other, Avery hadn't been to Shannon's house in over a year. She'd seen pictures of what Shannon was doing to the yard, though. God forbid Shannon invite her to drive the five minutes to see it in person.

Avery looked at Shannon, her heart doing its familiar trip-beat, but maybe it was less powerful than it had been. The skin around Shannon's dark-brown eyes crinkled, a familiar smile brightening her otherwise stoic expression.

"I got this for you." She held out a bag and Avery took it. "I've had it for a couple months. I saw it and thought of you."

Avery peeked into the bag and smiled. It was a blanket printed with avocados. "That's really cute. I love it. Thank you."

"It's soft, too. I know you love soft blankets. And avocados."

"I do." Avery set the bag down. "Thanks."

"You're welcome." Shannon glanced out at the yard before looking at Avery again. "I should get home. Thanks for letting me stop by."

"Yeah, of course." She bit back the "anytime" that threatened to pop out.

Shannon stepped forward and pulled Avery to her. She wrapped her arms around her, and Avery rested her head against Shannon's. They stood there, locked in as tight of an embrace as they could manage with that damn bulletproof vest separating them. Avery willed away the burn of tears in her eyes, not wanting Shannon to see she still had an emotional response to seeing her, to feeling her embrace.

When they released each other, Shannon pointed to her lower lip. "Still got that sore."

Avery hadn't been expecting that they'd kiss. In fact, she couldn't remember—okay, that was a lie, she knew very well that they hadn't kissed in over a year. It was the longest they'd gone without that kind of intimacy, so Avery had assumed the physically intimate part of their situationship had ended.

And it had, but Shannon, knowing how to keep Avery looped into their cycle, had to bring the possibility of a kiss to the surface, let it sit there and glow like an ember too hot to touch, just so Avery could receive yet another burn.

"Yeah," Avery said, feeling like an echo of herself. "Put more stuff on it."

"I will." Shannon looked at Avery long and hard, as if memorizing her. "I'll call you later."

"Thanks again." Avery pointed to the bag. "Talk to you later."

Shannon kept her eyes locked on Avery. "I love you."

Avery nodded, still worried about the potential of tears. "I love you."

Shannon waved as she walked back around to the front of the house. Avery watched her go, counting the seconds till her phone would ring and Shannon would say, like she always did, "It was good to see you."

Avery bit her bottom lip, then whistled for Houston. She'd like to not answer the phone, but she knew she would.

She always, always would.

"This," Fallon said, pointing at her plate, "is phenomenal. I never knew I liked vegetables this much."

Avery rolled her eyes, but Gavin soaked up the weird compliment. "I'm glad you like it. I found the recipe online this afternoon and had to try it."

"The sauce." Fallon moaned. "Did you make it from scratch?"

"Oh my God," Avery muttered. "Just fuck already."

Gavin grinned, nodding enthusiastically, seeming to have not heard Avery's little jab. "I did! It has over seven ingredients."

"Daddy," Thea said seriously. She was examining her plate with a discerning eye. "How many vegetuls are on my plate?"

"Just a few, sweetie. Do you like the sauce?"

"I don't think so." Thea poked at a piece of broccoli. "I don't like trees."

Avery stabbed the offending broccoli and avoided Gavin's glare. "The trees are a little crunchy, T. Try the little orange frisbees. They're nice and soft."

"No. I want sketti."

"See these little torpedoes?" Avery pointed her fork at the rice on Thea's plate. "They're kind of like sketti. I bet you'll love them."

Thea looked at her, untrusting and annoyed, but pushed some rice onto her fork and raised it to her mouth.

"Okay," she said around the food. "But sketti is better."

The three adults at the table watched to make sure Thea was continuing to eat before pulling their collective attention away from her.

"Seriously, Gav. This is incredible."

"Seriously, Fallon." Avery lowered her voice after mimicking Fallon's to a T, a skill she'd picked up in their early teen years. "Why don't you just hump him right here at the table?" Houston, lying at Avery's feet for once, huffed with annoyance.

"I apologize for my terribly uncouth sister," Fallon said to Gavin. She turned back to Avery, fire in her eyes. "Considering I saw a familiar car driving away from the house as I was pulling in, I imagine she's in a foul mood."

A part of Avery deflated, leaving her shoulders slumped. Fallon had always liked Shannon on a coworking level—not enough to forge a friendship with her, but she respected her professionally. She hadn't been thrilled when Avery started dating Shannon, and was far less than thrilled when their original romance imploded. Needless to say, Fallon remained not a very big fan.

"It was nothing," Avery mumbled, putting her fork down. Her appetite was slipping away.

"Hmm." Fallon leaned her elbows on the table and leveled Avery with a probing look. "Did her visit have anything to do with last weekend?"

Avery thought quickly, trying to remember if she'd told Fallon she hadn't spoken to Shannon last weekend. She was pretty sure she hadn't. After being open for the first three or four years of the back-and-forth, Avery had learned it was easier to keep it to herself. No one—least of all Fallon—understood.

"No," Avery settled on. When Fallon didn't respond, she looked up and saw a familiar and foreboding look on her face. "What?"

Fallon looked at Gavin, who was studying his brightly colored dinner plate. She seemed to make a decision, and looked back at Avery, compassion in her expression. "Aves, I saw her at McIntosh's wedding last weekend."

Avery swallowed. This wasn't shocking. McIntosh was on Shannon's platoon. Granted, Shannon had said she "probably wasn't gonna go," since she didn't like to attend social events with her colleagues. So, okay. A semi-lie that wasn't really a lie, more like an omission.

"Okay," Avery said, but as she did, she saw another flicker of emotion in Fallon's eyes. She braced herself, knowing what was coming.

"She was with Marie. They went together."

Avery pushed her plate away and Fallon immediately reached across the table and pushed it back.

"No, I'm done," Avery said, folding her arms over her chest.

"Yeah, you should be." Fallon's tone was light enough to carry kindness, but they both knew the words and the intention behind them were not light.

Thankfully, Gavin launched into a work story, pulling Fallon's attention away, letting Avery fade out right there at the table.

It was the piece that existed in the periphery of every single interaction between Shannon and Avery since the absolute beginning of their relationship: Marie, the ex-girlfriend, who had broken up with Shannon just days before she and Avery slept together for the first time. The timing looked ugly, and in a way it was. Avery and Shannon had admitted to having feelings for each other while Shannon was still in a relationship with Marie, but they'd held their boundaries for the weeks between the confession and the breakup. Although Marie didn't know about Shannon's feelings for Avery, the breakup wasn't amicable. Shannon had eventually admitted she knew it was coming, and things hadn't been good for some time. She also admitted that she still had feelings for Marie, and yes, Avery should have walked away right then and there, but she didn't, because she was already falling for Shannon, and she'd thought their connection was strong enough to move them both forward.

Three months into their relationship, Marie had come back. And Shannon had broken Avery's heart for the first time…only to try to take back her decision hours later, saying she'd made a huge mistake. It was all Avery needed to hear. And it was that moment, those words, that had set them off on the next seven years.

During that time, Marie was always present. Avery knew some specifics, but she was certain she didn't know everything. And why would she? She and Shannon were *not in a relationship*. Sure, they were having sex and saying "I love you" and exchanging Christmas presents and talking about the future they wanted to have together: but they were not in a relationship. They were friends, and oddly, their friendship had strengthened over the years, even through the hurt and disappointment.

But while they were friends, Avery grew to love Shannon more and more. Their emotional attachment strengthened, became a force of its own. It kept Avery entangled, even when she was hurting and saw the truth of the situation. Every time Avery started to slip away, Shannon's sixth sense fired up and she lured her back in. Neither was willing to walk away, despite a handful of arguments that always circled back to Shannon saying, "No one is making you stay."

But Avery was. Avery was making herself stay, telling herself for year upon year that eventually Shannon would get it. She would see that Avery was the right woman for her. She would finally find the strength to let go of her toxic connection to Marie, take time for herself, and come back, ready to fight for Avery and choose her every day. Avery was convinced this would happen.

And then, she'd hit a point where she had no choice but to admit to herself that Shannon could not let go of Marie. She didn't even want to. Little by little, Avery became aware of reality: Shannon was far more involved with Marie than she'd led Avery to believe. Shannon was doing life with Marie while keeping Avery in the background—her best friend to whom she was emotionally attached and with whom she had excellent chemistry and would never be "just friends" because their connection was far more than that.

Avery pressed her fingertips against the underside of the table. Shannon's silence last weekend had told her what she wasn't willing to say out loud: Yes, she was going to the wedding, and no, she wasn't taking Avery because she was taking Marie. Suddenly, the week prior—the intensity and consistency of their conversations, even the flirting—made a lot more sense.

Shannon had a way of building Avery up just to disappear... so that when she returned, Avery was still there, clinging to the reminder that they did have something solid, something good. Something powerful.

Avery blew out a frustrated breath. The worst part, in that moment, was feeling like a total humiliated idiot. Shannon knew Fallon would be at that wedding. Just as she had in other situations, she could let the news trickle back to Avery without having to be upfront and honest with her. Avery was getting very, very tired of that passive-aggressive bullshit.

More than that, she was fucking tired of being lied to. She clenched her jaw, remembering she wasn't being honest with Shannon either. She had no idea Avery was on a dating app. Avery didn't like lying, even if it was by omission, but it didn't matter because she'd blown it with the only woman she'd found remotely interesting and attractive.

Beyond *that*, the sick feeling in Avery's stomach reminded her that she wasn't ready to be involved with anyone else, anyway. She'd just hurt Nicole. And the last thing she wanted to do to someone—Nicole or otherwise, and frankly, Avery didn't understand why the image of Nicole's face kept popping into her brain—was what Shannon had done to her. What Avery had allowed to be done to her.

No, not what had been done to her. What Avery had chosen to accept, over and over again. In the name of love, of friendship, of possibility. Of potential. Of maybe someday.

Houston nudged her damp nose against her hand. Avery scratched her chin as she tried to take deep breaths. Something had to give, and soon.

CHAPTER ELEVEN

Brynn bent over and scooped up the drooly tennis ball from the ground. Nicole watched as she held it in front of Bronx, speaking quietly to him as his tail wagged with enough power to light up all of Balsam Lake. When she stood upright, Brynn arced her arm back and then thrust it forward, launching the ball into a long flight down the side of the dog park. Bronx wasted no time in racing after it, paws tearing through the muddy grass.

"And that," Brynn said, wiping her hands on her jeans, "is how you tire out a dog that has a seemingly endless amount of energy."

Nicole watched as Bronx reached the ball. He clamped his jaws around it and turned, trotting back to where his owner proudly stood. All too soon, the soggy ball was back at Brynn's feet.

"At least the sun's out today," Brynn remarked after tossing the ball again. She elbowed Nicole. "You're awfully quiet."

"I don't know what I did wrong," Nicole blurted. "I keep replaying the night in my head, and I know I should have just been upfront about—"

"Stop." Brynn rested her hand on Nicole's shoulder. "We talked about this, Nic. You didn't do anything wrong, and you don't have to announce that you're a widow the very first time you meet someone. Especially if you're not sure you want to date said someone."

"I know. I do, I know. I just keep hearing her speech in my head." She tugged her black beanie lower over her ears. "I could have prevented all of that if I'd just told her the truth."

"You said you didn't feel comfortable telling her about Ginny."

Nicole sighed. "Because of how she went on that tailspin about exes and divorces and emotional attachment. There was no way I was going to drop in a dead wife after she said all that."

"Sounds like Avery might have her own stuff going on."

"Yeah." Nicole nodded, stuffing her hands in the pockets of her jacket. It was warming up, slowly, but there was still a chill in the afternoon air.

She hadn't said much about her overall perception of Avery when she'd given Brynn the rundown of their brief evening. But Nicole felt validated that from the little she'd shared, Brynn had a similar takeaway.

"So it's just as well it was a disaster."

Brynn didn't say anything. She didn't have to; they'd already been over the fact that Nicole and Avery's first encounter wasn't a disaster. Nicole kept circling back to that descriptor, though, because it was the easiest way to explain it away. So they weren't a match. Fine. They couldn't even have a civil, open conversation about their romantic pasts. Also fine. They weren't attracted to each other, anyway. Extra fine. Totally fine.

"You have another woman seeking you out anyway, remember?"

Nicole snorted. She didn't know what to make of Colleen's surprise appearance at the funeral yesterday, nor did she know the intentions behind that random invitation. It hadn't felt flirty, more friendly than anything, but Brynn wasn't having it.

As she lobbed the ball for Bronx, Brynn added, "It won't hurt to see what happens."

"Right, now that I'm sexually cured."

Brynn burst out laughing. "Hey, that arrangement worked for both of us."

"You say that, but I still don't understand how it worked for you."

Brynn shoved her hands in the back pockets of her jeans, eyes never leaving Bronx. Nicole thought, not for the first time, that Brynn bore a striking resemblance to Tasha from *The L Word*, except Rose Rollins didn't have a cute gap in her front teeth like Brynn did. Otherwise, Brynn's light black skin and smooth black hair, along with her dark eyes and a wide, always amused smile, were almost a dead ringer for the actress.

"I like sex," Brynn said quietly, "in that I like making someone else feel good. I can take or leave the part where I feel good." She paused to throw the ball again. "It's the stuff that comes with sex that I'm not great at."

"The part where you meet someone, fall in love, get married, and have a relationship that's never fully connected, even when you're having sex?"

Brynn side-eyed her. "See, you do understand."

"I only know what it was like for Ginny. Or, I guess, for me and Ginny." Nicole scrunched her shoulders up to her ears. "We really did love each other. And I know she tried."

"You were her world, Nic."

"Yeah, see, that's where the problem is. I could never have been enough for her."

"No," Brynn said, waiting to continue until Nicole met her eyes. "You couldn't save her from herself. That's not the same as not being enough."

She held that thought before shifting the spotlight back to Brynn. "So it's like that for you? You don't think you'll ever be able to fully be with someone?"

"Because of how I am," Brynn said, nodding. "Yeah. It's like I can only go so far, or be so intimate—and not in a sexual way. It's not like I haven't tried." She smiled, but it was lacking real amusement. "I've got a couple exes who can tell you exactly how much I tried and just could not give them what they deserved. I got tired of disappointing people."

"And that's why the whole, um, sex thing worked for us."

"Yup. That was a need I could fill for you. The only need," she amended.

They were quiet for a moment, both watching Bronx try to befriend a couple mutts who were sniffing the grass near the fence.

"Well, that, and you're a good friend," Brynn said. "At least, you're a good friend to me. It's easy to be friends with you."

"Because of our common ground?"

Brynn laughed. "Nic, it's not like Ginny forced us to be friends."

A thought occurred to Nicole. "Wait. Did she—"

"No," Brynn interrupted. "She didn't make me promise to look after you. But she made sure I knew all about you, even though I never got the chance to meet you until her funeral." She took a deep breath. "She loved you. She loved you more than she loved herself."

"That was always the problem," Nicole murmured. "I know our marriage wasn't perfect. But it worked." She hesitated. "Most of the time."

"I think all marriages work most of the time. And the ones that don't end up in divorce."

"Or shared misery."

"Or that." Brynn picked up the ball Bronx had yet again deposited at her feet. "Don't second-guess your relationship with Ginny. You both did the best you could." She glanced at Nicole before continuing, "And her choices are not a reflection of how she felt about you."

"I know." Nicole took a step backward to get back into the sunlight and collided with a mountain of fur. "Oh, shit. Hello there."

The dog, a shaggy golden retriever, panted and pressed its body against her legs. It looked up at her, baleful eyes blinking, giving her no choice but to reach down and run her fingers through its soft fur. The dog huffed, a happy huff, and pressed harder against her legs.

"Houston, Jesus. You can't—oh. Hi."

Avery, who had been jogging over with an irritated expression, stopped short when Nicole looked up at her approach.

"Hey," Nicole said, still petting the dog, who apparently was named Houston, and was also... Avery's dog? Funny, she hadn't pinned Avery as a dog owner. "He's yours?"

"She," Avery corrected.

"Oh, sorry. I assumed Houston was a boy's name."

"That's not very evolved of you."

Surprised by Avery's attempt at a joke, Nicole coughed out a laugh. "So you like Texas?"

Avery looked insulted as she wrapped Houston's leash around her hand, over and over again until her knuckles lost their color. "Not really. She's named after Whitney."

"Nice," Brynn said, interjecting from a few feet away.

Nicole watched Avery size up Brynn, and despite the fact that she was still muddling through confused feelings about their first encounter, jumped in to explain. "Avery, this is my friend Brynn. Brynn, this is Avery." She panicked. "Um. Just Avery."

Brynn nodded at Avery. "Nice to meet you. I think I've seen you here before." She gave Nicole a pointed look, which she was quick to pick up on. Of course—Brynn had recognized Avery on the dating app because she'd seen her at the dog park. Brynn never forgot a face.

"Yeah, I try to bring her here as often as I can." Avery shifted from foot to foot. "She's not great at socializing with other dogs."

All three women looked at Houston, who was still happily leaning against Nicole's legs, gazing up at her with adoration. She was utterly oblivious to the other dogs milling around the park.

"I'm sorry," Avery said suddenly, taking a step forward before freezing, one hand stretching toward Nicole as though she'd hit an invisible barrier. "I can get her off of you."

"No, it's okay. She's sweet. And soft."

"She's a stage-five clinger," Avery said, a ghost of a smile lighting her face. "But only with some people. It's like she can sense when someone needs a little dog therapy."

Nicole swallowed the little lump in her throat. She'd been around Bronx plenty, but he had zero people skills. All he cared about was running, tennis balls, and treats. Houston was another story. Nicole had instantly felt calmer the moment Houston pressed her furry body against her legs. Now all she wanted to do was wrap her arms around Houston and rest her head on her soft back.

"She's special," Nicole said softly, looking at Houston. When she looked up, she found Avery studying her with a curious look scrawled across her face. Her eyes looked puffy, maybe from lack of sleep, and her face was a little pale aside from light red blotches on her cheeks. She was definitely missing her usual feisty spark.

Avery cleared her throat and looked away. "I think I scared your friend off."

Something about the way she said "friend" made Nicole's back stiffen. "Oh, she probably went to get her dog. He's very social. Sometimes overly."

The silence that settled between the two wasn't particularly comfortable. Nicole had a feeling Avery didn't buy the truth that Brynn and Nicole were just friends—sure, they'd been physically intimate, but Nicole was certain the only vibe they projected was platonic. Unless Avery was some sort of mind reader, there was no way she could have known. Besides, Nicole reminded herself, none of this mattered. They hadn't hit it off. She didn't owe Avery any kind of explanation about anything at all.

"She's coming back," Avery said, though it seemed like she was talking to herself, not Nicole. She looked at Houston, who was still attached to Nicole. "Houston, come."

Begrudgingly, the dog obliged, sitting next to Avery just as Brynn approached with Bronx, who beelined for Houston. The two dogs sniffed each other excitedly, Houston seeming marginally interested in this new potential friend.

"Looks like they like each other," Nicole said, purely to fill the silence.

Avery gaped as Bronx and Houston continued getting to know each other. "I've literally never seen her do this with another dog."

"Bronx is a friendly guy," Brynn said, smiling proudly. "He doesn't have the best manners, but he's always ready for a good time."

"Why does that sound like something you'd write on his dating profile?" Nicole shivered against the wind.

Avery laughed, then flushed, as though remembering that's how she and Nicole knew each other. She darted a look at Brynn, again seeming to size her up, then leaned down and hooked Houston back on her leash.

"We need to get going. It was nice meeting you." Avery nodded at Brynn.

"You too. I'm sure I'll see you here some other time." Brynn patted Bronx's head. "I know this guy would like to see Houston again."

"This is weird," Nicole said loudly. "Stop trying to get your dogs to date."

Avery smiled at that, a genuine smile that only made her prettier. Nicole bit the inside of her cheek. She did not need to go on thinking Avery was pretty. She scanned her quickly, trying to find a fatal flaw in her appearance. Of course, she came up empty-handed and, to add insult to injury, was caught when she made eye contact with Avery and found an amused look on her face.

"See you around," Avery said. With that, she turned and left, Houston trotting happily by her side.

"So that's Avery," Brynn said once she was out of earshot. "Interesting."

"I think she thinks we're more than friends."

"Of course she does. She needs to think that so her theory makes sense."

Nicole sighed. "Cool."

"I thought it didn't matter."

"Right." Nicole stared after Avery, watching the way her shoulders rounded into herself as she walked toward the parking lot. "I'm not interested."

CHAPTER TWELVE

Sundays were Avery's favorite day in the shop. They got decent foot traffic, people stopping by for a personal pick-me-up or a colorful apology for some wrongdoing the previous night, but the front of the store never felt busy. The weekend orders were usually wrapped up, freeing Avery to plan for the coming week. She purposely kept the store lightly staffed, preferring just herself and Zuri, adding more hours for Veronica and Jay during the holiday seasons.

This Sunday had caught Avery off guard. She'd miscalculated the time needed to assemble the intricate flower arrangements for Genevieve Longwood's big coming-out party next weekend. A mistake like that was entirely unlike Avery, and in her own mind, she was blaming everyone but herself. Outwardly, she muttered the error to Zuri before parking herself in the workroom.

Two hours later, she was stumped. She'd counted and recounted the table arrangements, coming up two short each time. Considering she was out of the flowers and the very specific glass vases used for the arrangements, Avery was perplexed. And annoyed.

Before she counted—an inevitably fruitless decision—for the third time, she stood in front of the iPad mini that's sole purpose was to provide the store with music. She'd had enough of the classical chill Zuri had put on when she'd arrived. Avery didn't feel like being soothed into a calmness coma—in fact, if she heard one more soaring violin solo, she was going to stab herself in the hand with pruning shears.

The opening chords of Nirvana's "Come as You Are" swept through the room, immediately easing some of the tension in Avery's shoulders. She turned the music up, wanting to drown in the 90s grunge playlist. When all she could hear was Kurt Cobain's scratchy voice and every one of her own thoughts had been sufficiently drowned out, Avery nodded, took a deep breath, and began counting yet again.

"Motherfucker," she growled shortly after. It simply did not make sense. She stomped through the room, flipping over boxes and digging through buckets of flowers.

"You good?" Zuri's voice barely came through over the punch of Nirvana still pounding through the open workspace.

"No, I'm fucking not," Avery said, kicking a box. "I'm missing two vases and two vases-full of flowers."

Zuri walked through the room, stopping at the table where Avery's handwritten plans were scattered. She picked up two pieces of paper before holding a third one out and pointing to a bright-pink Post-it on the top of the paper.

"What is that?" Avery narrowed her eyes.

"A note from Jay."

Avery stomped over to Zuri and grabbed the paper from her. Sure enough, Jay's chicken-scratch cursive (who wrote in cursive anymore?) explained the problem, which wasn't a problem at all: the numbers for the party were slightly lower than the planned numbers for the wedding, hence the two less vases in the supply drop off.

"Fine," Avery said, her tone etched with anger she couldn't stop from leaking out. "But that doesn't explain why I'm short flowers."

Zuri was already at the table where the completed arrangements sat. Avery watched as her long fingers gently pushed through knots of blooms. Nirvana melted into Alice in Chains, and soon, Zuri stepped back from the table, empty-handed.

"Do you want the truth?"

"Yes." Avery folded her arms over her chest. "I mean, I don't, but say it anyway."

"Five of these arrangements have more flowers than they should."

Embarrassed and confused, Avery didn't say anything. She was the only person in the shop who'd tended to those arrangements.

"But they look good. Not unbalanced. I say keep it."

Still not trusting her mouth, Avery turned and busied herself with cleaning up the leftover stems and leaves. She had another order for two large bouquets that she wanted to tackle. The requested flowers were tough to work with and challenging to pair with the right kind of filler. In other words, it was the perfect distraction from her ignorant error.

Zuri waited until Avery's workspace was clean before she launched her attack.

"Do you want to talk about it?"

"About what?" Avery spat.

"Whatever's boiling under your skin." When Avery didn't reply, Zuri went on. "The usual?"

Avery dropped an armful of fresh eucalyptus on the counter. "Partially," she admitted. "But there's nothing there that I'm not used to."

"Avery…"

"Don't," she said quickly. "There's nothing you can say right now that I haven't already said to myself. Multiple times." She pressed her fingertips into the cold metal of the counter. "And I'm working on it."

"How so?"

Great question. Avery wished she had a great answer. After Fallon dropped her cute little bomb about Shannon going to a wedding with her supposed ex, Avery had confronted Shannon. The answers she'd received were dodgy and gray, the usual when it came to confronting Shannon about what she was actually doing with her ex, who never seemed to fully be her ex at all... much like Avery wasn't her girlfriend or her ex, either. Neither had attempted a conversation after that shitty talk on Friday night. So, yes, it was the usual for Avery. She was brooding and stewing, just as mad at herself as she was at Shannon.

And she was "working on it" by giving herself distance from the situation, a.k.a Shannon. In the past, she'd accumulated a handful of less-than-proud moments of trying to force Shannon to talk to her. Call after call, texts amplifying with anger that morphed madly into sadness as they went unanswered along with the calls. Now, Avery took the colder, more passive stance: she ignored her. Well, she was *officially* ignoring her now that she'd called her that morning—just once—and listened to the seven rings before Shannon's voice announced she wasn't available but the caller could leave a message. Avery hung up before the outgoing voice mail message finished its spiel.

"I met someone," Avery said suddenly, surprising herself. She didn't want to get into the Shannon shit with Zuri, but this was an unexpected way of throwing her off track.

Zuri grinned and leaned against another counter. "That's what I call working on it."

Avery waved her off. "It's nothing."

"It's not nothing if you brought it up like that."

Knowing Zuri would stand there and silently wait for her to continue, she bit the bullet and explained. "We met on that stupid dating app. We had drinks at Looper's last week. And it wasn't great." She looked up. "But at least I put myself out there."

"A good step," Zuri agreed. But she didn't look convinced.

"What?" Avery gestured toward her with a stem of eucalyptus. "What's your face trying to say?"

Zuri hopped up onto the counter, swinging her long legs back and forth. "Keep talking."

Avery rolled her eyes. She tried to stay quiet, figuring it was best to keep her silly little thoughts to herself. But then Stone Temple Pilots came on and she cracked.

"There's a possibility that I was…uh, a bit of an asshole." She focused on the flowers, knowing Zuri was probably nodding in agreement. "I know it's a cardinal lesbian rule to avoid talking about your past relationships on the first date"—the word caught in her throat, but Avery pushed on—"but it came up. You know how it is."

"Yep."

"Okay, but she was weird about it," Avery said firmly. "This isn't a big town, you know that. So we have to have *someone* in common."

"Maybe you don't."

"Yeah, fine, maybe. But the way she wouldn't give me a straight answer…" Avery shook her head. "I think she was hiding something."

"And you called her out."

"Sort of. Lightly? I don't know." Avery blew out a breath, ruffling the fragile pink flowers of the Limonium in their steel vase. "I may have insinuated that she wasn't being honest because she's still emotionally attached to her ex."

"No you did not."

Avery cringed at the disappointment in Zuri's voice. "Well, when I say ex, I mean I may have also inferred that she was maybe separated, not divorced, and—"

"Stop."

This was precisely why Avery hadn't talked to anyone about Nicole. She knew exactly what Zuri was going to say, because she'd already said it to herself in the mirror. Several times.

"You put this poor girl through your own bullshit ringer, Avery."

"I know," she mumbled.

"Do you? Do you realize you projected all your shit onto her?"

"Yes," Avery said miserably, taking the shots because she knew she deserved them. "I know. I'm the one who's stuck in a fucked-up emotional attachment. I'm the one who can't let go of her past even though my past has made it very clear that she doesn't want to be with me. I'm the one who shouldn't even *be* on a dating app. I'm the asshole, Zuri. I'm the problem. I get it."

"Aren't you tired of it?"

Avery's breath caught in her throat. She nodded, then pushed out, "Yes."

"Good. Do something about it." With that, Zuri dropped to her feet and left the room.

Alone with her chagrin and misery, Avery leaned her elbows on the counter. Temple of the Dog was playing, reminding her that sometimes even too much love is never enough.

Seeing Nicole yesterday had left something in her unsettled. It's not that Avery had been kidding herself into thinking they'd never cross paths; Balsam Lake really wasn't that big, and it felt like once you met someone, you kept meeting them, especially when you least expected to.

And it's not like Avery had been unhappy to see Nicole. Something more like the opposite, if she were being honest with herself. But she knew she owed Nicole an apology. The Avery that had shown up at Looper's had been on the defense, only interested in protecting herself and keeping her walls thick and high, looking for a distraction from her own bullshit.

That, too, left Avery with a sour feeling in her gut. It was her responsibility to pack up her Shannon bullshit and move it to a less visible part of her internal landscape. She didn't want to use someone to help her with that process. And she didn't want to destroy someone while she continued working through the inevitable and necessary removal of Shannon from her life.

Avery twisted a broken stem around her thumb. It wasn't the right time for her to try to date. She wasn't even certain that she wanted to explore something with someone else. And not because she was waiting for Shannon to finally choose her—that transatlantic ship had sailed a Titanic-esque journey. It's more like she wasn't sure she would be chosen, period. By anyone.

But when she closed her eyes against the surge of emptiness, it was Nicole's face that came to mind. Intensely blue eyes beneath a faded black beanie pulled low, full lips smiling in a way that made Avery want to lean a little bit closer.

She blew out a slow breath, refocusing on the flowers in front of her. "Let it go," she said to herself and began moving the flowers and foliage around, waiting for the magic moment when the image in her head formed beneath her hands.

CHAPTER THIRTEEN

Bad days didn't happen as often as they had, say, a year ago. Nicole had been prepared for them then, almost too prepared. Expectant, maybe. She'd grown to understand that grief would erupt or trickle at any damn moment it pleased, regardless of what she was doing or thinking. One time, on a brilliant summer day, Nicole was in the middle of the lake (Balsam Lake, unironically named after the city) on her kayak. It had been a good day. She was in good spirits. But the moment she leaned forward to get her water bottle, her insides pinched with untethered memories and she burst into tears, right there in her kayak under the hot sun. Later, she replayed the moment endlessly, trying to pin down a thought or a feeling. Nothing came to mind, just the filmy recall of sadness that had overtaken her.

Moments like that had eased over time. Sure, anniversaries and other important dates were difficult, and if Nicole found one of Ginny's socks in her laundry (that kept happening, and she could not, for the life of her, figure out how), she got sideswiped with grief. But the knife had eventually stopped digging, leaving a simmer of anxious sadness in its wake. Nicole had learned to live with it, aware of its steady presence and thankful for the way it rarely reared its head at full power. Grief, it turned out, could simply sit inside of you, silent and unbothered.

And while it was generally quiet, today was not one of those days. Nicole had woken up with a heaviness in her chest that refused to break. She'd stumbled through her morning, using work as a distraction. After completing three projects and sending them off to her boss, she dropped into a chair and stared out the windows of her loft. She wasn't sure how much time passed, but when the numbness started to ease, she realized her nose was raw and her eyes were sore. The heaviness was still inside her, but it was more like fragmented pieces than an entire solid weight. That was progress, she thought, despite the fact that she hadn't made it out of the old sweats and long-sleeved T-shirt she'd thrown on when she got out of bed, and it had to be nearing six p.m.

The buzzing of her phone jolted her. Grief had a way of taking her far away from common things like cell phones and meals. Moving back into a space where other people existed was usually a challenge, but Nicole was relieved when she realized someone was trying to connect with her.

She lifted her phone and tried to smile. "Hi, Dad."

"Hey there, baby girl. Haven't heard from you in a few days, just wanted to check in."

Nicole rubbed the side of her head. Had it been that long? She didn't speak to her dad every day, but she normally didn't go more than a day without at least a text. "I'm doing okay. Just busy with work."

Hank made a noise that sounded like he was trying to laugh while someone was strangling him. "Lotsa people dying these days?"

"No," Nicole said quickly, then forced a laugh. "My full-time job, I meant. The company got a few new clients and my boss gave three of them to me."

"Look at you! Someday you'll run that place."

Typical Hank, cheering his daughter up the corporate ladder. She had no desire to rise even one rung above her current position, though.

"What's been going on with you? How'd that spice rack turn out?"

"Well, it spins." He chuckled, and Nicole heard the scratch of his beard. "Your mother thinks it could use some improvement."

Nicole stiffened. It was rare that her dad mentioned her mom. The only fights Nicole and Hank had ever had were all centered around Nicole's mom, or as Nicole more often referred to her, her father's wife.

She was her biological mother, but Nicole saw not a shred of that woman in herself other than their similar facial features and hair color. She'd worked hard as a teenager to *not* be like her mother, and that was before she became aware of her sexuality— the cherry on top of the mountain of her mother's disapproval. Growing up, Nicole never seemed to be able to please her mother. She had been an overweight child, uninterested in anything other than imaginary play and books. For Diana Callahan, who fancied herself a Northern Ohio Suburban Socialite (not that such a thing existed), Nicole was the opposite of what she'd wanted in a daughter. She had no interest in tennis, or fancy clothing, or even riding horses (the actual dream of several childhood friends). Even as Nicole shed her childhood weight and blossomed into a teenager with a perfectly average body who got above average grades, it still wasn't enough to get her mother off her back. Their relationship was fraught with arguments and cold silence, and Hank had too often been caught in the middle. When Nicole went off to college and returned home for Christmas only to tell her parents she was a lesbian, that was the final straw for her mother. Diana had left the house in a blind fury, leaving Nicole and Hank to sort through the aftermath.

Nicole couldn't bring herself to believe her father was truly happy being married to such a miserable woman, but he never complained. She imagined there was a side to her mother that she wasn't privy to. She was a good cook, Nicole could give her that. But kindness and warmth were not things that came easily to her mother—even when Nicole abruptly found herself a widow at the age of thirty-nine.

No, Diana Callahan hadn't even come to the funeral. Hank provided excuse after excuse, but Nicole knew the truth. Even though her wife was dead, Nicole was still a lesbian, and that was a piece of the family puzzle that could not ever fit.

"Well?" Hank prodded, bringing her back.

"Sorry, what?"

"I asked if you have anything you need me to make for you, but I think you have other things on your mind."

Nicole rested her head against the back of the chair, her eyes focusing on the high ceilings of her loft and the large fan that needed to be dusted. "I'm okay, Dad. I'm sure I can think of something I need."

"Kiddo, you don't seem okay." He sighed, and Nicole could hear the faint sound of a crackling fire in the background. She pictured him in the family room of her childhood home, the room he'd made into his personal den. "I'm sorry I brought up your mother. I know we don't—"

"No, Dad, it's okay. Really." She looked down and realized she had a blanket piled on her lap. She tugged it closer to her chin, needing the warm comfort. "How is she?"

He hesitated, clearly surprised. "You really wanna know?"

Nicole laughed then, a real laugh even if it was short and tight. "Not really."

"What's bothering you, Nic? And don't try to feed me lies. You might be four hundred some miles away, but I know how you sound when you're upset."

She snuggled deeper into the blanket. "I guess I've been thinking too much."

"You? Never."

"Always," she said, smiling sadly. "You know it'll be three years next month."

Hank was silent for a moment. Nicole imagined he was doing the math, even though she'd just done it for him. She wondered if the math, and the abrupt entrance of March, was what had knocked her off course all day. "Well," he said, his tone gruff. "I guess I'll start packing my bags."

"What? What for?"

"To come see you. I don't want you to be alone on that day."

Tears sprang into the corners of her eyes. On the one-year anniversary of Ginny's death, her dad had spent a week with her. He'd promised to do the same for the second-year anniversary...and then Diana had gone and scheduled a two-week Alaskan cruise without consulting Hank about the dates, leaving Nicole alone and her dad too many miles away. She had a feeling he still hadn't forgiven himself for that.

"Dad, you don't have to," she said, her voice thick. "I think I'll be okay."

He made some noise that probably had words in it, but Nicole couldn't make anything out.

"I have people," she continued, picturing Brynn. Avery flickered at the edge of her mental image, but she shook her head, shooing the image away. "I won't be alone. And besides, it's year three. It'll be easier."

"Well, you let me know. I'll be there if you need me. I won't be floating around in Alaska this year, that's for damn sure."

"You had fun, remember? You got to see bears. And moose." She squinted. "Meese? No, moose. Plural."

"I woulda rather been giving my daughter a bear hug," he said, his voice still gruff.

"Dad." Nicole laughed as tears slid down her cheeks. "I love you. You know that, right?"

"I love you, baby girl. Now tell me some good news. Is it warming up there yet?"

"Not really." There was a threat of a snowstorm the following week, typical March behavior for Pennsylvania. "I'm going to a party this weekend," she said, surprising herself with the admission.

"That so? You got a date to this party?"

Nicole blinked at the ceiling. Did she? "Kind of," she said, shrugging.

"Now wait a minute. You're out here meeting ladies and not telling your old dad about it? You know the rules, kiddo. Spill it."

Nicole gave Hank the outline of meeting Colleen over the unfortunate circumstances of her father's untimely death, being surprised to realize she found Colleen attractive, the snag of her being quite a bit younger, and the unexpected run-in at the funeral home last week. She tactfully avoided also having run into Avery that same day, not that she'd ever breathed Avery's name to her dad, but still.

Hank was chuckling when Nicole wrapped up the explanation. "Of all the places to meet a woman."

"Comes with the territory."

He full-out laughed at that. She may have looked like her mother on a very superficial level, but her personality was all Hank—dark, twisted humor included. "So what are we thinking? Girlfriend material?"

Nicole nearly choked. "God, no! It's just a date. Not even a date. We're just…going somewhere together." Again, Avery hovered at the edges of her memory. Nicole frowned. Avery had no business being in her brain. She was irritated that she hadn't heard from her after their run-in at the dog park, which was ridiculous considering they'd never even exchanged phone numbers. Nicole pressed her phone harder against her ear. She hadn't looked at the dating app for a while. Was Avery still on there? *Stop it*, she commanded herself, turning her focus back to her dad.

"I know it's been about a thousand years since I went on a date, but I think going somewhere together is about as date-y as you can get."

"Okay, fine. Whatever. It's not a big deal." And deep down, Nicole knew that was the truth. Maybe Colleen could be a bridge to getting Nicole fully back on her dating/sexual-being feet. Or maybe she'd just be a friend.

"It's okay if you're not ready," Hank said warmly. "There's no rush."

"It's not that." Nicole sighed, ready to unload the weight that kept dragging her down. "I'm nervous, Dad. Of making the wrong choice." *Again*, she thought.

Hank cleared his throat. A good twenty seconds passed before he began speaking, and as soon as he started, Nicole knew with certainty that he'd been holding on to this for a while.

"You didn't make the wrong choice with Ginny. You two— Nic, it was very obvious that you loved each other very much. I know your relationship wasn't perfect, but come on now, kiddo. No relationship is. You worked hard at it, and I know you gave it your all."

"But was I happy?"

"I think you were. You were until you weren't."

Nicole sucked in a breath. "Do you think we'd still be married if she hadn't died?"

"You know, I've actually thought about that."

She laughed. "I figured."

"And I know you have, too. But there's no answer, Nic. You either would be, or you wouldn't be. It's impossible to know."

"Right," she said. "I think if we'd both started putting in the same amount of effort, we would have made it."

"But was Ginny capable of doing that?"

Nicole shook her head. "Not with how she was. If she'd…" she trailed off. "I don't think we would have made it."

"And that's okay. Who knows, maybe her death is easier to move past than the divorce would have been."

"God, Dad." Nicole laughed. "That's dark."

"Well, think about it."

She did, briefly, before coming to the realization that she'd rather think about it when she got off the phone. He had a good point, though—one she hadn't previously considered.

"Here's what I want you to remember. You listening?"

"Of course I am."

"Good. You loved Ginny. Ginny loved you. Love is one thing, Nic. True commitment and effort is another. And you need it all to make a marriage work."

"All that and more," she said lightly. Her stomach growled, reminding her that an absurd amount of time had passed since she last ate.

"You gonna go feed that empty stomach?"

"You heard that?"

"Loud and clear." Hank laughed. "Go get yourself some dinner. And call me tomorrow, would ya?"

"I will." They said their goodbyes and Nicole ended the call, dropping her phone onto her lap.

Suddenly desperate to avoid being alone with her thoughts, she picked her phone up and tapped on the dating app. A girl had to eat, after all, and surely there was no harm in seeing if someone wanted to join her and absolutely not talk about anything other than safe, superficial topics—never mind that extending such an invitation over an app kind of guaranteed the person wouldn't see it right away, which *then* guaranteed this was a sure dead-end attempt. But it was an attempt nonetheless. Nerves swam in Nicole's empty stomach as she pressed the little white envelope, opening her messages.

She sat upright, staring at her phone. She blinked several times. Where Avery's profile picture had once been now sat an empty circle. Their conversation was still there, and Nicole cocked her head to the side, wondering how long that unopened message from Avery had been waiting.

She pressed again, opening the thread of stilted communication. There, at the bottom, was Avery's newest message.

Hey. I'm deleting my profile but I wanted to tell you instead of disappearing without a word. Turns out I'm not ready to date. If you ever want to hang out at the dog park with me and Houston, here's my number.

Nicole bit her lip. Beneath the phone number was one final sentence, time-stamped just two hours earlier:

Sorry if this is weird, I have no idea what I'm doing.

She snorted. Well, they could agree on that.

Below Avery's message was the announcement from the dating app that this user account no longer existed, and the messages would be deleted in twenty-four hours. Before she could overthink her reasons, Nicole took a screenshot, securing Avery's phone number in her camera roll.

The mixed messages were bold and clear: I'm not ready to date but here's my phone number. Avery could play it off as just wanting to be friends—but she hadn't even said that. At least she had the maturity to admit that she had no idea what she was doing.

Nicole put her phone down on the coffee table and stood up. She might be starving for food, but she could do without Avery's confused and confusing communication. Dinner for one, yet again.

CHAPTER FOURTEEN

Avery leaned over and adjusted the trail of moss sweeping from the small, round fishbowl being used as a centerpiece. She'd questioned Genevieve Longwood's choices from the moment they'd started planning the flowers for her now-cancelled wedding, but Avery had to admit, her ideas had come together in an unusual but captivating manner.

Arranged loosely in the fishbowl were handfuls of dusky-pink garden roses. They rested casually against plumes of silver sage fern. Genevieve hadn't wanted much filler, explaining that she liked a bare approach to centerpieces (something Avery had never before heard a bride-to-be say). But Avery had talked her into sprigs of white wisteria—not too much, but enough to give a fuller appearance to the arrangement. The wisteria worked surprisingly well with the trailing moss that spread over the rim of the bowl, curling over the pristine white tablecloth. The end result was a soft explosion of muted colors and diverse textures.

"You hate it, don't you?"

Avery grinned, watching as Veronica hurried past her to place another centerpiece on a table. "Nah. It's just not my favorite."

"I think it's cool." She adjusted the moss to flow in a carefully curated haphazard way. "And it pushed you out of your comfort zone, so that's even cooler."

Avery scoffed. "I think it's the fern that's bothering me."

"Yeah, you usually avoid that kind." Veronica stood back, hands on her hips, and appraised their work. "It does look vaguely like lettuce."

"Exactly! And lettuce—"

"Has no place in flower arrangements." Veronica grinned as she walked past. "Girl, I know. It's like the cardinal rule of working for you."

Avery tried to protest, but Veronica was gone, heading back to the van to bring in the last two centerpieces. While she waited, Avery took a long, studied look around the room.

Genevieve had stuck with the original location for her wedding reception—a medium-sized event space at a golf course—and her former bridesmaids, now demoted to just friends and party organizers, had done a wonderful job sprucing up the place. It looked appropriately festive but not over the top. The design scheme matched the flower arrangements, continuing the soft urban vibe Avery had worked hard to cultivate. Not a rainbow was in sight, giving no hint that this had morphed from a celebration of a heterosexual union into an enthusiastic "I called off my wedding and now I'm officially announcing that I'm a lesbian" party. Avery appreciated that bit of class, though she expected nothing less from Genevieve.

"Hi! You're still here!" Speaking of, Genevieve rushed in with a smile bright enough to light the entire room. "Oh my God, Avery." She stopped in the middle of the room and spun slowly around. "This is absolutely amazing."

Avery took in the moment. Her work was generally finished before a wedding ceremony even ended, so she rarely got to see her bridal clients enjoy the work that she put into the reception. Genevieve's reaction was genuine, making her wish she got to witness this moment more often.

She cleared her throat. "So you like it?"

Genevieve laughed and stopped spinning, settling her gaze on Avery. "I love it. Every inch of it." She swept over to the nearest table and leaned in to inspect the centerpiece. "Ooh, these are just perfect. You were right about that white stuff. It brings it all together."

Avery stifled a laugh, silently apologizing to the wisteria for being referred to as "white stuff."

Veronica came back in, and Avery helped her arrange the final two centerpieces while Genevieve continued floating around the room, oohing and aahing each time she found something delightful. Her joy was likely contagious, but Avery's armor was thick. She could, however, appreciate seeing someone so fully happy, especially considering Genevieve had essentially blown up her life in order to embrace her own happiness.

Avery cleared her throat again, annoyed. She'd been on the brink of tears for days and refused to believe it was because she still hadn't heard from Shannon—now a full week of silence. It was the usual pattern: both were avoiding confrontation and raw, honest conversation. But the change was that Avery *wanted* to be honest. She wanted to say the things she'd been holding deep inside for years. She wanted to lay it all out there and then—

And then what? She certainly knew the answer, but she despised it. Hated that she still, after all the time and chaotic back-and-forth bullshit, wanted Shannon to choose her. To fight for her.

Beneath that, though, sat a new, tightly knotted feeling. Avery knew it was time to let go. She hated that, too—hated that she hated the truth of it—but louder than the whisper of self-hatred was the primal scream of finally wanting to fight for herself.

Genevieve's excited gasp echoed through the room. Avery blinked and looked up to find her raising her arms as she stood beneath one of the hanging arrangements. She looked like a Greek goddess in a long, flowing white dress with her blond hair braided back into an ornate style. The wisteria-laced greenery swung gently above her, just brushing the tips of her extended fingers. She was a painting waiting to happen.

"These are perfect!"

Avery took a step back as Genevieve rushed over to her at full, newly gay speed. She was literally glowing and Avery wasn't sure if it was from delight or really excellent self-tanner.

"I can't thank you enough," she said, her voice excited and warm. "This is exactly what I was hoping for. I just hope everyone loves it as much as I do."

There it was, the tiny glimmer of anxiety she'd been expecting. Genevieve's coming out was a big deal, after all, and her parents weren't planning on attending this soiree. Genevieve had dropped that into conversation a few days ago. She'd changed the subject immediately, but Avery knew sadness when she heard it.

"They will," Avery said. She knew she wasn't the best at reassuring people, especially in situations like this. It was one of many reasons she preferred to remain in the background of her job. "The people who will be here love you and want you to be happy. All this decor bullshit is just an aesthetic bonus." She spread her arms out. "Like a party for the eyes."

Genevieve hiccupped out a laugh as she pressed the heels of her hands against her cheekbones, seeming to try to push them into her eyes. Avery must have looked alarmed because she quickly explained, "Trying not to cry," before releasing her cheekbones and fanning her hands in front of her eyes. "A party for the eyes. I love it."

Avery nodded and shuffled back and forth. Her work here was done, but finding a way to—

"You'll stay," Genevieve announced, cutting off her mental exit plan. "You have to."

"Oh, no, I—" Avery looked down at her outfit. While she'd "classed up," as Zuri said, and worn black Dickies cargo joggers and a dark green crewneck sweatshirt instead of her usual work overalls, she was definitely not dressed for this event.

"You're perfect." Genevieve grabbed her hands. "Stay! I insist."

Avery squirmed internally. There was a laundry list of reasons why staying wasn't the best idea, and her appearance, which clearly stated she'd been wrestling with flowers all day, was at the top. She wasn't sure what her hair looked like but knew it was approximately thirty-seven steps below Genevieve's fancy braid.

"No, I real—"

"Oh, I'm doing it again!" Genevieve laughed and dropped her hands. "I wasn't flirting with you, I swear!"

"I didn't think you were," Avery got out before Genevieve went on.

"I'm still learning how to lesbian. It's so complicated! How are you supposed to know when a woman is flirting with you? I mean, women are just so *nice* and they compliment you, but that doesn't mean they want to sleep with you!" Genevieve laughed through a big exhale. "I think I need a lesbian mentor." She narrowed her eyes at Avery.

Veronica cut in, obviously trying not to burst out laughing. "Trust me, G. This is not the one you want to mentor you."

"Hey!" Avery protested.

But Genevieve had gotten distracted by voices at the doorway. She squealed and was off, hurrying to the entrance to begin greeting the first arrivals to her joyous coming-out party.

About an hour later, Avery was huddled in the corner near the bar, nursing a beer, trying to be invisible. There was a large fake palm of some sort in front of her, and it seemed to be doing its work in cloaking her since no one had approached.

The room wasn't full by any means, and Avery knew a good portion of the planned wedding guests had been replaced by friends and gay friends-of-friends, but there was still a nice crowd. She hoped it was enough to convince Genevieve that she truly was loved and supported.

The lady of the hour was making her rounds. Her glow had increased somehow—was it an additional application of self-tanner? Avery would never know—and even from her slightly hidden position away from the hubbub, Avery could feel the buzz of excitement in the room. It was a happy celebration, and while there were hordes (an exaggeration, but it felt that way to Avery) of lesbians frolicking about, she felt little more than a sense of dread.

It wasn't that she didn't find anyone attractive. She did, actually, and had watched two women to see if they appeared to be paired up with anyone (one for sure was, the other was still a mystery). It was the perfect environment to seek out someone new, even just for conversation and maybe a little flirting. She could test the waters easily, and with little risk. She could, in fact, *try to move on.*

But Avery stayed in the corner, buoyed only by the one woman who was both cute and seemingly unattached. She wouldn't approach her. She wasn't sure she even wanted to. But it was nice to think about, at least. Nice to imagine she could... if she wanted to.

A laugh rang out from several feet away. Avery angled her head, curious. There was something about the laugh that sounded familiar, but the laugh paired with the environment seemed highly unlikely.

"What?" Avery whispered as her eyes settled on Nicole, who was leaning against the bar. "Why are you here?"

She wracked her brain as she backed out of sight, searching for a connection that made sense. She and Nicole were both quite a bit older than Genevieve. That, and Nicole didn't seem particularly connected to the queer community in Balsam Lake. It was something that both intrigued and bothered Avery; she had gone over their initial conversation many times, trying to match the little she knew about Nicole to how they'd never crossed paths before that night at Looper's. Well, besides their virtual path-crossing on the stupid dating app. Aside from that, Avery had met Nicole's friend—and been further thrown by the fact that, aside from seeing Brynn at the dog park a few times, she didn't *know* her. It was all throwing potholes into the congested highway of Avery's theory that every lesbian in Balsam Lake was connected in some way, and that annoyed her.

"Who are you hiding from?"

She jumped even though Nicole had whispered. And there she was, standing next to Avery.

"You're annoyingly good at sneaking up on me," she said without thinking, trying to slow her pulse.

"I think it's more like, you're not great at paying attention to your surroundings." Nicole paired the barb with a toothy smile.

"That's fair," Avery mumbled. She brushed her free hand over her sweatshirt, still self-conscious about her outfit.

"So?" Nicole prompted.

"What?"

She nodded once toward the crowd. "Who are you hiding from?"

Myself, she thought. "No one. I, um, wasn't planning on staying. Hence my outfit."

Nicole appraised her with a sweeping glance that Avery had to admit she enjoyed. "I like your outfit. It suits you."

Heat warmed her cheeks. The compliment was gentle and low-stakes. It snuck its way past Avery's dented armor and nestled somewhere south of her heart. "Thanks," she managed.

"Oh," Nicole said, recognition dawning on her face. "You did the flowers?"

Avery nodded and watched as Nicole turned to fully take in the room. When she looked back at Avery, her bright blue eyes were sparkling.

"They're incredible. They feel like they fit the vibe of this party. You're really good at what you do." She closed her eyes briefly and shook her head. "Sorry if that sounded weird."

"Not at all," Avery hurried to say. "Thank you. I love what I do so it means a lot when other people love what I do, too."

Nicole watched her for a moment, then said, "You're sure you're not hiding from someone?"

Avery laughed. "No. I just feel super out of place."

"I get that," Nicole said quietly. She looked like she wanted to say more, but she turned her gaze back to the party.

Avery swallowed. There was something about Nicole that she couldn't put her finger on. She was beautiful, of course. Her black hair was partially pulled back, highlighting the soft angles of her face. Unlike Avery, Nicole was dressed for the occasion, in sleek black pants and a black button-down shirt that must have been a women's cut because it expertly fit her curves. Avery smiled, wondering if Nicole owned anything that wasn't black, but also hoping she didn't, because she happened to look amazing in the color.

Beyond Nicole's physical beauty, there was something about how Avery felt when she was nearby… She didn't want to think about that too much. And yet she'd sent her that weird goodbye message on the dating app, kind of expecting a reply before she deleted her account. Maybe *wanting* a reply. Or a text, since Nicole had her number. But a few days had passed and there had been nothing. Now that Nicole was standing next to her, Avery had all the chances in the world to just *say* something to her—and she was choking on everything she believed was better left unsaid.

"I should get back to—" Nicole cut herself off.

Just as Avery was pushing past her fears, reality slid back into place. Nicole wasn't there alone. Of course she wasn't, and that explained why she was there to begin with. She must have been there with—*with?*—someone. Sure she was, Avery thought. Look at her! She's gorgeous and she has a complex but interesting personality—*shut up*, Avery commanded herself.

"Okay," she said quickly. "Have fun."

Nicole bit the inside of her lip. "I don't think it's a date," she blurted, then immediately flushed a deep pink that only enhanced her beauty.

Avery heard her, she really did, but the well-oiled wheels of her distrusting brain were already spinning into action. "It's cool."

"Avery, I—"

"It's cool," Avery repeated. As the words left her mouth, a tall, blond woman who looked like the older, slightly more cultured version of Genevieve approached them.

"This looks like a serious meeting," she said, smiling easily as she looked between Nicole and Avery.

Nicole's blush deepened. "Oh, we were just—"

"I'm Avery," she said, extending her hand.

"Colleen," the other woman said, shaking Avery's hand. "Nicole was telling me how you two ran into each other at the funeral home. We"—she gestured toward Nicole—"also met through death." She laughed.

Avery glanced at Nicole, who looked like she'd rather be embracing death in that moment than be a part of this odd and awkward conversation. She tried like hell to dissolve the tug of empathy.

Colleen must have sensed the strangeness, because instead of trying to create more conversation, she touched Nicole's shoulder lightly and said, "I'm going to find our table. It was nice meeting you, Avery."

She vanished as easily as she'd arrived, leaving them in their strange, strangled bubble of confusion. *Not a date, my ass*, Avery thought angrily. Yet she couldn't help but notice the way Nicole hadn't taken her eyes off Avery the entire time Colleen had been with them.

"Do you think we—"

Avery didn't need to hear any more. She twisted the beer bottle in her hands before stepping around Nicole. "I'm actually going to head out soon. I hope you have a good time."

Before she could hear any protests, not that she believed there would be any, Avery hightailed it out of the room, only pausing to say goodbye to Genevieve.

CHAPTER FIFTEEN

Restless, Nicole kicked at the covers of her bed. She'd made the critical error of not getting up when she'd woken with a start at six thirty. That was too early for a Sunday, so she'd lazed in bed...before accidentally falling back asleep. She knew it was a bad idea; that weird window of sleep was when she had her worst nightmares, most of them paired with false awakenings that kept looping her back into the nightmares.

This morning's had featured a buried memory of a disagreement she'd had with Ginny just months after they'd started dating. It was the kind of argument that was laughable later, but in the moment had felt like the end of the world—or at least the end of their dating relationship. The nightmare had skewed the truth of the disagreement, and thanks to the false awakenings, Nicole's subconscious had made her reenact it four times before she managed to shake herself awake.

She'd expected that hours had passed, and when the clock announced it was only seven fifteen, Nicole laughed harshly before pulling her pillow over her face. She wouldn't let herself fall back asleep, but like hell was she going to get up.

By seven thirty, restlessness was driving her crazy, and she tossed her down comforter to the floor. It didn't deserve that treatment, but she had to project her anger somewhere.

She glanced out the windows as she padded toward the kitchen. The sun was out, full and bright. She poured herself a large glass of water and drank it while standing in the kitchen, staring across the open space and out the windows. She had to get outside today, no matter how deceiving the sun was in relation to the real-feel temperature.

After checking the weather on her phone, she dressed for the chilly morning. She didn't even mind the cold; her lungs needed that cleansing rush of chilled air.

She steered herself in the direction of the lake. It was a little under two miles from her apartment, a solid round trip for a morning walk. Part of the reason Nicole had chosen her apartment was that proximity. She liked being able to both walk to the lake and have a super quick drive when she wanted to kayak.

Downtown was deserted, unsurprising for this early on a Sunday morning. The streets would begin to populate later as brunch began. If the sun stayed out and the temperature actually hit fifty degrees as predicted, there'd be some brave outdoor drinkers in the afternoon. But for now, the streets were hers, and hers alone.

As she walked, she replayed the repeated nightmares. She and Ginny hadn't fought a lot over the span of their relationship, but their arguments were always difficult for Nicole because the two women processed their feelings in entirely different ways. Nicole was a talker, and Ginny was an avoider. Before they moved in together, if there was an unresolved conflict or a drop in communication, Nicole would spend days thinking Ginny was totally over her and didn't want anything to do with her, only for Ginny to pop back up like nothing had happened. It had improved only slightly when they lived together. Ginny, it turned out, could put incredible distance between them even when they were sleeping in the same bed every night.

Nicole shivered, but not from the cold. It still amazed her, nearly three years after Ginny's death, how her perspective of her relationship, of her marriage and her wife, continued to shift. Identifying the negatives were impossible for that first year post-death; everything had been viewed through rose-colored glasses. And then, like a sudden wind shaking crisp leaves off weathered trees, the less-than-grand elements of their time together strode onto the memory scene. That was an interesting part of grief, one Nicole hadn't been expecting. She also didn't like it. It felt like she was casting years of her life in an ugly glow. She didn't want to remember the bad. It felt wrong, disrespectful. But finding a balance that honored the good *and* the bad was a challenge she faced nearly every day.

She always had the choice between painting Ginny in a savior light or casting her as the villain. The truth rested somewhere in between the two extremes, but Nicole sometimes found herself avoiding the reality of who Ginny was and what their relationship had been like. Her death had left Nicole grieving not only what they'd had, but also what they could have had. In a dark twist, she sometimes wondered if Ginny would be alive if they'd never met.

Nicole shook that thought off. She'd caught a ride on that hurtful train more times than she'd like to admit, and Brynn had told her repeatedly that her role in Ginny's life had nothing to do with Ginny's fate. It was a hard, jagged pill to swallow, and more times than not, Nicole rolled it around in her mouth, wishing it would dissolve and she could forget about it for good.

As she walked, the image of Avery sitting in front of her at Looper's popped into Nicole's mind. Shame lined her throat—a silent judgment. Still, nearly three years later, she hesitated to disclose that she was a widow. Maybe if Ginny's death had been later in their relationship, later in her life, Nicole wouldn't struggle so much with the admission. But, she reminded herself, being a widow under the age of forty-five was a strange, lonely club. Nothing about it was easy, and sometimes, admitting her membership in the club was the hardest part.

As the lake came into view, Nicole felt her muscles loosen. She hadn't realized just how badly she needed to see the sun shimmering over the surface of the lake. Despite her love of books and the indoors as a child, there had always been something curing about being in nature. Nicole had often gone on long walks with her dad. Sometimes they talked about random things, sometimes they solved the world's problems, and other times they were silent. She missed those walks, and wondered if maybe her dad could come visit next month after all.

The macadam path that encircled the lake was dotted with a few human forms in various states of exercise: an older couple walked, a group of four young women ran, and Nicole could just see the wheels of a bike in the distance. She was sure there were others elsewhere on the three-mile loop.

Suddenly tired—more mentally than physically—she walked to a bench near the water and sat down, pulling her knees to her chest and hugging her legs as she looked out over the gently lapping waves of the lake.

She didn't want to erase the last ten—nearly eleven, she realized with a groan—years of her life. And she knew a part of her would always hold on to that grief, even if it was tucked deep into a corner of her heart where the light didn't reach. Every experience she'd had with Ginny from the moment they'd met at a Cowboy Junkies concert in Philadelphia when they were both thirty-one years old had brought Nicole to where she was right now. The good and the bad. The amazing and the confusing. The incredible and the traumatic. It was all a part of her, no matter when she moved on, no matter who she someday loved.

Nicole dropped her head back to rest on the back of the bench. Love. It was still a crazy concept to her, dangling so far out of reach that she could barely see it. Optimism had never been her forte, but she reserved a small space inside herself for hope. For maybes. For cautious what-ifs.

On cue, Avery surfaced in her mind yet again. Nicole smiled, remembering how cute she'd looked at Genevieve's party, even if discomfort had been radiating off her. Nicole wished she'd asked Avery to sit with her and Colleen because when she went looking for her not ten minutes after they'd parted ways, Avery had disappeared. The disappointment had been palpable, even if she'd had an overall pretty good time with Colleen. Avery hadn't left her mind all night. She wondered where she'd run off to, whom she'd been avoiding (Avery hadn't convinced her otherwise), and how it would have been if they had gone to the party together.

That was the thought that had kept Nicole awake once she'd gotten home. It was a silly thought. Inconsequential and irrelevant.

"Yeah, keep telling yourself that," Nicole said quietly. She released her legs and kicked them out in front of her, then swung them back and forth a few times.

While Avery wasn't surrounded by red flags, her flags weren't exactly green, either. There was something impenetrable about Avery—something Nicole imagined she may not want to know the truth of. But there was a crack in Avery's armor. Every time their eyes met, the crack widened. And while Nicole had absolutely no desire to come at Avery's walls with a sledgehammer and a garbage bag, she also couldn't quite give up on her, even if Avery's confused interactions seemed to say she just wanted to be friends.

Fine, Nicole thought. *I can do friends.*

It was then that she remembered the awkward moment the previous night when she'd opened her big mouth without a plan for explaining who Colleen was. It was like Avery had shut down the moment Nicole tried to explain she wasn't on a date, which, okay, Nicole didn't even need to explain that. She had nothing to explain to Avery, because *they* certainly weren't dating.

Annoyed and frustrated, she stood up and dusted off her leggings. This was one of the many reasons why she'd repeatedly told herself—and Brynn—that she had no desire to date. It was all so confusing, so gray. She needed a damn manual to explain the ins and outs.

"And you're not even dating her," she said aloud as she began the walk home.

On a whim, and, if she were being honest, curiosity, Nicole paused outside of The Twisted Tulip. She was a little sweaty despite the continued chill in the air; her irritation had propelled her faster than she'd intended. But that didn't matter. Even *if* Avery was working first thing on a Sunday morning, there clearly was nothing going on between them, so Nicole's sweat wasn't a factor that needed to be considered before she pushed open the door and stepped inside the warm shop.

And, okay, wow, it was really warm in there. Nicole wiped her forehead, then her mouth. She pulled her sweatshirt away from her body and yanked it back and forth a few times, trying to air herself out. She wrinkled her nose. Was that smell coming from her? Oh, God. It was. She hugged her sweatshirt to her torso, hoping she hadn't stunk up the room.

Just as she was making her way to the display case, a shuffling of feet made her look up toward the back of the room. A Black woman with broad shoulders and long, impeccable braids came through a doorway. She smiled easily.

"Morning. Anything I can help you with?"

Nicole nodded. "I'd like to make a bouquet."

"Cool." The woman nodded toward the display case. "It's freshly stocked. Feel free to grab whatever you want."

Nicole's eyes wandered over the bursts of colorful flowers in the case. She had to hand it to Avery—The Twisted Tulip had an impressive selection. And everything looked impossibly fresh.

The bell over the door rang, and Nicole lost herself in the flowers, glad the woman had been distracted by the new customer. She had zero bouquet-making experience, but she wanted to put something together that felt right to her. Having another person's input didn't feel right. Not today, anyway.

Nicole sadly eyed an empty black bucket. That was the same spot she'd found the most perfect pale-pink peonies weeks ago. The edges of the petals had been slightly darker, something that had surprised her as the flowers continued to bloom. She'd loved them and was terribly sad when they started to droop.

A noise prodded her out of her flower reverie, causing her to turn around. There stood Avery, barefoot and in overalls. Nicole smiled immediately, recognizing the sound as bare feet slapping against the concrete floor. Somehow, the impracticality of being barefoot in a flower store fit seamlessly with what Nicole knew of her personality.

Avery, though she was staring at Nicole, hadn't said anything. Her greenish-brown eyes blinked several times. She had a strange look on her face, one Nicole couldn't decipher. But what Nicole could recognize was what Avery was holding in her hands.

"Oh," Nicole breathed, stepping closer but keeping enough distance so she wouldn't scare Avery off, back to wherever she'd come from. "That's exactly what I was looking for."

"These?" Avery said, her voice a little hoarse. She cleared her throat. "You were looking for these?"

"Yup." Nicole stepped aside, giving her a clear path to the empty black bucket in the display case.

"You like pink peonies?" Avery asked as she gently placed the bunch of flowers in the bucket.

"They're my favorite. But only when they're a really, really light pink." Nicole stood next to her, still keeping a respectable distance. She studied the new arrivals before selecting four.

"They're my favorite too," Avery said. She didn't meet Nicole's eyes, but at least she wasn't scurrying away. "I probably shouldn't have a favorite. That's kind of like having a favorite child in my position."

Nicole laughed. "I won't tell."

"That's kind of you." Avery took a step back from the case. "I should get back to work."

Nicole nodded, trying to think of something to say that would keep Avery right where she was. Before she could find the words, the other florist spoke up.Nicole nodded, trying to think of something to say that would keep Avery right where she was. Before she could find the words, the other florist spoke up.

"Can you grab a vase for her?"

Avery spun to glare at her coworker. "What?"

"A vase," the woman repeated.

Avery huffed and pointed to the wall behind the desk. "What kind of vase do you want?" she muttered, not looking at Nicole.

"Oh. Um, I don't want one." She looked between the two women. "Can I just have this wrapped in paper?"

"Of course. Zuri would be happy to do that for you."

Zuri, she of the luxurious braids, grinned at Avery. "Actually, Avery is much better at wrapping." With that, she walked away and disappeared into another area of the store.

Nicole debated leaving, but she really wanted the damn flowers. When Avery turned to her, eyes focused on the wall behind her but with one arm extended, Nicole placed the flowers in her hand. Avery turned away as soon as the stems made contact with her palm.

"I could probably wrap them myself," Nicole said.

Avery, now behind the counter, looked up. She looked like she wanted to laugh but couldn't quite get it out. "Do you have flower wrapping experience?"

"Not one bit. How hard can it be?"

She smiled. "Honestly? Not hard at all."

Nicole relaxed a bit. At least Avery's enormous wall had lowered enough for her to not be a defensive asshole.

"I am curious as to why you don't want a vase," Avery continued as she carefully wrapped brown paper around the flowers Nicole had selected.

The image of the living room cabinet that housed probably ten vases slipped into Nicole's mind, but it popped like a soapy bubble when she realized what Avery had just said. "What did you say?"

Avery looked up. "I said, I don't know why you don't want a vase."

A laugh burst from Nicole. "You're not serious."

"It's a perfectly rational question."

"No, not that." Nicole kept laughing, barely managing to get words out. "You said *vaz*."

Avery rolled her eyes. "And?"

"It's pronounced *vase*."

"So say you." Avery slid the paper-wrapped bouquet over. "We cultured folk prefer the French pronunciation."

"But," Nicole sputtered, "that's not even how it's pronounced in French."

Avery stared at her for a beat, then cracked a grin. "So you're telling me all this time I thought I sounded fancy, but I really just sounded like an idiot?"

Nicole shrugged. "Kind of?"

"Well," Avery said, putting one hand on her hip. "I can't say I'm going to stop saying *vaz* but I'll do my best not to say it around you."

Biting the inside of her cheek, Nicole replayed the words. She heard the implication, but coming from Avery and her dictionary of mixed signals, didn't want to put too much stock into it. And yet...

"Can you take a break? For coffee?" Nicole blew out a breath. "I mean, do you want to have coffee? With me? Now, maybe? If you can."

Avery watched her carefully, then raised her arm and pointed to a spot behind Nicole. As she turned, Nicole couldn't help but laugh.

CHAPTER SIXTEEN

Embarrassment seized Avery at the sound of Nicole's laughter. She wanted to disappear into the concrete floors. A beautiful, intriguing (yeah, she could admit it now) woman had just asked her to take a break and get coffee with her, and what had Avery done?

Pointed, like a moron, at the beverage station in her own damn flower shop.

Nicole's voice jolted her out of her overlapping emotions. "I love it. What all can we make?"

She sounded genuine, which allowed Avery's fierce self-protection to soften. Just a little. She wiped her hands on her overalls before joining Nicole at the beverage bar.

"Pretty much anything. We have every milk you can imagine, too." Avery leaned forward, trying her best not to get too close to Nicole, who was radiating warmth and an earthy scent Avery liked very much. "Syrups, too."

"What's your favorite?"

Avery shifted back, trying to keep a modicum of distance between them. She hadn't expected to see Nicole first thing this morning. She certainly wasn't upset about it, but after their little run-in yesterday and the thoughts that stalked her all night, she was more unsteady than ever around this woman she barely knew.

And couldn't stop thinking about.

It wouldn't be a big deal, of course, if Avery hadn't spent the last seven years thinking about only one woman, and now that Nicole had slid her way into Avery's brain, she was taking over all these spaces that Avery was absolutely certain could never be inhabited by anyone but—

"Avery?"

She pinched her thigh through her pocket. *Get it together, asshole.* "I'm pretty simple. I usually make a vanilla latte with almond milk."

Nicole was studying her, but Avery kept her gaze locked on the espresso machine.

"I actually don't drink coffee," Nicole said, and it was then that Avery could have slapped herself for not being courteous, for not *making basic fucking conversation*, and asking Nicole what her usual drink order was. "I'm more of a tea girl."

"We have tea." Avery squatted down and opened the cabinet where they kept the tea and extra mugs. "Pick your poison."

"Earl Grey, if you have it. Two bags."

Avery popped back up with two Earl Grey tea bags dangling from her fingertips. Nicole held out her hand and Avery dropped them into her palm.

"Tazo," Nicole said, nodding appreciatively. "That's my favorite."

"So do you just drink straight tea?" Avery asked as she opened the container of ground espresso and scooped some into the portafilter. She twisted it into place and set a mug beneath it, then hit the switch.

"Sometimes. Have you ever heard of a London Fog?"

"Can't say that I have."

"It sounds fancier than it is." Nicole leaned against the counter. Avery did her best to avoid ogling her, because she really looked ridiculously cute in her winter workout outfit.

The woman could rock a beanie like it was no other lesbian's business, that was for sure. "It's just Earl Grey tea and a milk of your choice, plus some vanilla syrup. Some people add lavender, but I'm strictly a fan of smelling lavender, not ingesting it."

"And what's your milk of choice?" Avery moved to the mini fridge and opened it, gesturing to the array of choices.

"Wow, you really aim to please here." It looked like Nicole was blushing, but it was overly warm in the shop so maybe she was just flushed in general. "Soy, please."

"Do I need to heat it?"

"Actually, no." Nicole watched as Avery grabbed a mug and filled it with steaming hot water from the espresso machine. That water could burn hell, it was so hot, and Avery carefully set the mug down for Nicole to drop in the tea bags. "The milk helps cool the tea."

Avery poured almond milk into a small metal pitcher and placed it under the steam wand. Frothing milk was an instant conversation killer, and she took a moment to regroup. It wasn't a big deal that Nicole was here. She clearly liked flowers, and The Twisted Tulip had excellent flowers. And she liked tea drinks. Avery snuck a look over, watching as Nicole carefully squirted three shots of vanilla syrup into her oversized mug.

It was possible, too, that Nicole liked something about Avery, but she couldn't imagine what in the entire fuck that could be, so with a deep breath, she resolved to simply enjoy having a morning caffeine boost with a very pretty woman who happened to like flowers.

"You're a professional, huh?"

Avery smiled as she wiped down the steam wand. "I was a barista for a couple years in college. If nothing else, I know how to make espresso drinks, and how to keep the machine clean."

"And yet you'd never heard of a London Fog." Nicole shook her head, exaggerating her disappointment. "Shameful."

"My deepest apologies." Avery stirred her drink one last time before tossing the wooden stir stick into the trash. "Wanna sit?"

Nicole met her eyes, and Avery was once again mesmerized by how blue they were. She'd never considered herself someone who paid much attention to people's eyes, but Nicole's were unavoidable. They practically glowed with blueness, if that was even a thing.

"I'd like that."

Avery led them over to the armchairs and waited for Nicole to choose one before sitting down across from her. They sat quietly, sipping their drinks and avoiding eye contact. Distantly, Avery recognized the sounds of Zuri working in the back room.

"You know," Nicole said, setting her mug down on a side table. "I looked for you last night, but you'd disappeared."

Avery ran a hand over her forehead. She flashed back to her conversation with Zuri, who had so kindly forced her to face the truth of projecting all her bullshit onto Nicole. She didn't want to do it again, so she thought carefully before she spoke.

"I never intended to stay," she began. "So I finished my drink, thanked Genevieve, and left."

Nicole watched her, seeming to know there was more.

"You looked for me?" Avery asked before raising her mug to her lips.

"Yeah, I did."

She tried not to smile. "Why?"

Nicole shrugged. "I thought it would be fun to hang out."

There was more, Avery was sure of it, but she let it go. Sort of. "But you…were with someone."

Nicole shook her head immediately. "See, I knew you'd assume that."

"How is that an assumption? She literally came over while we were talking."

"And did I introduce her as, like, my *date*?" Nicole raised her eyebrows.

Avery shook her head, not trusting her mouth.

"Okay then. Because she wasn't." Nicole sat back in the chair, seeming proud of her point. But Avery wasn't convinced.

She waited a beat before pressing, but gently. "So she was just a friend? That you went to a coming-out party with?"

Nicole narrowed her eyes. "Why are you so curious about who I may or may not be dating? And why do you seem to think I'm dating the entire town?"

Fair questions. Avery had a wicked jealous streak, and she had no right whatsoever to be privy to Nicole's dating life, but she could not shake the veil of her past that hung stubbornly over this...situation. She didn't think Nicole was lying to her, but she continued to believe there was something Nicole was purposely hiding. Perhaps if Avery ventured out on her own honest limb, she might get something back in return.

She swallowed, hard. The discomfort radiating through her entire body was palpable and she contemplated running to the bathroom to vomit, but she hated throwing up, so maybe she could just scream at her reflection in the mirror until all her lingering internal demons gave up their fight.

"I, uh, have a hard time trusting people." Avery nodded once. "And that's kind of the tip of the iceberg."

Nicole's eyes were focused on her. She didn't move when she said, "I'm listening."

Avery leaned forward, resting her elbows on her knees. "Because of past experiences, I have this thing where I have a hard time believing that people are being honest with me. Like they're always hiding something, intentionally or not. But mostly intentionally."

She avoided Nicole's eyes as she continued, "That first night we met, I wasn't fair to you. I know I was pushing you about your past and kinda, I don't know, went on a weird tangent that was totally about my own shit." She pushed her thumbs into her cheeks. "For what it's worth, I felt terrible about it. *Feel*," she quickly amended. "I feel terrible about it. Still."

"Well, you should." Nicole's voice was firm but not angry. "You were an asshole."

Avery nodded. "I'm sorry. I was. And you didn't deserve it. Just like you don't deserve me being weirdly jealous and trying to figure out who all these women are in your life." She shook her head, eyes focused on the floor. "I know it's none of my business."

After a moment, Nicole said quietly, "I'm sorry that someone treated you in a way that has made you doubt others."

Avery squeaked out a noise that was almost a laugh. "You have no idea."

"You don't have to tell me," Nicole said. "But if you ever want to, I promise I'll listen and I won't judge you."

Avery finally looked up. Nicole's expression was full of compassion. It was almost overwhelming, but the newly understanding energy between them steadied her. Still, she couldn't help herself.

"So, Colleen…"

Nicole laughed. "Okay, Avery. Listen. Colleen's dad died, and I met her because her mom hired me to help with the eulogies." She must have noticed Avery's confused expression, because she nodded. "I'll explain that later. Anyway, I ran into her at another funeral—actually, the one where I saw you—and she asked me to go to Genevieve's party with her." Nicole shrugged. "I didn't know if it was a date or not, but once we were at the party, it became quite clear to me that Colleen is into Genevieve, and I was just there as a fun person to hang out with. Or maybe a wing woman, though I'd be a terrible wing woman."

Avery wrinkled her nose. "Don't you think they kind of look alike?"

"Oh, totally. Had you stayed last night, you could have witnessed the very awkward flirting that turned into a hardcore make-out session." Nicole grinned. "Blond hair everywhere."

"Can't say I'm sorry I missed that." Avery ran a finger over the edge of her mug. "You didn't have to explain, by the way. Not for my sake, I mean."

"I know. But I have no problem explaining something if it clears things up. Or makes you feel better."

A funny feeling stirred in Avery's gut. She put her mug down and sat back in the chair. "So you're not dating anyone?"

When Nicole didn't answer right away, Avery looked up to find her biting her bottom lip. A strand of black hair had escaped the loose bun at the base of her neck and was grazing her rounded cheek, just barely touching the corner of her lips. A wave of pure attraction whooshed its way through Avery's body. The longer Nicole stayed silent, however, the more it dissolved.

Just as Avery opened her mouth, Nicole held her hand up. "Avery. Wait." She took a deep breath and leaned her head against the back of the chair as she exhaled. "I should have told you this when we first met, but to be honest, I've never had to do it before. Not like this, anyway. And I didn't know how." She raised her head and met Avery's eyes. "It's a timing thing, I guess? I don't know when I'm supposed to say it."

"Just say it," Avery said. The wave had churned into a new sensation, one she was eager to get rid of.

"I'm not dating anyone. I haven't dated anyone in a really long time." Nicole clasped and unclasped her hands. "I was married," she continued. "And now I'm a widow."

Of all the things Avery had been prepared to hear, that one hadn't made the list. She clenched her jaw, her insides churning with proper embarrassment. God, she'd been such an asshole that first night. She hadn't even considered that Nicole could be carrying something so heavy. She'd just jumped right to projecting her own ideas of the worst—when this was the *actual* worst, but for Nicole.

"I was such a dick to you," Avery said. "I am so sorry."

Nicole nodded. "I can't argue that. But also, you didn't know."

"No," Avery said, shaking her head. "I didn't know, but that's not an excuse. I just—fuck, I threw all my shit at you, and you were probably sitting there thinking, 'This bitch has no idea.'"

"Kind of." Nicole smiled.

A thought struck and Avery felt the color drain from her face. "Was I your first date? After, I mean?" At Nicole's nod, Avery groaned. "Why are you even talking to me?"

"Because," Nicole said.

Avery eyed her. "Because why?"

She shrugged. "I'm not sure of that yet. So, just because."

That, at least, was something Avery understood. She looked at Nicole, who gazed back as she sipped from her mug. It wasn't often that Avery was at a loss for words, but in this case, she didn't feel the need to speak just to fill space. While she would continue beating herself up for being so inconsiderate, she felt some level of peace now that the air had begun to clear between them. She winced. One side of the air, anyway.

But while Shannon and that long experience had certainly shaped parts of Avery that she was dying to reform, she didn't want to spoil...whatever this was by unloading her years of mixed signals onto Nicole. Shannon had no place here. Avery wasn't sure that *she* had a place here either, but she was slowly coming to accept that her path was going to continue to cross Nicole's until one of them stuck a sturdy fork in the road.

Someday, she thought. Someday she'd open that box—not all the way, just enough to establish that she hadn't been dating either but she also hadn't been completely single for the past seven years.

"I should let you get back to work." Nicole was already standing, smoothing her hands over her sweatshirt.

Avery didn't want her to leave, but she couldn't think of a valid reason to ask her to stay. "Right. I have a job to do."

Nicole laughed as she handed Avery her empty mug. "Does it get busy on Sundays?"

"Actually, it does. We're only open until four, but we get a decent number of customers in the early afternoon."

"That makes sense. Main Street really comes alive after eleven or so." At Avery's inquisitive look, Nicole continued, "Oh, I live here. In the lofts up the street."

"The ones with the massive windows?"

"Yup. Perfect for people-watching."

Avery nodded appreciatively. They were beautiful lofts, mostly because the developers had retained as much of the original building as possible. "Then you should come in for flowers more often." She jerked her head up. "Because you live so close."

"Maybe I will." Nicole's expression had softened into something sweet and open.

Avery took a few steps back, holding the mugs close to her chest.

"Avery," Nicole said, following the word with a genuine laugh. "You don't have to be afraid of me."

"I'm not," she retorted. It was a blatant lie, but one Avery couldn't dive into at the present moment. She took two steps forward, keeping a professional distance between them. "But I should get back to work."

Nicole nodded. Then, seeming to flip a moment of hesitation into a spark of inspired desire, she closed the distance between them. With her hands firm on Avery's upper arms, she leaned in and kissed Avery's cheek.

"Thank you," she whispered.

Before Avery could react, Nicole was gone, only wisps of her earthy scent remaining as proof she'd ever been there. Avery was rooted to the spot, feeling the gentle press of Nicole's lips on her cheek over and over again.

After several minutes with nothing but the acoustic chill music to keep her company, Zuri's voice interrupted her trance. "So, that's the girl."

Avery could only nod.

"She's cute."

Another nod.

"You good?"

At that, Avery snapped out of it and brushed past Zuri on the way to the workroom. "No," she said. "I have no idea what I am."

CHAPTER SEVENTEEN

Nicole slid her finger over the silver picture frame on her desk. She wasn't sure why she kept that particular photograph there, right where she had to see it every time she sat down to use her computer. It wasn't even the best of the wedding photos; it was a little blurry and didn't capture the beauty of her or Ginny.

But it was perfect. Or, if not perfect, it was symbolic. It held a truth that Nicole had never allowed herself to see when Ginny was alive. And once she was gone, the truth of this photo was all Nicole could see, all she could understand.

The picture was black and white, a favorite style of both women. Their backs were to the camera and they were walking away. Their hands were linked just by their pinkies and ring fingers, and it looked as though they were pulling apart. Ginny's profile showed her wide, laughing smile as she locked her eyes on Nicole. But Nicole wasn't looking back at her wife. She was staring straight ahead, determination evident in her stride. It was impossible to tell if she was smiling (she was pretty certain she had been; her cheeks had ached the next day from smiling so much), impossible to even imagine what expression her face held.

They had loved each other, that much Nicole knew for sure. And the bigger truth, the one Brynn had confirmed, was that Ginny had loved Nicole far more than she had loved herself. It wasn't wrong, and it wasn't shameful. It didn't take away from all that they had shared, and it didn't diminish the love Nicole had—*still* had—for Ginny. All that love was the truest thing about their relationship.

It was also proving to be the hardest thing to let go. Nicole traced her finger over the image of their bodies. She'd come a long way in her grieving process, finding ways to move through feelings rather than sit and drown in them. There were piles of feelings she'd let go of, more she imagined she would wade through even at her happiest moments. And she would always miss Ginny—the truth of her, and the hopes of her.

But none of that had to hold her in this space of grief, of loss, of loneliness. Of missing out.

Maybe missing out, that is. She couldn't be sure she was missing out on anything, but—

Avery.

Nicole sighed and dropped her hand from the picture frame. She kept circling back to Avery, and for the life of her, she couldn't figure out why. There was some kind of quiet magnetic pull that dragged Avery into her mind every damn day. Simple thoughts: what was she doing? What flowers did she get delivered that day? What was her favorite book? Who the hell had hurt her so badly and how could Nicole locate the person and yell at them until she was blue in the face?

She'd known from the start that there was a darkness to Avery. And she could tell that Avery did her best to shield that from her, but Nicole was tired of the protection. More than that, she was tired of not knowing if she should even bother thinking about possibly pursuing Avery. In their limited conversations, Nicole was giving and sharing, but she saw she was alone in that. Avery, aside from the little she'd shared yesterday, was a closed book. Nicole saw it and respected it; not wanting to scare Avery off, she'd been proceeding with caution.

And after throwing all her carefully curated caution into the wind yesterday, Nicole was even further from knowing what to do. She didn't make moves like that—sudden, unplanned. Truth be told, she wasn't the "first move maker." Sure, it was only a chaste kiss on the cheek. It wasn't like she'd lunged at Avery and smothered her mouth with kisses. But Nicole tended to let the other person take the wheel when it came to that initial nerve-wracking physical connection. This position was new and slightly uncomfortable. Plus, seeing as she'd fled the scene of her well-intentioned crime immediately after making her move, she had no idea how Avery had reacted to it.

She eyed her phone then pushed it to the corner of her desk. Nicole hated when the ball was in her court, and considering that Avery had no way of contacting her... Ball, court, free throw on deck.

Nicole picked up her phone, opened the middle drawer of her desk, and tucked it in before closing the drawer tightly. She had work to do.

Two hours later, she rubbed her eyes and leaned back in her desk chair. She'd crammed a day's worth of work into a few hours and her body ached from being in the same position for too long.

Standing up, she reached high over her head and tilted to the right, feeling little pops in her spine, then to the left. She shook out her arms and walked out of her alcove office. Now that her "real" work was done, otherwise known as the work that paid the bills, she needed a break before plugging in to the "fun" work.

She stopped in her tracks. When, exactly, had she started referring to eulogy writing as "fun"? Nicole shook her head. Apparently, death had a strange way of reshaping a person's perspectives.

After a quick late lunch of ham rolled up in muenster cheese and a handful of black olives, Nicole returned to her desk. She glanced at the wedding photo and, after pressing her fingers to her lips, touched Ginny's profile. Then she gently laid the frame face down.

"Okay," she said aloud, cracking her knuckles before placing her fingers on the keyboard. "Time to learn about cats."

Having grown up without pets, Nicole was entirely indifferent toward animals. She acknowledged that they were cute and soft, but she didn't feel the need to have a furry companion. The elderly woman whose eulogy she was working on, however, had loved cats. Like, *really* loved cats.

Nicole shuffled through her notes. Yes, the family had talked at length about how much Arlene, the deceased, had loved cats. Unfortunately, her husband, Harold, had felt differently, and after their single orange cat died, he'd put the kibosh on adopting any more. Arlene's love of cats had been passed down to her daughters and her grandchildren, however, so she always had a cat or six in her life. Just not in her home, except for that one time her granddaughter had brought her new orange kitten over, and much to everyone's surprise, Harold had delighted in playing with the little wild creature. Apparently, he was quite happy to see it go back home, too.

After learning about the connection between cat owners and their beloved furry demons (in short: cat owners really wanted to believe their cats loved them, but cats were ninja assholes who conned them into thinking there was mutual love and adoration), Nicole set to work on a few drafts for eulogies. It was always a little odd, writing about someone she'd never known. A eulogy was supposed to come from the hearts of people who had known and loved the deceased, so to bring Nicole in to write did seem, well, weird.

She preferred to think of herself as a memory guide. As she knew all too well, death had a way of blocking memories for the survivors. It sometimes helped to have an outsider, someone who wasn't connected to the family, to guide them through stories and anecdotes that were buried beneath the immediate grief. By doing nothing but listening, Nicole was able to pull out snippets that would come together to form a well-rounded speech that honored the deceased.

When Ginny died, Nicole hadn't wanted to give a eulogy. The idea felt like fire running through her veins, pooling in her gut in a rolling inferno. But as she sat in her shock and grief in the days immediately following her wife's death, Nicole realized that she knew her in ways that no one else did. And for as angry and heartbroken as she was, Nicole still wanted to honor her. She wanted people to know who Ginny was to her—who she would always be to her.

That was the refrain she'd looped in her brain as she stood in front of a crowd of people and read Ginny's eulogy. She couldn't remember what she'd felt like, or how she'd sounded. She didn't know if she'd made mistakes while reading, or if she'd broken down in tears at any point. It was all a blank spot in her memory. Reading a eulogy for a deceased wife just wasn't something a thirty-nine-year-old woman should ever have to do, and it was as though her brain understood that and decided to black out the event.

But Nicole had done it, and even now, was glad she had. It had turned out to be a critical step in her grief journey.

Fully distracted from the cat-lover's eulogy, Nicole found herself Googling "loving someone after losing your spouse." She knew there wasn't a concrete timeline for things like that, and she was more worried about self-judgment than anyone else judging her; and honestly, she barely even *liked* Avery, but she was curious. The idea of loving someone again—like really, truly falling in love and cherishing that connection with someone else—still made her want to hide under her bed. But it no longer felt completely unattainable. Or impossible.

Nicole wrinkled her nose. One thing was certain: she would never again be in a relationship with someone who didn't love themselves. Nope, not happening. Next time, she wanted an equal. Someone who was confident and secure in their skin, who knew who they were and loved who they were, even on bad days.

Next, her fingers betrayed her by typing "how to figure out the right kind of partner for yourself," and she judged herself for the odd phrasing but couldn't figure out how else to write it. She snorted as she scrolled through the various links that promised ways to figure out "the perfect match." For so long, she'd believed Ginny was her perfect match. They had fallen so fast and so hard; their chemistry was the best she'd ever experienced. Within a month of dating, she couldn't imagine being with anyone else. Ginny was it. But even in the haze of feel-good moments and love-drunk hours, Nicole had felt the tremors of inconsistency. She compromised and gave in and rolled with the punches, even as the punches (theoretical, that is—Ginny had never laid an angry hand on her) grew bigger and more worrisome. She accepted that there were aspects of Ginny that she would never understand, particularly the effects of her time serving overseas in the Army. But Nicole believed her love would carry them both through to happiness.

She lingered her cursor over an article that claimed to be able to "break the patterns of dysfunctional attraction." Nicole narrowed her eyes as she looked at her screen. Dysfunctional attraction sounded terrible and sexy. She should definitely avoid that. She scrolled on, hoping to find the article or blog that would explain everything to her.

A few minutes later, she leaned back in her chair as the soft tendrils of a realization crept in. She didn't need the Internet to explain anything to her; she just didn't believe in happily ever after. No one could blame her for that, either. But that wasn't a good enough reason to hold herself back from life, or women. She could date whomever the hell she wanted to date. She wasn't tied down to anyone, or a certain type of someone. The world was open for her to dip her toes, ankles, whole-ass legs into if she so desired.

Nicole yanked open her desk drawer and pulled out her phone. After unlocking it, she reached up and stood the picture frame up.

"You can be here for this," she said to Ginny's image. "You're not holding me back anymore." She paused. "Actually, I'll check back with you on that in a couple weeks."

Before she lost her momentum, Nicole opened her messages and created a new one. She stared at the blank screen for a few minutes, trying to figure out how to sound breezy and determined at the same time.

Finally, she typed: *Hey, it's Nicole. I know it's last minute, but any chance you're free for dinner? I've got a craving for fried pickles.*

Her finger hovered above the screen. "Do it," she whispered, then pressed send. Satisfied and terrified, she put her phone down and pushed it to the back corner of her desk. It was only three thirty. She assumed Avery was working and probably couldn't reply right away. Plus, Nicole had given her a nice window to reply before it became too late to make dinner plans.

With a nod, she turned her attention back to Arlene and her love of cats.

By six p.m., Avery hadn't responded. Nicole, meanwhile, had drafted notes and sent them off to Arlene's family. Now, her stomach was rumbling and she could no longer avoid the truth: Avery was blowing her off.

Or, okay, maybe that was harsh. Maybe she was busy. Maybe she already had dinner plans and didn't know how to say that, so she ignored Nicole instead. Maybe she'd had a bad day and wasn't paying attention to her phone.

"Oh, no," Nicole said, walking through her apartment. "We are not making excuses for her."

She looked at her phone one more time, just to make sure she hadn't missed a text or even a call. Nothing.

"That is fine," Nicole said. "Absolutely fine."

She clicked on Brynn's number and held the phone to her ear. "Hey. Did you eat yet? I think I need to talk."

CHAPTER EIGHTEEN

Houston yawned and pressed her front paws against Avery's leg. When Avery looked at her, Houston tilted her head and gave one of those soul-searching looks that reminded Avery how damn empathetic her dog was. She'd gotten pretty good at hiding her emotions from Gavin and even Fallon, but Houston always knew what she was feeling.

"I know," she said quietly, scratching Houston's ears. "I'm trying."

With an enormous yawn that suggested Houston had done far more than lounge around the house all day, the dog nuzzled her nose into Avery's leg. A heavy, grumbly sigh followed. Avery shook her head. She was an empathetic dog, yes, but also an incredibly dramatic dog.

What Avery didn't have to explain to Houston was the tense line she was currently walking with Shannon. In the week and a half that had passed since Avery had confronted her about the wedding, there had been little communication between the two. Par for the course; Avery wasn't surprised. What did surprise her was that she wasn't having an emotional reaction to the silence. She had, briefly—the first two days of silence rotted in her gut, nudging her between sadness and anger. But after that, Avery had felt…calm. A little empty and a little bereft (and a lot angry, more and more as the days passed), but settled.

Loud giggles filtered up from downstairs. Avery smiled. She was familiar with the sounds of Thea chasing Gavin through the open concept living-dining-kitchen area. It was a daily activity for the two. Thea referred to it as "exercise" and thought it was her civic duty to help keep her daddy in shape. Neither Avery nor Gavin would ever break it to her that the reason Gavin was in such good shape was because he'd adjusted his work schedule so he could hit the gym before picking Thea up from preschool.

Idly, Avery wondered if Gavin would ever tell Thea the truth about her birth mother, Naomi. She was getting old enough to start asking questions and so far, Gavin had been dodging them with a skill Avery hadn't suspected he had. Of course, the truth was that no one knew the truth about Thea's birth mother. Naomi had literally left one morning and never came back. Avery suspected mental health issues, but Fallon was convinced there was a much seedier, darker story behind Naomi's disappearance. Whatever the case, a week after she'd disappeared, Naomi had contacted Gavin only to inform him that she'd signed over all parental rights to him. Since then, there'd been nothing. Gavin never spoke of her, so by default, neither did Avery. But she had a feeling that at some point, Thea would start asking questions no one could answer.

In many ways, Avery had stepped in as a bonus mom. She was perfectly happy to help take care of Thea. Gavin didn't ask for much help, so it never felt like she was in a true "mom" position. That was a role she'd never aspired to. Kids—whether or not she carried them—had never appeared in Avery's picture of what she wanted in her life. She wasn't against them, and believed that if the right woman came along and she happened to have children, then that would be, well, fated. But on her own, the idea of being a mom wasn't something that appealed to her.

If she were being honest, that was one of the reasons she'd stayed attached to Shannon for so long. There wasn't a rush on Avery's biological clock, so she didn't see how she was wasting time by continuing on in her situationship. Granted, there was the mountain of other issues, namely the one about not getting her needs met, that should have propelled her away from Shannon, but Avery felt no sense of urgency, only complacency.

She leaned her head back against the edge of her bed. Her butt was getting sore from sitting on the floor, but Houston looked comfortable and she hated to disturb her.

She shut her eyes. She knew she had to call Shannon back and was dreading picking up the phone to do so. They'd had an ugly conversation earlier that afternoon, and Avery had cut it short because she was at work. There were things she needed to say, however, so she'd called Shannon back when she left the shop around three. Shannon, as usual, didn't answer. Avery had put her phone on do not disturb—both to lessen her anxiety and to send Shannon directly to voice mail if she called back. Yes, it was passive-aggressive, but Avery was beyond the point of caring. When she'd seen Shannon had called her back at five fifty, Avery had held off on calling back. This back-and-forth was emblematic of one of their many patterns, and Avery knew what came next.

What she wasn't sure of was whether or not she was strong enough to break the pattern.

"Just do it," she whispered before picking up her phone. Her stomach curled in on itself, causing a ripple of anxious emptiness to swirl through her body.

"Hey," Shannon said. Avery startled, not having expected her to answer on the first ring... Or at all.

"Hi." Avery cleared her throat. "So, I think we need to finish our conversation from earlier."

"Okay."

Avery waited a few seconds before realizing, as usual, Shannon wasn't going to be the one to move the conversation forward. "Okay. I just..." Avery looked down at Houston, who was asleep now and oblivious to her owner's distress. "What are we doing, Shannon?"

The sigh that came through the phone would have knocked Thea over had she been standing nearby. "We've been over this."

"Yeah, we have, but then something happens or someone says something and it gets confusing again."

"You keep getting confused. Because you don't want to hear what I say to you."

The skin on Avery's arms chilled. It wasn't the first time Shannon had thrown this at her, this not-entirely-incorrect-but-still-hurtful statement. Avery listened to everything Shannon said, and she believed her…but the wires kept getting crossed and words were misconstrued when laid next to actions and then there were the wisps of memories overlapping with misplaced hope—Avery knew she was at fault. But she wasn't alone in that.

"I do hear what you say. But what you say—"

"Doesn't match what I do. I know."

"Can you just explain to me why you took her to the wedding?"

Shannon was silent. Avery knew she was pushing her luck. Marie was an off-limits topic between them. But Avery simply could not understand why Shannon insisted upon choosing Marie, and not her, especially when she'd repeatedly told Avery how destructive her relationship with Marie had been.

"No."

Avery leaned forward, shaking her head. "Are you back together with her?"

Another sigh. "It's complicated."

"No, it's really not. That's a yes or no answer."

After a moment, she said, "We talk. And we see each other. We spend time together."

And go on vacation together, and go to weddings together.

Even without the omissions Avery's brain so helpfully supplied, Shannon's words weren't a surprise. But they still struck a chord of pain deep inside. "So you're in a relationship with her again."

"I didn't say that. It's not that simple."

Avery bit the inside of her cheek. "It is, Shannon. Just answer me."

"I did answer you. You just don't like the answer I gave you."

She wanted to scream. The urge was so powerful that she allowed herself a moment of imagining a scream so loud that Shannon's eardrums would burst from the over-the-phone impact.

"I don't know what we're doing," Avery said quietly. "I've told you that I can't be friends with you if you're in a relationship with her. It's too hard."

Shannon went silent again. Avery figured she would. There was only so much lying by omission a person could do in one phone call.

"I've told you, Aves. You and I will never be just friends."

There it was. The line that had kept Avery hooked for years. To her, it meant much more than the words implied. Avery heard "someday we'll be together," when really, all Shannon was saying was that their friendship held love and attraction—two things that could continue or fade over time, two things that didn't guarantee any kind of happy ending. Two things that were simply the end result of years of friendship tangled with incredible chemistry. Two things that did not spell forever.

For once, Avery didn't want to bury her head in the sand and continue under this guise of friendship. If she really thought about it, her friendship with Shannon wasn't bringing much to her life—or, at the very least, it wasn't adding anything that she couldn't find in another friendship. The root of the connection was an emotional attachment (many thanks to the therapists who posted on TikTok and gave her free therapeutic awakenings) that was so ingrained in every inch of Avery's body that she'd gotten to a point where she didn't *want* to let go. Because it felt impossible.

But letting go of the physical—or, in their case, the phone calls and text messages and random visits every couple of months—didn't mean Shannon would cease to exist. It didn't mean Avery couldn't still love her and care about her from afar, and silently. But setting the boundary and letting go would build a buffer that Avery desperately needed. She didn't want to be hurt anymore; she didn't want to continue holding on to the possibility that someday Shannon would wake up and—

She sat up from her slouched position, still holding the phone to her ear.

Maybe she didn't *want* Shannon to wake up.

"I—" Avery cut herself off, distracted by her thoughts. She knew she wasn't "over" Shannon, so to speak, but this...this was new.

"I love you, Avery. I know my actions don't always line up with that. But I love you, and that has never changed."

"Right," Avery said, coming back to the conversation. "And I love you. But maybe...maybe we need space."

"I don't need space from you," Shannon said quickly.

Avery disagreed but she wasn't in charge of Shannon's decisions. She was, however, in charge of herself and making decisions that benefited her emotional state.

"It just feels like we're moving in different directions. I want to move forward," Avery said, still unsure of what that looked like but knowing the statement was true, "and you keep moving backward."

Shannon sighed. It was a sound that Avery wouldn't mind never hearing again.

"I need some time," Avery said, pushing the words out before they absconded along with her courage. "Time to myself."

"So, what? No calls, no texts?"

"Right. Nothing."

"That's what you want?"

"That's what I *need*," she clarified. She didn't want to not talk to Shannon, but someday, she hoped, she'd reach that point. For now, she had to focus on what she needed...especially since she'd lost sight of her needs seven years ago and was starting to realize she didn't want to be in that untethered space any longer.

"Okay." Shannon sounded far away, the only evidence that she was feeling any kind of emotional response to Avery's request.

"Okay," Avery repeated. "I...Okay. I love you." Force of habit, force of truth. Avery closed her eyes.

"I love you. Bye."

When Avery set her phone on the floor, she waited for the rush of emotions to flood her. Minutes ticked past and nothing happened. Slowly, her stomach began to untwist. A ribbon of relief twirled up, circling her heart and squeezing tightly.

"You can do this," she said, opening her eyes. "You have to do this." She nodded. "You *want* to do this."

And somewhere in the recesses of her stubborn and persistent love for Shannon, Avery knew it was true: she wanted the space. She wanted to breathe without wondering when Shannon was going to call. She wanted to experience life without her, even if it hurt a little.

But more than anything, Avery wanted to prove to herself that she was strong enough and determined enough to let go of something she'd held on to so tightly that she'd lost feeling in her fingertips. It would take time, she knew, but she was closer than she'd ever been before.

A thought occurred to her and she picked up her phone, scrolling to her messages. After having her phone on do not disturb off and on all afternoon and evening, there were twenty-some unread texts waiting. Most were work-related, but there was one from an unknown number, sent early that afternoon.

Avery scanned it before opening it, her heart sinking a little. It was Nicole, asking if she was free to meet for dinner. Avery glanced at the time, confirming that she'd gone too long without responding and now looked like a total asshole—plus, it was too late to make a hurried plan to meet up, *plus* she wasn't in a super frame of mind...

She put her phone back down, resolving to text Nicole first thing in the morning and apologize for blowing her off. In the meantime, Avery needed a distraction—preferably the kind with pigtails and a habit of dropping letters from her words. She patted Houston, who woke up with a mighty yawn, and the two of them trooped downstairs to hang out with a four-year-old and her dad.

CHAPTER NINETEEN

It was oddly warm in the funeral home. Will had once told Nicole that he tended to keep the temperature a little lower than necessary, mostly because of the heat that crowds of mourners produced. The last thing anyone wanted was to be in a stifling room with a dead body.

Nicole pulled her dark-gray sweater away from her body, trying to usher air in to cool her rapidly overheating body. The snag, she assumed, was that it was unseasonably warm outside. Speaking of… Nicole turned and looked out the windows. It was gorgeous outside. She was a little annoyed that she'd agreed to come to this funeral. She'd much rather be out by the lake. It wasn't quite warm enough to kayak—not yet, but soon—but the temperature and cloudless sky promised a relaxing and comfortable respite by the water.

She checked her watch. It was only eleven. Hopefully she could be at the lake by two at the latest.

"Shit."

Nicole turned at the sound of the expletive to find Will hovering in the doorway. He looked panicked and annoyed and was tugging his tie away from his throat.

"It's broken," he added, gesturing to the air around them. "I was hoping it wasn't warm down here, because it's boiling upstairs."

"It's a little tropical," Nicole said. "Is the heat running nonstop?"

"Yep." Will crossed the room, straightening chairs on his way. He cast a look at the casket. "I hope Arlene liked warm climates."

Nicole coughed out a laugh. From what she'd learned from the family, Arlene had indeed loved the warmth. She'd spent hours sunbathing when she was younger. Rumor was that she used to lather herself in baby oil and stretch out in the family's large backyard, roasting and toasting until her skin was golden brown. She'd passed that love of the sun down to her daughter, then to her granddaughter. So, Nicole thought, the family would probably be just fine with the warmer-than-usual room.

"I have the HVAC people on the way," Will said, moving toward the doorway. "Hopefully they get here before someone passes out from heat exhaustion."

Nicole peered out the window again. The family was arriving and, judging by the smiles on their faces, seemed to be in good spirits. Arlene had lived a long ninety-six years of happy life. She'd suffered a bit of dementia in the last handful of years, but her family had never left her side. As a bonus, they were the type of family that found humor in everything. Truthfully, they hadn't needed Nicole's help with the eulogies. The grandkids had plenty of great ideas, they were just a bit noncommittal and needed guidance with structuring their thoughts and memories.

It was a weird thing to say, but even though she very much wanted to be out in that gorgeous weather, Nicole was looking forward to this funeral. She kind of wanted to hang out with the family afterwards. Judging from her interactions with them, their post-burial luncheon would be entertaining.

A blur of movement in the parking lot caught her eye and she squinted, half-excited, half-petrified. Maybe petrified was extreme, but scared didn't quite cover the feeling. Whatever it was, it seemed to be the appropriate emotional response to seeing Avery for the first time since she'd thrown herself at her, then sent a text that Avery—days later—still hadn't responded to.

But Nicole quickly put that aside when she saw the look on Avery's face. That was the expression of a woman who was trying like hell not to show how stressed she was. Nicole scanned the parking lot and realized Avery was alone and, if she knew her funeral timings correctly, running late.

Without considering anything other than the desire to help someone who clearly looked like she needed it, Nicole exited through the side door and approached Avery in the parking lot.

She tried to avoid admiring Avery's ass as she leaned into the van and moved flowers around. But it was unavoidable; Avery had a really nice ass. Nicole tilted her head for a better look. She didn't know how she hadn't noticed this until now, but now that she'd seen it, she didn't want to stop seeing it.

"What the fuck!" Avery exclaimed when she turned around.

Nicole felt her cheeks heat up. "I'm sorry," she said immediately.

Avery stared at her, curious confusion scrawled across her features. "What were you doing?"

"Oh—I—" Nicole sputtered. "Waiting?"

"For what?"

"Um. For you to…turn around?" She tried to smile.

"Mmhmm." Avery looked like she was fighting a smile. "Did you come out here to help me? Or just stand there and pretend like you weren't staring at me?"

"I wasn't," Nicole protested. She put her hands on her hips. "Besides, you had your back to me, so you wouldn't even know if I *had* been staring at you, which I definitely was not doing."

"Likely story." Avery gestured toward the van. "So then you're here to help me."

"Yes."

Avery cracked a smile. "That's nice of you." She turned around again but kept talking. "Zuri was supposed to meet me at the shop, but she got held up at her other job. Then I couldn't find two of the arrangements because—okay, I don't know why, but someone put them somewhere where they shouldn't have been. And now," she said, turning around with an armful of flowers, "I'm late and in a mild panic."

Nicole held out her arms. "Load me up."

Avery's stressed smile shifted into something more genuine. Nicole watched the way it brought all of Avery's features together. Her eyes were more green than brown, and the sun was illuminating little flecks of gold in them. Nicole bit the inside of her cheek, noticing how Avery's freckles seemed to be shimmering across her adorably crooked nose. She wanted to know what Avery looked like with her hair down, but as usual, it was pulled back up into a messy bun with errant curls popping out from all angles.

Nicole swallowed. She should absolutely not be imagining running her hands through Avery's hair. There was no reason for her to picture looping curl after curl around her fingers, giving them a little tug when Avery said something funny or ridiculous or—

"Nicole?"

"Yes!" She straightened up, avoiding eye contact. "Here I go." She turned and hurried back into the steamy safety of the funeral home, hoping she and the flowers wouldn't wilt upon entry.

She was dismayed at the wall of heat that met her as soon as she stepped into the room that was now holding not only Arlene in her casket, but also some of her family. Nicole glanced down at the beautiful flowers in her arms, hoping they were resilient.

"Thanks," Avery said, her voice low and startlingly close to Nicole's ear. "Can you, um, distract the family or something?" She stepped away to unload her arms.

"Yeah, of course." Nicole held out her arms and allowed Avery to scoop the flowers from her. She paused to watch Avery begin to assess her situation, and, fighting the urge to help her but also wanting to lighten her stress by getting out of her way, Nicole moved toward the family members who were lingering near the casket.

"Hi, everyone," she said with a smile. "How are we all doing this morning?"

The family immediately enveloped Nicole into their conversation. But even as she talked with them, she was distracted by knowing that Avery was in the same room. Every so often she'd catch a glance of her moving around with stealth not unlike a cat, hidden by underbrush, stalking its prey. The flowers seemed to magically spread themselves out by their own volition.

Just as Avery was silently attaching the casket spray to the top of the casket, which was actually the edge of the side, since the casket was open, Arlene's daughter, Carol, gasped. Avery, awkwardly standing behind the casket with her hands still tangled in the flowers, froze.

"Oh! I almost forgot!" Carol moved quickly to a bag sitting on the floor by a cluster of chairs. "Where should we put him?"

The grandkids, Jeff and Kristin, started laughing. Relieved that the family was indeed embracing the humor of the situation, Nicole grinned. She glanced at Avery, whose face had gone white. She was staring down into the casket. Nicole felt a pang of empathy for her; a dead body, regardless of a person's attachment to it, was jarring.

"Put him in the casket with her," Jeff said.

"Yeah, he can—here, give him to me." Kristin, with the item secured in her hands, moved toward the casket. She looked at her grandmother. "Hey, Nana. I'm just gonna snuggle your little guy right…here." She stepped back and admired her work. "Perfect."

The family dissolved into laughter, some of it mingled with tears. Nicole looked back at Avery, who was still void of color and still staring at Arlene.

Nicole tried to be invisible as she stepped around the back of the casket and put her hand on Avery's back. "Hey. You okay?"

Avery didn't say a word. Instead, she dropped her shoulders and shook her head a few times. Nicole watched as Avery came back to life, working her deft fingers through the casket spray and the wires that kept it in place. At least, Nicole hoped they'd keep it in place—she'd been to one funeral where the elderly wife of the deceased, caught up in an animated conversation, had leaned against her husband's casket and the spray had come tumbling down onto the deceased. Thankfully, that family had a great sense of humor too.

With a loud exhale, Avery stepped away from the back of the casket. "Sorry about that," she mumbled.

"Nothing to apologize for. This time," Nicole added, hoping for a smile.

She was rewarded with one, though it wasn't as exuberant as she'd hoped.

"How are you just…around dead bodies all the time?" Avery looked directly at her. "Wait. You never actually told me why you're always in funeral homes."

Nicole angled her head toward the back of the room. "Come with me. I'll explain." She took one step then turned abruptly, nearly colliding with Avery. "Wait. Are you finished with the flowers? I don't want to take you away if you have more work to do."

A shade of pink not unlike the peonies they both favored dusted her cheeks. "I'm good."

Nicole wanted to admire the blooms of color on Avery's face but instead, she turned and led them to the back of the room, then out into the hallway. She gestured to a pair of armchairs and they sat down.

Avery dropped her head into her hands. "Sorry," she said, her voice muffled. "I don't know what just happened to me."

"Well, you saw a dead body." Nicole shrugged. "Happens to the best of us."

She peeked out through her fingers. "Not to you."

"Avery," Nicole said softly. "You can't compare my experience to yours. I see a dead body once a week, especially this time of year."

Avery shook her head, some more curls springing free, and sat up. She twirled her pointer finger in a circle. "Time to explain, because I'm really confused."

"I don't have an official title," Nicole began, suddenly nervous. Sure, her dad and Brynn knew what she did, but this was the first time she was explaining it to someone who didn't know her well—or what she'd been through that brought her here. "Basically I help people write eulogies."

Avery stared at her. "That's it?"

Nicole laughed. "Wow, thanks."

"No, I didn't—sorry. God, I apologize to you a lot." Avery pressed her fingers against her cheeks, which only increased the spread of blush. "If you write eulogies, why are you at funerals? Isn't that a behind the scenes thing?"

"Yup. And I don't go to every funeral. There have been a lot lately. I don't know why." Nicole looked over at Arlene's family. "Death is weird and wild. Families lean on funeral directors more than you'd think, and Will—you know Will?" At Avery's nod, Nicole continued, "I've known him for a long time, pretty much since I moved here. His brother was in the same platoon as my wife."

Avery's expression hardened, and Nicole could practically see her walls shoot up. "Platoon? In BLPD?"

It took Nicole a second to decipher the acronym for Balsam Lake Police Department. "Oh, no. They're not cops. They were in the Army. I mean, Will's brother is still enlisted. My wife… not so much."

Avery took a moment, then nodded. Her defenses seemed to lower, but Nicole tucked that response to "platoon" into her back pocket. She'd circle back to it someday. Maybe.

"Anyway, Will recommends me to families. Some of them like me to be here for the funerals—but I only come to the ceremonies that are small and held here." Nicole grimaced. "I don't do churches."

"Me either," Avery said quietly.

"So we've got that in common." Nicole dug her fingers into the side of the cushion, wishing she hadn't said that. "And, yeah. Sometimes the families ask me to be here for the service, mostly for extra moral support."

Avery nodded. "That's interesting."

"It's weird, you can say it. But it's my kind of weird. It's actually really fulfilling to help people in this way." Nicole studied Avery. "You can ask questions, if you want."

"I do have one," Avery said, her words coming slowly.

"Shoot."

She cleared her throat. "You still call her your wife?"

Nicole sat back in surprise, then shrugged. "Yeah. She's not my ex-wife, so I can't say that. Sometimes I call her My Dead Wife. But it's easier, once people know she's dead, to just say my wife."

An indecipherable look passed over Avery's face. "You do not call her 'my dead wife.'"

"Why not? That's the truth." Nicole watched Avery, waiting for some kind of reaction. All she got was a mixture of confusion and curiosity. She wanted to dig into that, but she also had a job to do. "Do you want to come listen to the eulogies? They're pretty good."

"That's quite a pat on your own back."

Nicole laughed and stood up. "What can I say, I know what I'm good at."

Avery made a noise as she stood up. As they walked toward the Monocacy Room, the room where Arlene's service was now underway, Avery did a double take into a side room.

"Whoa," she said, stepping toward the room. "What's this?"

"The show room!" Nicole said. "It's where funeral directors take families to select caskets and to plan for other funerally things."

"So many caskets," Avery said under her breath. "Why are they so little?"

"They couldn't fit all the options in here if they were life-sized."

Avery cast a look at Nicole, her eyes dark with amusement. "Don't you mean death-sized?"

"Oh my God." Nicole pressed her hand against her mouth, hoping her laughter didn't reach Arlene's friends and family. "You did not just make a death joke."

Avery shrugged. "I think you're rubbing off on me."

Nicole bit back a smile as they walked into the Monocacy Room.

CHAPTER TWENTY

For the life of her—and the irony of that statement was not lost on her—Avery could not figure out why she was voluntarily standing in the back of a room that currently housed the body of a dead person and that person's family and friends. It's not that she was freaked out by death. Okay, fine, maybe a little—but, like, the normal amount of freak-out. Avery hadn't yet lost someone very close to her. Both of her mom's parents were still alive, and she'd never known her biological father's parents. Her stepgrandfather had died when she was in elementary school, but she hadn't known him. She'd gone to the funeral, though, and it had been nothing like what was happening in front of her now. His funeral had been grand, way over the top, in a cold and formal church. This ceremony, held in a small room that seemed perfect for the remaining connections of an elderly woman, was comfortable and inviting.

So inviting that Avery was still standing here.

She snuck a glance at Nicole. It was only fair, Avery thought—Nicole had seen her at work several times, so this was Avery's chance to see Nicole do her thing. Now that she understood what Nicole's funeral home connection was, she was less confused and more intrigued. Superficially, it made sense, since Nicole's full-time job, if Avery remembered correctly, had something to do with writing. So maybe writing was just Nicole's thing, and she used her talent to—

Avery whipped her head to the front of the room. She could have sworn she'd just heard a meow, but unless one of the attendees had a weird habit of randomly making cat noises... "What was that?" she whispered to Nicole.

"The cat," Nicole said, as though it was the most natural answer in the world. "Didn't you see them put it in the casket?"

"No!" Avery craned her neck to see, but a group of people were blocking her view. "What the fuck is happening?" she hissed.

Nicole covered her mouth as she laughed. "Arlene—that's our deceased—loved cats. But her husband didn't, so she hadn't had one in a long time." Nicole looked at Avery. "You'll learn the rest in the eulogy. I think it's the one her granddaughter is giving."

Avery shifted her weight from foot to foot. She had a thousand more questions, but they were silenced as Will Conway approached them.

"Avery!" he said happily, but quietly. "Welcome to our sauna!"

She hadn't realized how hot it was until then. She'd assumed it was her body's reaction to being around Nicole, but she also hadn't wanted to think too much about that, so she'd stopped thinking about the heat entirely. "Is it always like this? I'll have to adjust my future flower selections."

"No, it's usually just right." He glanced at the family. "Thankfully they don't seem to mind. It should be fixed within a half hour." Looking back at Avery, he continued, "The flowers are amazing. Are you okay with me recommending you to families as the main provider?"

Avery stood up straight, pride flowing through her limbs. "Yes. That would be great."

"Wonderful." Will winked at Nicole. "Making her stay to hear your hard work?"

"She needed the full experience," Nicole said, nudging Avery's arm with her elbow. "Nothing like a good funeral hazing ritual."

Avery looked between Nicole and Will. "You two are weird."

"Comes with the territory," they said in unison, then exchanged an amused look. Will slapped Avery on the back before he disappeared.

"Just in time," Nicole said softly, moving closer to Avery. "This one's my favorite."

Distracted as she was by Nicole's closeness, Avery managed to focus most of her attention on the granddaughter's eulogy. Through it, she learned that when Arlene moved into the assisted living facility, she was coherent. As time went on, however, her mind started to get hazy. On the recommendation of a nurse, Arlene's daughter had gotten her a mechanical cat. And Arlene had fallen in love.

"Alexander the Second is here today," Kristin, the granddaughter, said, gesturing to the bizarrely lifelike orange cat sitting in the casket. "We thought about keeping him, but I know my nana would want the little guy to be with her."

As she continued speaking, Avery turned to Nicole. She startled, having forgotten how close they were standing. She could smell Nicole's shampoo. A whiff of coconut and bergamot nearly made her swoon.

Nicole turned her head and suddenly they were eye to eye, or nearly so, since Avery did have a few inches on her. Avery took a sharp inhale. She remembered with distinct clarity how Nicole's lips had felt on her cheek. She fought not to drop her gaze to said lips, though it was tempting.

"You good?" Nicole whispered, her bright blue eyes searching Avery's.

"Yeah." Avery cleared her throat, hoping that would rid her tone of its sudden huskiness. "Uh, I was just wondering about the cat. Are they really leaving it in the casket?"

Nicole nodded. "I think so."

On cue, the cat meowed, causing ripples of laughter in the small group. Avery looked up just in time to see the cat move its head back and forth, then give a swish of its tail.

"I don't have words for this," Avery whispered.

"Welcome to my world," Nicole said.

"But you do have words for this." Avery gestured to the front of the room, where another eulogy was beginning. "Technically."

Nicole shrugged. "I think it's easy for me to help them because I'm removed from the death. When we have distance from painful experiences, we're able to be more rational and clear-headed. It's easy to write with emotion, but editing demands a quiet mind."

Avery stared at Nicole. In no way, shape, or form had she assumed she *knew* Nicole, but she was slowly realizing that there were many layers to this woman. Layers that she wanted to peel back. Slowly and carefully, but purposefully.

"Too much?" Nicole said, wincing.

"No." Avery shook her head. "That was really deep."

"I have my moments."

As the eulogy wrapped up, Nicole excused herself. She took a few steps, then looked back at Avery. "If you can wait a couple minutes, I'll walk out with you."

Avery nodded. She still had no idea why she'd stayed, and now she was wondering what she thought she was doing with Nicole... Nicole, who was far more than Avery had imagined her to be—or, more accurately, more than Avery had given her the space and time to show. Nicole had experienced her own intense heartbreak, and Avery knew she was in no shape to get involved with her; she truly believed all she could offer someone was eventual heartbreak.

And the thought of hurting Nicole—of causing her any pain whatsoever—made Avery's stomach turn. She'd been through the ringer with Shannon. Yes, she'd chosen to stay, chosen to continue communicating, chosen to lean on the side of "maybe someday." But the hurt that Avery had accumulated over the years hung over her like a thick veil. She needed to lift that veil (and throw it into the fire, honestly) before getting too close because the last thing she wanted was to do to Nicole what had been done to her.

But she stayed. She watched as Nicole interacted with the family. They seemed thankful for her, and gave her plenty of hugs. Though she was in the back of the room, Avery caught a snippet of a joke that sounded like, "See you next time!" followed by one of Arlene's grandkids commenting on how dark their family humor was.

When Nicole returned to Avery, her cheeks were flushed and her eyes were bright. She was carrying a bloom of happiness that tugged Avery closer to her.

"Ready?" Nicole asked.

Avery nodded. "I can tell you really like doing this."

Nicole fixed her eyes on Avery. "I do. Thank you for saying that."

She shrugged. "I can see it written all over your face."

In the silence that settled between them, there was nothing but gentle intrigue and appreciation. Avery had absolutely no idea what to do with any of that, so she turned abruptly and headed for the exit.

A burst of laughter from the front of the room stopped both of them, and they turned toward the commotion.

"Was that—?"

"Oh my God."

Sure enough, as Will and his team continued pushing the now closed casket out of the room, baleful mechanical meows echoed from within. Most of the family members who remained in the room were laughing so hard they were crying.

"Poor Alexander the Second," Nicole said.

"I feel worse for the people who walk near her gravesite and hear random meows coming from the ground."

Nicole burst into laughter. "I hadn't thought about that. Remind me not to go to that cemetery anytime soon."

Avery held the door open. "I get that you're into death, but do you...do you also hang out in cemeteries?"

"Okay, first of all, I understand the confusion but I'm not 'into death.'" Nicole cast a sideways glance at her as they walked toward the parking lot. "I like helping people handle death. Big difference."

"So you don't go on midnight strolls through cemeteries?"

"No, you weirdo." Nicole laughed a little. "Though I do wear a lot of black, so I can see how that's misleading."

"I've noticed." In fact, Avery had distinctly noticed how the black pants Nicole wore looked very, very good on her.

"Avery." Nicole's voice was firm, but she heard the underlying hesitation in it.

"Yeah?" She leaned against the delivery truck, wondering how dirty it was and if she'd come away with filth on her shirt.

Nicole looked at the ground, then farther down the parking lot before settling her eyes on Avery, who was momentarily stunned by how blue they were under the beam of sunshine.

"I texted you the other day."

Shame immediately spiraled through Avery. She'd never replied, though she had meant to. Before she could respond, Nicole went on.

"I get that, like, we're not dating." Her blue eyes dimmed. "Or whatever. I don't actually know what we're doing. But if you don't want me to text you, why'd you give me your number?"

"It's my fault," Avery said, already feeling the disappointment of having inflicted even the smallest bit of hurt onto this incredible, fascinating person. "I didn't purposely ignore you. I didn't see your text right away, and when I did, I told myself to reply, but then I got caught up with other things…" She cringed internally, remembering that day and how she'd been busy playing passive-aggressive with Shannon. "There's no excuse. I suck."

"You don't suck." It was too kind, but Avery didn't feel like arguing. "But you can be a bit rude."

Avery laughed. Nicole's blunt honesty was refreshing as hell. Avery had a feeling she'd never be in the dark if they dated, or more than dated. It was a comforting—no, exciting—thought.

"You're right. And yet again, I'm apologizing to you." Avery held her stare. "I'm sorry."

"We really need to get out of this pattern," Nicole said. "Hopefully next time we run into each other, neither of us will have a reason to apologize."

Something internal tugged, but Avery brushed it off, knowing what it was. But she wasn't ready to throw herself into something with Nicole. She wouldn't deny the attraction any longer, but she couldn't help feeling like Nicole would be a rebound.

And though Avery knew she had barely scraped the surface of learning who Nicole was, she knew enough to firmly believe that this woman was worthy of so much more than being a rebound from a shitty situationship.

"On that note," Nicole continued, "I'm gonna get out of here so I can enjoy this weather." She hesitated as she played with her key ring. "Do you have to go back to work?"

Avery would have loved to ditch work for the rest of the day and see what kind of trouble she and Nicole could get into, and since she was the boss of her business, she could absolutely do that. But fear trickled and dripped down her throat, convincing her she wasn't ready.

"Yeah, I do. Enjoy the sunshine for me?"

The smile that lit up Nicole's face was intoxicating and Avery felt it trickle into the quiet, dim parts of her heart. She knew she'd be picturing it for the rest of the day.

"I will. Bye, Avery."

"See ya," Avery said to Nicole's retreating form. She waited until Nicole got into her car and drove away, then slumped against the side of the van.

* * *

It was after six by the time Avery got home. While she was hanging out at the funeral home, Zuri and Veronica had fielded three brides-to-be (none of them Genevieve Longwood, which Avery was relieved to hear as she was convinced Genevieve was going to throw herself into her first lesbian relationship and race to the altar). She'd spent the rest of the day playing catch-up with paperwork, phone calls, and calendars, making sure they could fit in all three weddings.

When she pulled into the driveway, she wasn't surprised to see Fallon's car. Avery wasn't convinced there wasn't something going on between Fallon and Gavin, though neither would admit it if questioned. There were sparks there, Avery could see, but she knew Gavin's priority was Thea. And Fallon... Well, Fallon was unpredictable when it came to relationships. Her track record was actually worse than Avery's, and neither of them could blame that on their parents, who had a great relationship.

"You smell like a legit pile of dirt," Fallon announced when Avery walked into the kitchen. "I smelled you the moment you opened the door."

"I can't believe you can smell me over your unmistakable odor of self-importance," Avery retorted. She dodged Fallon's incoming punch with ease. "Gettin' slow there, Knight. Better hit the gym twice a day instead of just once."

"At least I have muscles and don't need someone to help me carry *flowers*."

Avery glared at Fallon, whose every feature was lit up with devious excitement. "The fuck are you talking about?"

"Language," Gavin warned from the stove.

Thea, however, was fully absorbed in an animated show, and was far enough away that she probably couldn't hear Avery's growl. She was also lying on the floor and using Houston as a pillow, which explained why the traitorous dog hadn't greeted her owner at the door.

"Sorry," she said anyway. Honestly, the amount of times she'd said that damn word lately. Avery turned back to Fallon. "I ask again, what the *fuck*," she whispered, "are you talking about?"

Gavin sighed heavily and Avery knew she'd have a vegetable thrown in her general direction if she didn't clean up her mouth.

"I was on the road today," Fallon said. She was sitting at the counter, a can of Fegley's Space Monkey next to a half-empty glass. It was Fallon's one beer a night, and she'd chosen a good one. Avery's mouth watered despite her irritation. "And I happened to drive past Conway Funeral Home. I saw your van, so I slowed down, and what did I see? Little sister dumping a shit ton of flowers into the arms of some innocent stranger."

Avery wasn't sure which angle to attack first: the little sister dig, which Fallon was obsessed with despite the fact that they were a mere month apart in age; the ridiculous insinuation that Avery couldn't carry her own damn flowers; or the reference to Nicole as an "innocent stranger."

Gavin made the decision for her. "Wait," he said, turning from the stove. "You let a random person touch your flowers?"

"Oh," Fallon said, leaning back on the stool. "Excellent point. Who is she?"

Avery rubbed her hand over her forehead. She was going to have a hell of a time getting out of this one. It was common knowledge—and another thing Fallon made fun of her for—that Avery detested when others touched her flower arrangements. She had gotten to the point where she was mostly okay with Zuri's touch, but Veronica was still on probation. There was no way Fallon or Gavin was going to buy any lie Avery spouted about who Nicole was.

"A friend," she settled on, helping herself to a can of Space Monkey. "And that's—"

But it was already too much. Both Fallon and Gavin were staring at her, their jaws practically on the floor. Before Avery could begin to dig herself out of the hole she was rapidly descending into, Fallon snapped out of it and clapped several times.

"Does this mean what I think it means?"

Avery shrugged. She knew exactly what Fallon was referring to, but talking about Shannon was the last thing she wanted to do. "I cut off communication," she said, hoping that was enough. She paired it with a stare that she hoped would shut her sister down.

The kitchen went silent except for whatever was bubbling on the stove. Avery watched as Fallon and Gavin exchanged a look. Gavin nodded, then turned back to his cooking. Fallon, unfortunately, turned her attention back to Avery.

"You know," she said, her voice unusually gentle, "I've always liked Shannon, Aves. She's a great cop."

"Yeah, I know."

"But I hate the effect she's had on you." Fallon sipped her beer. "I know how hard you tried to make it work, even just as friends. And I know it must be hard, not talking to her. But I'm really proud of you for doing that."

Avery nodded. She didn't trust her voice, or her words. Plus, she rarely saw this side of Fallon and didn't want to jinx it.

"Have you blocked her number?"

"No." Avery sighed, her shoulders dropping. "I will. I'm just not quite there yet."

"You'll get there." Fallon clapped once. "Now, you need to tell us about this new *friend* whom you've conveniently never mentioned before."

"Well," Avery said dramatically, "*I* haven't mentioned her. You did."

Fallon stared at her, her glass halfway to her mouth. "So? Spill it."

"There's not much to spill." Avery sat down at the table. She knew the only way to get Fallon off her back was to give her some information. "We met, I was an asshole, we've run into each other a few times since. That's it."

"Is she cute?" Gavin asked, but he was looking at Fallon.

"From what I saw, yes. Very." Fallon looked back at Avery. "Are you still being an asshole?"

"Trying not to be."

"Well, that's something." Fallon clapped again.

"What the fuck's with the clapping?" Avery asked, her voice hopefully quiet enough not to reach Thea's ears.

"It's new," Gavin said, his back to both women. "And she won't stop doing it. Much like you won't stop cursing."

Fallon clapped in response, then changed the topic to something boring like stocks. Avery didn't care about money talk, plus she wanted to get out of Fallon's line of fire. She slipped out of her seat and headed into the living room. Houston started wagging her tail immediately, and Avery sat down next to her, running her hands through her soft fur.

"Hey, Thea Bea," Avery said, tapping her on the forehead. "How was school?"

"Shh," she said, pointing at the TV. "Dis is a good part. Be quiet like Houston."

"Okay," Avery whispered. At least one person in the house wasn't dead set on interrogating her. She lay down next to Thea and Houston and let the sounds of the cartoon turn her mind to mush.

Avery picked up and put down her phone about six times before she finally opened her texts. She glanced at the clock. It was almost nine p.m., and she wasn't sending anything that could sound like a booty call, but she didn't want Nicole to think it was—or, okay, maybe part of her did, but then—

"Oh my God, fucking knock it off," Avery said, tapping out her planned message.

Hey, she typed. *Like I said in the message I sent with my number, I have no idea what I'm doing. But I thought maybe we could plan to see each other...instead of randomly running into each other. Would you be up for that?*

Avery blew out a nervous breath after she hit send. It wasn't her finest, or smoothest, move, but it was a move. She tapped her fingers against the dining room table. Nicole didn't have to respond at all, but Avery believed she would. However, it was entirely likely that she wouldn't respond tonight.

Avery was exhausted, but a surge of anxious energy was making her restless. She whistled for Houston as she stood up, and the dog scampered down the stairs, probably from where she'd been lying guard at Thea's bedroom door. She skidded over the floor and stopped at Avery's side.

"Walk?" she said softly.

Houston quivered, then sat down, still shaking with excitement. Avery secured her leash and they set off into the evening. They made it a single block before Avery's phone vibrated.

"Let's see what she said, buddy."

Yes. I'm definitely up for that.

Avery grinned into the darkness. Her grin faltered when she remembered that she truly did not know what the hell she was doing, but did know she liked how she felt when she was with Nicole.

And that, she figured, was an excellent start.

CHAPTER TWENTY-ONE

There was a small crowd of middle-aged people hanging near the door to the building that housed Lumber Jane's, the female-owned axe-throwing business where Nicole had agreed to meet Avery. As she approached the group, she scanned them to make sure Avery wasn't among them, even though she was certain she would have immediately recognized her hair. Sure enough, the group was Avery-less. Nicole stopped a few feet from the door and turned toward the street.

A flicker in her brain wondered if axe throwing was really the best idea for a sort-of-maybe date with someone who was obviously shouldering some dark emotions. Then again, maybe it was just what Avery needed.

She'd been surprised when Avery texted two nights ago. She'd definitely felt the attraction sparking between them at the funeral home. And judging by the looks she'd caught on Avery's face, Avery felt it, too. But Nicole couldn't figure out where she stood with Avery, so the sudden proposal to plan to meet up instead of leaving it to fate that kept throwing them together

(Nicole's interpretation of Avery's text, of course) had brought a new round of questions to mind.

Tumbling through the hailstorm of questions, one certainty scrawled across her brain in bright red cursive: Avery had no idea what she was doing with Nicole.

Which left Nicole with only one task: to protect herself as she waded through this attraction. She could do that. She didn't love the idea of it, but she couldn't deny the pull she felt. She didn't *want* to deny it, either.

Besides, she was still going through her own grieving process. Slow and steady (if they could get to steady) was perfectly fine with her. Anything rushed would definitely be very, very—

"Hey. You made it."

Nicole looked up, her firm thoughts of moving slowly tossed to the side with abandon. God, Avery was pretty. She wore a smile that was genuine but tinged with caution. Nicole wanted to kiss that caution right off her face.

Chill, she commanded herself. "Hey," she said, hoping her voice was level. "Yeah, I've never been here before. Have you?"

Avery shook her head. Her hands were stuffed in the pockets of a beat-up black leather jacket that almost went at odds with what Nicole knew of her, but somehow looked perfect on her.

"Nope. But we have to make a deal before we go in."

Nicole tilted her head, curious. "Go on."

The caution was evaporating from Avery's smile, which set off tiny fireworks in Nicole's diaphragm. "Loser buys pizza."

A quick mental mapping reminded Nicole of a coal-fired pizza restaurant that was a five-minute walk away. "Stoke?"

An emphatic nod was Avery's only reply.

Nicole stuck out her hand. "Deal." She kept her cool when Avery took her hand and shook it, a shake that was firm and gentle all at once. A part of herself that she'd assumed died right along with her wife went ahead and swooned. She was certain her cheeks were heating with a furious blush, but thankfully Avery walked toward the building, leaving her to fan her cheeks as she followed.

Inside, the building was vibrating with life. Nicole looked around, shocked to see a bar. The idea of alcohol and axe throwing didn't seem brilliant, but the number of people walking around in official Lumber Jane's T-shirts was significant, so she assumed the alcohol-axe ratio was well managed.

She continued perusing the scene as Avery checked them in. There were a decent amount of people there with a wide range of athletic abilities. But the crowd wasn't boisterous or obnoxious; everyone seemed to be enjoying themselves in an excited but contained manner. The axe-throwing pens (Nicole had no idea what else to call them) lined the outside walls of the room, leaving a large area in the middle with long high-top tables and stools. Nicole perked up when she spied games on the tables. She loved nothing more than a good game of medium-sized Jenga. Giant Jenga was fun, too, but she'd bruised one too many toes playing that one.

"Okay, we're good to go." Avery returned to Nicole's side. Her nervous energy was palpable and Nicole watched as she tried to surreptitiously scan the room. "Want a drink?" she asked, eyes still tracking their surroundings.

"Actually, yeah. A beer would be great."

Avery continued looking around as they approached the bar. It almost seemed like she was looking for someone—or maybe looking to make sure someone *wasn't* there? Nicole had no idea, but by the time they'd gotten their beers and walked to their assigned axe-throwing pen, Avery had relaxed.

"Welcome to Lumber Jane's!" an ebullient woman said as they settled in. "I'm Eva."

"Nicole," she said, then pointed. "And this is Avery."

"Great! Have either of you been axe throwing before?" At their shaking heads, Eva grinned. "Awesome. I'll walk you through everything. Who wants to go first?"

Avery and Nicole looked at each other. Caught in the softness of Avery's stare, she swooned internally again.

"You can go first," Avery said. "I'll happily watch."

"So you can get all the good tips before you start?" Nicole shook her head. "Can't fool me, Avery."

She held up her hands in mock innocence. "I'm just trying to be chivalrous."

Nicole did her best to shoot her a mean glare, but it likely fell flat, as Avery grinned and nodded toward the pen.

"Show me what you can do."

The words sizzled through Nicole's body and she turned away, thankful for the break in eye contact. Her plan to protect herself was melting at an unprecedented rate.

Eva was waiting for her, axe in hand. "Let's do this!"

Nicole focused her attention on Eva's instructions, doing her best to ignore the fact that Avery was just a few feet behind her, leaning on the high-top table that separated her from the pen. Nicole tried like hell to forget how good Avery looked in something as simple as jeans and a long-sleeved T-shirt. And she really, really tried to erase that hot leather jacket from her mind.

She dutifully threw her axe time and time again, trying to work out the mechanics of stepping, lifting, and throwing. It was a weird combination of physically easy and mentally challenging. Each time she thought she'd nailed her throw, the axe died a sad death before hitting the board. But when she thought for sure she'd thrown a dud, that baby sailed right to the board and hit a mark.

Lesson over, Nicole returned to Avery and handed over the axe.

"That was impressive," Avery said before she left.

"It was not."

"Maybe not your throwing," she said. "But your determination."

"I'm nothing if not determined."

Avery dropped her glance, just for that millisecond of a blink, to Nicole's lips. When they locked eyes again, Avery's were dancing with something Nicole hadn't seen until that moment.

"I've noticed," Avery said. She moved away from the table and walked up to Eva.

"Shit," Nicole breathed, watching. If Avery had no idea what she was doing or what was happening between them, Nicole was going to have to spell it out for her.

Physically.

The thought tumbled through her, spotlighting shimmers of tenderness and arousal. Okay, fine, so the attraction had bloomed into something much bigger. Something palpable.

She did her best to shake it off and focus on watching Avery throw the damn axe, but of course the woman's hotness increased by approximately fifty percent when she was throwing a deadly weapon at a wooden board. Her long legs seemed to know exactly how far to step. Each time she raised her arms over her head, axe secured in her hands, her shirt rose just enough for Nicole to admire that wonderful ass. And when she retrieved her axe, she looked back at Nicole every single time. Her smile was full, her eyes bright.

Nicole was so distracted by Avery's strength and beauty that she missed the part where she should have been taking tips from how seamlessly she threw her axes. So when Eva set them up with a couple games to play, Nicole was doomed to failure.

"I hope you're enjoying your height advantage," she grumbled after losing a second round of Around the World.

Avery laughed, the axe dangling at her side. "I think your height has the advantage. You're just letting go too early." She grinned. "I'd coach you but I'm worried you'd chop my head off."

"After losing so fantastically, the thought is tempting." Nicole tapped her finger against her chin.

"Noted," Avery said. "Let's play Twenty-One instead. Maybe you'll have more luck."

"So kind of you," Nicole said as she swept past and took the axe. Avery stopped her by holding on to the axe, forcing Nicole to meet her eyes.

"Wanna know my secret?" Avery said, her voice low.

Nicole eyed her. "Yes. Tell me."

Avery moved closer, positioning her mouth right next to Nicole's ear. She inhaled deeply before she spoke, sending shivers down Nicole's arms. "Channel every ounce of shitty feelings you have inside of you, and toss them out when you let go of the axe."

"Is that really what you're doing?" Nicole whispered.

Avery moved a bit away. Her expression hardened and she shrugged. "Kind of. Just try it." With that, she moved behind the table, leaving Nicole with the axe hanging loosely from her hand.

Thoughts and images coursed through her mind as she turned back to the target. She no longer considered her grief "shitty," but she knew Avery hadn't intended to bring those two concepts together. Nicole, a naturally forgiving person, just didn't have a whole lot of shitty feelings to latch on to.

Oh. She paused. There was one. She'd buried it beneath the sadness, often feeling wrong or mean for attaching to that particular emotion. But it was still there, simmering.

With a deep breath, Nicole unlocked the tightly shut part of her heart that held knots of anger. She felt the rush immediately, a volcanic flood of blistering, thick ire. She shivered despite the overwhelming internal heat.

"Fine," she murmured, aiming her body at the target. "Here's a shitty feeling for you."

The axe hit with a resounding thud. Nicole stood, hands on hips, admiring it. It wasn't a bullseye—she could fine-tune her aim another time—but it had stuck and earned her five points.

The sound of clapping pulled her back, and she turned to see Avery watching her with admiration.

"I knew you had it in you."

Nicole scoffed as she picked up her beer. "You have no idea."

Avery passed her a curious look but didn't question. She moved toward the pen and threw her axe. When she turned, Nicole expected to see celebration over the bullseye she'd just nailed. Instead, Avery's face had darkened. The life had gone out of her eyes and every muscle in her body looked rigid. But then, as she strode toward Nicole, the hardness eased into something much softer. With a start, she realized it was sadness.

She congratulated Avery, all the while thinking just how much both of them held inside that neither had any idea about.

"You did put up a good fight." Avery leaned back in her chair. Whatever storm of emotions had momentarily overtaken her during axe throwing had drained back out. "Even if you lost every game we played."

Nicole held up a hand in protest. "Listen. I never said I excelled at athletic things."

"Oh," Avery said. "You mean to tell me you weren't a three-season athlete in high school?"

"Have you looked at me?"

Avery appraised her, warmth radiating on her face as tingles erupted yet again in Nicole's body. "I certainly have."

"Well then," Nicole said haughtily. "Not exactly the body of an athlete."

"Athletes can have all kinds of bodies," Avery pointed out. "But—" She cut herself off, suddenly very interested in her water glass.

"But what?"

Avery hesitated. "Before I answer that, can we clarify something?"

Nicole nodded.

"Is this—are we, you know?"

As much as she wanted to save Avery from her awkward fumbling, Nicole was enjoying her vulnerability too much. So, she waited her out. It didn't take long.

"Nicole," Avery said. "Are you really going to make me say it?"

"I sure am." She looked up. "Oh, lucky you. Interrupted by pizza."

The waitress set down their food. After Nicole assured her that they had everything they needed, she left, and Nicole raised her eyebrows at Avery.

"You were saying?"

But Avery had taken the opportunity to take a huge bite.

Nicole watched in amusement as her eyes watered and she fanned her mouth. "Patience really isn't your forte, huh?"

"Actually," Avery said after she managed to swallow the steaming-hot pizza, "I've been told I'm too patient."

Nicole leaned forward, careful to keep the sleeves of her sweatshirt out of her pizza, even though it was a faded black and wouldn't show the vibrant red sauce. "Maybe you could start being less patient and more direct."

The same expression that had clouded Avery's face at Lumber Jane's blinked on and off now. "Maybe," she said, though it sounded reluctant.

Nicole took the pizza, now cool enough to safely eat, as a fated sign that she should stop pushing. There was obviously a wound there, something unspoken and simmering, and she didn't want to be the one to poke it too hard. After all, Avery had been the one to ask her to hang out tonight. If she wanted to know whether or not it was a date, she could ask when she was ready.

"So if you didn't play sports in high school, what did you do?"

Nicole finished chewing before she replied. "Not much, honestly. I've always preferred the company of books to that of people."

"That doesn't surprise me."

"No? Why's that?"

Avery shrugged. "You don't seem like the type of person who needs to be around other people. You've got that fiercely independent thing going on." She shrugged again. "I could be wrong, but that's what it feels like to me."

"You're not wrong," Nicole said slowly. "People can be very draining."

Avery nodded. "I get that. I lived by myself for a long time, and then my buddy Gavin moved in with his daughter. The company is nice, sometimes, but it's hard when I want the house to myself and they're there." She cringed. "That sounds bad."

"No, I get it." Nicole paused, wondering if she should hop on the train that was at the forefront of her thoughts. Why not? "Did you feel like that when you lived with someone you were in a relationship with?"

Avery offered a crooked smile. "I've never done that."

"Seriously? You've never shacked up with someone? Not even U-Hauled?"

"Nope." She looked quite proud of herself. "I had a couple relationships in my twenties that managed to avoid that. Thankfully," she added. "And then I was engaged."

"Wait a minute," Nicole said, holding up both hands. "You were *engaged* and you never lived with the person you were engaged to?"

"Correct."

"You do realize that's a little odd."

Avery nodded as she chewed on a piece of crust. "Yeah. But I also realized that was a pretty clear sign that I didn't want to marry her."

Nicole wanted to ask so many more questions, but she had a feeling this sudden openness could stop as quickly as it had started.

"I actually bought my house when I was engaged," Avery continued. "Obviously that didn't go over well. But that relationship was dying before I bought the house."

"When did it end?" Nicole held her breath, hoping that was a gentle enough prod.

Avery wiped her hands on her napkin before lifting them to her hair. She pulled her hair tie out and chaotic waves of dark-red hair fell across her shoulders. Just as quickly as they'd fallen, they were scooped back up into another messy bun.

"About ten years ago."

Surprised, Nicole blinked several times. She'd been silently putting the pieces together, trying to understand the darkness that sometimes shrouded Avery. But ten years... It just didn't seem logical that she'd still be hurting over a relationship that had ended so long ago—and one that she seemed to have closure and clarity about.

Then again, the heart wasn't known for being logical.

"Since then," Avery said, her voice wavering between firm and agitated, "I've pretty much been alone. So when Gavin and Thea—that's his daughter—moved in, I felt less alone. In a way," she added, then seemed to regret it.

Nicole heard an omission in the words, but judging by the expression on Avery's face, now was not the time to press for more.

"Thanks for sharing that with me," she said instead.

Avery looked surprised. "You're thanking me?"

"Well, yeah." Nicole weighed her words before speaking. "You don't seem very open, so I appreciate that you felt comfortable sharing some of your past with me."

Some of the lively color faded from Avery's face. She nodded and picked up another piece of pizza. Nicole accepted that for what it was—a silent "that's enough for now"—and took another bite herself.

"Where'd you park?"

Nicole pointed to the parking garage down the street. "Over there."

"I'm around the corner." Avery looked around, then started walking toward the parking garage. "I'll walk you to your car."

"You don't have to," Nicole said, falling into step with her. "This area is pretty safe."

"I'll feel better knowing you got to your car safely."

She didn't protest. As they walked, the sounds of the city— Weston, about seven miles from Balsam Lake—buffered them. Sirens wailed from blocks away. They walked past a bar that had its front door thrown open. Music from a subpar cover band rushed out into the street. Drunken singing bounded out with it, threaded through by screeches of laughter.

Avery bumped into her, muttering "Sorry" before putting a little more distance between them. Nicole didn't want more distance but felt she had to respect what Avery seemed to need.

And, right. Nicole's sole job was to feel the attraction while protecting herself. Got it.

She stole a glance at Avery, who looked tired but content, as though their time together had stolen some of her energy but also rounded out some of her sharper edges.

"What level are you on?"

"The second." Nicole stopped them at the door. "Avery, you really don't have to walk me up. I'll be okay."

Confusion creased Avery's face. "Do you not want me to walk you up?"

Nicole scuffed the toe of her boot against the sidewalk. "I guess my answer depends on the answer to the question you never finished asking when we were at dinner."

After a long pause, Avery brightened. "That's right. The pizza stole my moment."

"Kinda seemed like you wanted it to," Nicole said, keeping her tone light.

"I wasn't mad at the pizza for barging in like that." Avery smiled. "Okay. We're adults, right?"

"Yes. Definitely."

"So this doesn't have to be weird?"

Nicole shook her head. "Let's avoid weird."

"Okay. Then this was a date, right?"

The shred of tentativeness in her voice made Nicole smile. "Yes. It was a date."

Avery nodded. "Glad we got that settled." She gestured to the door. "Would you like me to walk you up?"

"Actually," Nicole said, taking a step closer, "let's say goodbye here."

"Goodbye." Avery turned to walk away, and Nicole grabbed her arm, laughing. When she turned back around, Avery grinned and tugged Nicole closer until their bodies connected in a hug.

Nicole took shallow breaths, not wanting to disturb the moment. Her body was warming from her toes up, every inch that was connected to Avery fueling the flames. As they stood, locked in an embrace, Nicole remembered Ginny saying how their bodies "just fit together."

She'd always believed her because she'd felt it too. But this, the way Avery's arms were tight around her back, the way Nicole's arms looped around Avery's waist and nestled against her lower back—this fit, too. Nicole rested her cheek against Avery's shoulder. She could definitely get used to their small height difference.

Just as she was wondering if she would need to make the move, Avery shifted. Before she could react, Avery gently held her chin in place and leaned down to kiss Nicole's cheek.

"My turn," she whispered, then stepped back. "Good night, Nicole."

Nicole turned to watch her walk away. She was fading into the hubbub of the street by the time Nicole responded.

"Good night, Avery."

CHAPTER TWENTY-TWO

Avery was trying her absolute best not to let her irritation show. After all, it was her literal job to put up with the whims and fancies of indecisive brides—and to do it with a smile on her face.

She couldn't muster up a smile while seated across from Liana Chastain. There was something about the woman that put Avery on edge every time she walked into the shop. Part of her wished she'd turned down the wedding, but it was a big job, which meant big money. Liana wanted flowers not only for the wedding and reception, but also for the rehearsal dinner, and she was currently pitching the idea of Avery making take-home bouquets for all the single women who would be attending.

"And roses!" Liana clapped her hands, the glare from her aggressively large engagement ring nearly blinding Avery. "The bouquets need to be loaded with roses. Is there a good color to show, like, the fact that they're single?" She giggled, and it nearly sounded coquettish, but the underlying arrogance prevented it.

"Is that mean? I don't want to be mean! But I would love for everyone at the wedding to know these gorgeous girls are single and ready to mingle!"

Avery stopped herself from picking up the nearest medium-weight object and throwing it at the woman. She chose to step away from violence and embrace the challenge. "Wait. I thought these were take-home bouquets."

"They are, but it would be nice if they were on the tables when the guests arrive at the reception," Liana said, as though it was the most logical explanation possible. "That way they can have them during the reception so people can know they're single *and* they have something to take home to remember the night by!"

Veronica leaned forward. Avery was so caught up in Liana's unhinged ideas that she'd forgotten Veronica was sitting next to her.

"I love this idea, Liana, I really do. But let's think about practicality for a minute." Veronica went on with a very sound explanation, and Liana's eyes glazed over.

"I just need to clarify something," Avery said during a lull in Veronica's explanation. "Is this a wedding or a singles mixer?"

Liana laughed loudly. "A wedding, of course!" She crossed her arms over her chest, a defiant glint in her dark-brown eyes. "But I feel so bad for my single girlfriends. I'm sure it'll be really hard for them to watch me get married to the most incredible man while they sit there, alone. I thought this would be a nice way to help them find someone."

Avery sighed. "That's very thoughtful of you. I think Veronica and I can work something out that will make everyone happy." She knew Veronica was gawking at her, but Avery had no energy to fight this situation. She stood abruptly. "Let me go get some samples for you. Feel free to continue sharing ideas with Veronica. I'll be right back."

She escaped as quickly as possible. Brides didn't normally have this much of an effect on her—and she'd worked with her fair share of entitled or clueless women. Liana's little crusade to help her single friends was laughable, at least superficially, but it was bumping against a buried hurt inside of Avery, and she needed a breather.

Back in the workroom, Zuri was putting together an anniversary bouquet for a local business. Avery smiled, idly wondering who would do the flowers for her shop's anniversary. It seemed silly to provide them herself. Maybe she'd stick with balloons.

"Not a fan?" Zuri's voice was a soothing balm, low and melodic. Avery's agitated and defensive attitude immediately started to alleviate.

"She's a lot," she said, hoping that would suffice. "I just needed a break."

Zuri nodded as she clipped the stems of a handful of bright yellow ranunculus. They were the superstars of the arrangement, and Avery was thrilled with the intensity of their color.

"I didn't go into this business for the weddings," Avery mumbled as she leaned against the table at which Zuri was standing. "They're so stressful. Brides have all these expectations and wild ideas." Avery pulled the elastic out of her hair and ran her fingers through her curls.

"You help them curb their ideas. The end result is always great, Avery."

"Yeah." She couldn't argue. Her weddings really were incredible. "But still. I just wanted to put flowers into bouquets and make people happy."

"You do make people happy."

Avery snorted. "Name five."

Zuri assessed her, locking eyes until Avery looked away. "We're not talking about business anymore, are we?"

Dipping her head down, Avery used her long hair as a shield. She hadn't told anyone she went out with Nicole (again? It seemed like a better idea to qualify last week's outing as their first date and let their Looper's evening ride off into the sunset without a label) and something was keeping her from owning up to it now. She knew the bulk of it was fear. She'd gotten so accustomed to that emotion that when it wasn't wrapped around her like a well-worn blanket, she felt naked and exposed—and vulnerable.

In the week since they'd last seen each other, Nicole and Avery had done plenty of texting. They'd both been wrapped up with work, but there seemed to be an unspoken agreement that they both wanted to go out again. Nicole had made a comment about taking things slow, and Avery had emphatically agreed.

So slow that they hadn't yet made plans to see each other… But that could be solved with a single text.

Avery straightened as she wound her hair into a loose topknot. "It's not my responsibility to make people happy." She tapped on the counter. "Personally, that is."

Zuri grinned. "Damn right."

The door swooshed open and Veronica rushed in. "You're up," she said, pointing at Avery. "That woman is exhausting."

Zuri held out her hand and Avery slapped it. It gave her just the bump of confidence she needed.

"Oh," Veronica said, hiding a grin. "Her mom is here now, too."

After collecting an armful of various flowers, Avery shot daggers from her eyes as she backed out of the workroom. "I could kill you," she whispered menacingly.

She left to the sound of Veronica calling out some kind of retort-threat. Avery smiled despite the budding stress. She was lucky to have such great coworkers: not only were they excellent flower arrangers and overall businesspeople, but they were also able to handle her twisted sense of humor and wayward murder threats.

"Okay," Avery said as she walked back to the storefront. "I've got samples for you."

Liana squealed and the woman sitting next to her smiled appreciatively. Avery relaxed instinctively. Liana's mother looked nothing like her—but more importantly, her energy was totally different.

"Hello," the woman said, extending her hand. "I'm Hilari Chastain, Liana's mother."

"Avery Pullman." She shook Hilari's hand. "It's nice to meet you."

"You as well. Your flowers are beautiful," she said, smiling warmly. "My good friend's daughter, Colleen Bankhurst, won't stop raving about the flowers you provided for her girlfriend's coming-out party."

Avery did her best not to laugh. Genevieve was actually dating Colleen? She couldn't wait to tell Nicole. "That's very kind of her."

"I wasn't there," Liana said. Avery couldn't put her finger on Liana's tone, but she didn't love it. "Heard it was a blast, though."

There it was: pompous exclusion. She didn't peg Liana for a homophobe, but she had a feeling that even though Colleen's mom and Liana's mom were friends, that generational branch of compatibility hadn't extended down to their daughters. Avery looked more closely at Liana. She was probably right between Genevieve and Colleen, age-wise, and Balsam Lake wasn't that big. Maybe some leftover high school drama, Avery thought. The idea cheered her up.

The bell over the door rang, pulling her from her useless trail of thoughts. She did a double take when someone came in wearing a black beanie tugged low. She wouldn't be surprised if Nicole was stopping by, but when she looked closer, the woman who'd come in looked nothing like her.

"Hi," Avery said brightly, turning away from Liana and Hilari. Her smile widened as the door opened a second time and another woman walked in, bouncing a ring of keys in her hand. Avery's gaydar was pinging off the charts and her heart slowly soared, wondering if finally—

"Hi," the second woman said easily. "We'd like to set up a time for a wedding consultation."

Avery's heart shot off into the stratosphere. She'd been waiting for this moment: her first lesbian wedding. She nearly tripped over herself as she walked to the sapphire blue armchairs, motioning for the women to follow her.

"I can get you set up with that." With perfect timing, just as Avery excused herself from the Chastain women, Veronica came back into the storefront. Avery wiggled her eyebrows, hoping to translate some silent message. Veronica shot her a snarky grin and headed to Liana and her mother. Relieved, Avery turned to her newest brides to be.

"I'm Avery," she said, trying her best not to bubble over with excitement. "Why don't you start by telling me about yourselves? Then we'll set up our first official meeting."

Later, after Zuri had helped close up shop, Avery leaned back in her office chair, going over the highs and lows of the day. She would get through Liana Chastain's wedding with a whole lot of help from Veronica—and Zuri, even if she had to drag her into it. It would work out, even if she was forced to make those ridiculous "I'm Single!" bouquets.

She hadn't spent much time with the lesbian couple, Maya and J.C. But the ten minutes or so of chatting with them had filled her with an excited sense of purpose. She knew marketing herself as an LGBTQ+-only wedding-flower provider would not provide enough income, but it was tempting. At the very least, she was hopeful that Maya and J.C.'s wedding would help bring her shop more exposure in the local gay community.

Avery leaned back further, testing the limits of her chair. Meeting Maya and J.C. had reminded her of the little bomb she'd dropped on Nicole about her former engagement. So much time had passed since the dissolution of that relationship that her ex-fiancée no longer crossed her mind very much at all, and the fact that she'd so easily told Nicole was an even surer sign that the whole situation was so far in Avery's past that she officially no longer had feelings attached to it. However, there was a bit of stigma knotting her thoughts: she didn't want her past to come across to Nicole as an indication that Avery was a commitment-phobe.

The truth was that for a period of time, she had genuinely believed that she wanted to marry her ex-fiancée. She'd loved her very much, and they'd had a good friendship. But their pieces were mismatched, corners trying to jam themselves into round openings. Fortunately, they'd ended their relationship before they went through with the marriage, which would have complicated their breakup in ways Avery preferred not to think about.

What did make her laugh, especially now that she worked with brides-to-be, was that Avery and her ex had sent out save-the-dates, secured a venue…and then nothing more. Absolutely no wedding planning happened. And yet, at the time of their breakup, they were scheduled to be married *in a month's time*. What the fuck they were thinking, Avery had no idea—she could only assume her ex-fiancée had at some point had similar realizations post-breakup. But they didn't speak, which was definitely for the best.

Avery rolled her head to the side, looking out the window in her office. She liked that she had definitively known that she did not want to marry her ex-fiancée. She didn't love that she couldn't yet say the same about Shannon.

It was the what-if. The possibility. The *potential*. Avery shook her head. She'd been trying so hard to let go of all of it, but Shannon had a deep hold on her that was frustratingly difficult to disengage. When she really thought about it, though, marrying Shannon wouldn't have solved their problems. It would have likely created more of a different variety.

The thing that kept her hooked was that if they were married, Shannon would be her wife. There would be no mistaking who Shannon loved, to whom she was devoted. Everyone would know it was Avery, and there would be no more uncertainty, no more questioning. No more ex-girlfriend clinging to the side of their boat.

But Avery also knew marriage wasn't the answer. It wouldn't magically solve the issue of Shannon refusing to let go of her past. Marriage was a label, a descriptor, a ring that could be taken off. It didn't erase people, feelings, or experiences. It wasn't a solution.

And it wasn't a guarantee of forever. Avery swallowed as she thought of Nicole having been married, thinking it was forever, only to lose her wife. And not even through divorce: through death. If either of them deserved to be more jaded about the permanency of love, it was certainly Nicole.

Avery pushed herself out of her chair and gathered her things. It wasn't a competition, she reminded herself as she walked through the shop, double checking the lights. They each had their battle wounds and every ripple of scarred skin was worthy of acknowledgment. It didn't matter how messy and inexplicable the scars were; Avery had a feeling Nicole was the exact right person to understand.

She nodded as she locked the door to her pride and glory, resolution lifting her shoulders as she walked to her car.

It was still light out when Avery let Houston tug her out the front door for an evening walk. She'd turned down Gavin's offer of company. She wanted to be alone for her next step in moving forward.

Houston trotted along, lifting her nose to catch scents. Avery kept her phone in her left hand. She was going to make a call, but she wanted to make sure she was ready before she hit the button.

"Okay," she breathed after she and Houston had covered a couple blocks, slowing their pace as she hit call and brought the phone to her ear.

"Well hello," Nicole said. The smile in her voice lightened Avery's mood instantly.

"Hey. Is this an okay time to talk?"

"Yeah, absolutely. I'm just reading."

Avery smiled. "Anything good?"

"I'm not sure yet," Nicole said. "I wanted to DNF after the first chapter, but the second chapter was an improvement, so we'll see."

"What the fuck is DNF?"

Nicole laughed. "Book nerd speak for 'did not finish.' I used to push through books even if I wasn't enjoying them, but I recently discovered the beauty of tossing them aside if they're not working for me."

"Well, yeah, sounds like a waste of time otherwise."

"Exactly. So, what's up? Any flower crises today?"

Avery paused at the corner, debating which way to turn. Houston decided for her, leading them toward the street where there were no dogs running around in fenced-in yards. "You wouldn't even believe it if I told you."

"I'm all ears."

"I'll tell you all about it another time." Avery bit her bottom lip. Now or never. "I actually wanted to talk to you about something else, but I need to do it now so I don't lose my nerve."

Nicole was quiet a couple seconds before saying, "Okay. I'm all ears for that, too."

Of course she was. Avery dropped her gaze to the ground. She wasn't sure if she deserved someone as, just, *good* as Nicole. She'd never questioned her self-worth this much and knew it was a by-product of what she'd gone through with Shannon, which made her anxious and angry all at once.

She tempered her feelings and plowed ahead. The need to be honest was loud and refusing to let go.

"Remember how I was talking about some of my old relationships?"

"Yes."

"And how I maybe got a little dodgy about the last ten years? Since I split with my ex-fiancée?"

"Yes."

"Okay. This is—I don't know how to explain it." Avery clenched her teeth.

"Just say it, Avery. If I have questions, I'll ask."

She looked toward the sky before speaking. "I literally hate to use this term but it's the only way I know to describe it. I was basically in a situationship. For the last seven years or so." She waited for an interjection or a laugh from Nicole, but there was just silence, the sound of an incredibly patient person listening to her crank open her dented box of regrets. "There were relationship-things that happened and were talked about, but I was single. So I wasn't alone, but I was alone. If that makes sense."

"It does."

"Do you want to hang up on me?"

Nicole scoffed. "Why would I want to do that? This is just part of your story, Avery. Keep going, I'm listening."

"I don't want to get into all the details right now," Avery said. She could feel herself slowly deflating, the initial burst of energy from the admission starting to wane. "But I wanted you to know that—I don't know." She blew out an exasperated breath. "It's been really hard for me to let go of her because we never had the kind of relationship I wanted, mostly because her ex was always in the picture. So I feel like I swim in a sea of what-ifs."

"So poetic," Nicole said. Avery heard the smile in her voice, thankful it was that instead of sarcasm. "But I get it."

"It's hard."

"I can imagine. And for the record, I'll listen to whatever you want to tell me about it. And I'll never make you share something you don't want to."

"How are you just so—so nice? About everything?"

Nicole laughed and the sound brought a smile to Avery's face. "Believe me, I'm not nice about everything. But when it comes to your heart and what it's been through, of course I'm going to be nice about that."

"And not hold it against me?" Avery winced, waiting for the response.

"Why would I?" After a pause, Nicole said, "Are you still involved with her?"

"No." The word came so fast, so easily, Avery was thrown. "I haven't blocked her number, but I did cut off communication with her."

"Okay. That's a good step."

Avery heard the miniscule change in Nicole's tone, but didn't bring it up. She couldn't blame her; she just didn't want to hurt Nicole, even if it was with honesty.

"I was thinking about her when I was throwing axes," Avery said.

"Ah," Nicole said. "I wondered what was going through your brain."

"Not in a sweet way," she quickly added. "And not in an I-want-to-throw-an-axe-at-her way, either."

"You were channeling your shitty feelings."

"Yeah." Avery smiled. "Believe me, I've got a fucking stockpile of hurt feelings from over the years, and I was finally able to kind of, I don't know, turn them into strength."

"Then I'd say axe throwing did its job."

"Definitely a solid start," Avery said. They were both quiet for a moment, then Nicole spoke.

"Correct me if I'm wrong, but I think you're realizing that your situationship is dead in the water."

"Wow, don't hold back, Nicole."

She laughed. "Am I wrong?"

Avery thought about it before responding. "No. You're right. It's just the letting go despite knowing that that's so fucking hard. I don't get it."

"I do. You haven't properly mourned the loss."

"Oh, trust me, there's been plenty of mourning over the last seven years."

"I believe you, but maybe there's more."

Avery shook her head in disbelief. She felt herself smile and again was struck by how effortlessly the coolness of Nicole was seeping into the sun-scorched cracks of her most blistered internal corners. "You're probably right."

"I usually am," Nicole said, confidence bright and heavy in her tone.

"I'm learning that."

"Good." She cleared her throat. "Now, I know just the thing to help you start to really let go of this. Are you up for it?"

"Uh, what is it?"

"I'm not telling you that, because you'll overthink it and then when we do it, it won't be organic, which will defeat the purpose. So. I'll ask you again. Are you up for it?"

Avery grinned. "Yeah, I am. Unless it's some kind of weird cult-joining situation."

"That comes later. Are you free tomorrow at all?"

She ran through her Sunday schedule in her head. "I work until three. Free after that."

"Great. Are you a shower after work kind of person?"

"Trust me, you'll want me to shower after work."

"You're so considerate. How about you come over at five? I'll text you my address."

Avery nodded, forgetting that Nicole couldn't see her. "Sounds good. Do I need to bring anything?"

"Just your heart," Nicole said, her voice gentle. "That's it."

"I can do that," Avery said, echoing her gentleness. "Thanks, Nicole."

She laughed. "Don't thank me yet. I'll text you later, okay?"

Avery nodded again. "Okay. See ya."

"Bye, Avery."

Phone tucked back in her pocket, Avery blew out a long, heavy breath. She couldn't say she felt better, necessarily, having begun to open up. There was so much more she should say— wanted to say, if she really thought about it—but for once, she was leaning into patience and trusting that it would take her where she needed to go instead of where she stubbornly believed she wanted to go.

CHAPTER TWENTY-THREE

"Lovely weather we're having." Brynn looked around the small entryway before she shook the sleeves of her rain jacket.

"Thanks for the extra shower," Nicole said drily, brushing the droplets from her own jacket, which was practically dry. As usual, she'd arrived at the restaurant well before Brynn, who didn't seem to have a punctual bone in her body now that she was out of the Army. Nicole's early arrival had allowed her to avoid the sudden downpour that was currently drenching the streets.

"No one made you stand so close to me."

"Excuse me, *I* was standing here first." Nicole made a dramatic show of continuing to flick the rain from her sleeves. "*You* chose to stand close to me."

"Missed you too." Brynn pulled her into a side hug that lasted about as long as the blink of an eye. "I'm starving. Is our table ready?"

"Now that you're here, yes." Nicole approached the hostess, gesturing for Brynn to follow. Soon after, they were seated in a cozy booth next to the wall of windows.

Broken Yolks was Nicole's favorite brunch haunt. She couldn't count the number of times she'd been there with Ginny. At one point, they'd had a favorite waiter who knew their orders inside and out. Since Ginny's death, though, Nicole had struggled to come in. She'd made it once, by herself, and nearly suffocated in anxiety afterwards. That, and she hadn't been able to order her favorite—Belgian waffles with blueberry compote and a side of extra-crispy bacon—because Ginny wasn't there to do their usual split/share and it felt wrong to have the meal to herself.

Now that the three-year anniversary (an odd way to title it, but Nicole didn't know what else to call it) of Ginny's death was approaching, she'd felt a renewed need to reclaim Broken Yolks. It was too soon to take Avery, so she'd been thrilled when Brynn agreed to meet for Sunday brunch.

Nicole looked around, pleased that the decor hadn't changed. Broken Yolks was comfortable and eclectic; pretty much nothing matched, but it somehow worked. The walls were a bright orange that was barely visible beneath the art scattered over every available surface. The owner made a point to feature pieces from local artists, but he had a soft spot for creations that were breakfast-themed. Case in point, a large painting of avocado toast being hoisted to an open mouth by toy forklifts hung across from where Nicole sat.

Brynn pushed a menu toward her, and she immediately pushed it back. Brynn raised her eyebrows. "I thought you said you hadn't been here for a while."

"I haven't, but I know what I want."

"What if the menu changed?"

That horrifying thought hadn't occurred to her. She shot Brynn an annoyed look as she picked up the menu. Seconds later, she tossed it back to the table. "Nothing's changed, thank you very much."

Brynn grinned as she continued looking over her options. "You get the same thing every time?"

Nicole hesitated. She hadn't worked out if she wanted to try to re-create the brunch she'd always had with Ginny or if she wanted to try something new. Since she was with Brynn, she knew she was safe to revert back to familiar habits…but part of her wanted to break out of the old pattern. Begin to forge a new path and all that.

"I used to," Nicole said slowly. "But I have two ideas in mind. Whichever comes out of my mouth when we order is what I'll get."

Brynn put her menu down and turned her full attention to Nicole. "Why do I feel like that carries way more weight than just a breakfast option?"

"Brunch," she corrected, smiling. "But also, yes."

"And you dragged me out in this monsoon," Brynn said, jerking her thumb at the windows next to them, which were currently being slammed by sheets of rain, "to bear witness to your new *brunch* selection?"

Nicole thought about kicking her under the table, but settled for throwing a balled up napkin. "It's more than that."

"I figured as much."

They paused the conversation to place their orders with a waiter Nicole had never seen before—but of course she hadn't, since she hadn't walked into the restaurant in well over a year.

"Okay," Brynn said once they were alone again. "So was that your regular?"

Nicole grinned. "Nope. I've never had the huevos rancheros." She paused. "Not gonna lie, though, I might get a Belgian waffle to go because they are incredible."

"No judgment." Brynn leaned back in her chair, watching Nicole carefully. "Cut to the chase, Callahan. What's going on?"

"Avery," she blurted, unable to keep it all locked inside. Nicole was a loner at heart but sometimes she missed being close to people she trusted. Case in point: figuring out this Avery situation was way too much for one brain.

"Dog park girl?"

"Yes." Nicole allowed herself a moment of remembering that day and the way Avery's dog had seemed to sense her need for comfort. "We went out. On an actual date. Or, I guess, a re-do date."

A grin split Brynn's face. "And?"

"And...Honestly, Brynn, I'm not sure." Nicole picked up a raw sugar packet and fidgeted with it. "There's definitely an attraction there. Nothing's happened," she added.

"But you feel the potential for something to happen?"

Nicole nodded.

"And you're freaking out about that?"

"Actually, no. That's not what it is." She looked around the restaurant before continuing, "I knew there was something—"

A flash of lightning lit up their table yet they both jumped at the following clap of thunder.

"When did April showers become April storms?" Brynn asked as she stared out the window. With a start, she looked back at Nicole. "Oh. Whoa. It's April."

Nicole nodded. The raw sugar packet was so damp in her hands, she was about to have a slick of sticky sugar on her palms. "It's April," she echoed.

They looked at each other, the road of unspoken words stretching between them, vowels and consonants laid to waste in the brush lining the potholed surface. Nicole tried to take a deep breath but found she couldn't. Instead, she settled for shallow gulps as she watched a squall of emotions storm over Brynn's face.

Finally, she spoke. "Do you want to talk about it?"

Nicole shook her head. "Nope. Not today."

"Nic..."

"No, Brynn." She shook her head again. "It's a couple weeks away yet. I don't want to focus my attention on something that's unavoidable." Nicole held her stare. "What I need to talk about is Avery."

"Okay," Brynn said after a moment. She leaned back so their waiter could set down their meals. Brynn wasted no time digging in, and Nicole knew that was her way of resetting.

"Happy with your new choice?" Brynn asked after they'd eaten silently for a while. She was nearly finished with her eggs Benedict.

"Extremely." Nicole set down her fork, ready for a break and a talk. "So, Avery." At Brynn's nod, she continued, "I like her. I like how I feel when I'm around her. I know that in the grand scheme of things, I barely know her, but I like what I'm learning. Her walls are higher than mine, but she's started opening up to me. Little steps."

"I like little steps." Brynn wiped her mouth. "Little steps make big paths."

"Did you just make that up?"

"I did."

"That's terrible." Nicole grinned and shook her head. "Leave the fancy word stuff to me, okay?"

Brynn smiled as she loaded her fork with eggs and Canadian bacon. "What are you learning about Avery?"

"Well," Nicole said. Although this was the whole point of the conversation, she suddenly didn't feel great about sharing Avery's business. Nicole didn't know specifics, however, so she didn't think she was breaking any great confidences between them.

"I got the sense that she was holding something back," Nicole began. "Not the first time we met. She was too busy being a defensive asshole then, which, yes, I have called her out on. It was one of the times I ran into her at the funeral home. I could just tell there was something deeper in her that she was trying like hell to hide."

"Ever the detective."

"It's not like that." Nicole pushed a piece of chicken chorizo around her plate. "More like a common feeling. Something we shared, but I couldn't put my finger on it."

Brynn held her coffee mug in front of her mouth. "Is she a widow?"

"No." Nicole bit the inside of her cheek. "But she's definitely dealing with grief, even if she's not aware of it."

"Nic, just say what her deal is. I'm not going to hold it against her."

Nicole wasn't entirely sure about that. "She spent the last seven years in what she referred to as a situationship. And she said she cut off communication, but I don't think her feelings have been cut off."

Brynn's coffee mug landed on the table with a firm thud. "Then why are you still talking to her?"

"I knew you'd question that."

"How could I not?"

"I know," Nicole said evenly, keeping her cool just as Brynn was. The nonemotional element of their friendship was something she valued, and so different from any other friendship she'd had over the years. "She told me last night that it's been a sea of what-ifs—her words, not mine—because the other woman's ex has always been in the picture."

Brynn rolled her eyes. "Lesbians. Okay. So what happens if you and Avery get into a relationship and her ex-situation comes back, promising she's done with her ex?"

The huevos in Nicole's stomach turned to lead. She'd thought of that; it was one of many tempestuous thoughts that had rolled through her mind after hanging up with Avery last night. And she had no idea what would happen. So she shrugged.

"Nic, I gotta say, you really have a thing for wounded women."

She chafed at that but couldn't argue the point. "Hear me out," she said. "Avery's got her stuff to work through, right?"

Brynn nodded.

"Do we honestly think I'm completely over losing my wife?"

"I think you're pretty damn far in the process, so far that you're definitely interested in someone else and thinking about what could happen if you began a relationship with that someone else." Brynn's expression grew serious. "And maybe you won't ever be completely over it, Nic. You'll just keep learning new ways to live with it."

Nicole swallowed around the lump in her throat. "Okay, yeah. But what if Avery is exactly who I need right now? Since she's working through her own healing process—and Brynn, I really do believe she is—and I'm still working on mine, there's no risk of us getting super attached to each other. We can date, see where it goes, but keep working on ourselves and keep our hearts locked down so we don't fall for each other."

Brynn wrinkled her nose. "That's the most ass-backwards theory I've ever heard."

"I think it's brilliant."

"Well, I'm here to burst your bubble. Nic, you can't control whether or not you get attached. You can both try to keep it casual, but unless one of you is incapable of connecting on an emotional level"—she pointed to herself—"then someone is going to get attached, and someone is probably going to get hurt."

"I didn't get attached to you," Nicole pointed out.

"Yeah, because you weren't emotionally available then." Brynn raised her eyebrows. "You've healed that part of yourself. That's why you were able to stop sleeping with me. You didn't need that emotionless connection anymore. Whether or not you want to admit it to yourself, I can tell you're interested in Avery on an emotional level. The fact that we're even having this conversation tells me that."

"Is that the worst thing?"

"I don't know."

Nicole blew out a breath. "Yeah, me either."

"When are you seeing her again?"

Nicole smiled. "Tonight. She's coming over."

"So much for not getting attached."

"It's not like that," she protested. "I'm going to help her with the letting-go process."

"Oh my God," Brynn groaned. "That's not your job!"

"I know." Nicole smiled despite herself. "I'm not doing it for her, or making her do something she doesn't want to do. But you have to admit, I'm pretty good at helping people figure out how to hold on to what's important while letting go of what needs to be let go."

Brynn stared at her, then shook her head with a sigh. "Yeah, I can't argue that. I just don't want to see you get hurt."

"I don't want to get hurt," she said firmly. "And we both need to trust that I'll see myself out if I sense that's starting to happen."

It took a minute, but Brynn finally agreed. Satisfied, Nicole sat back and dug back into her huevos rancheros.

Just as Avery knocked on the door, Nicole was finishing an internal freak-out about how she would be seen through her apartment. She still hadn't gotten around to doing much decorating, and the spots of blankness were irritating her. She didn't want Avery to think she lived in this very monochromatic, neutral world, but it was way too late for an emergency redecorating.

"Hey," Nicole said as she opened the door.

Avery smiled nervously. "Hey. I brought these for you."

Nicole took the bouquet. She'd been wondering if Avery was the type to bring flowers to a woman. Now she had her answer, though she suspected it wasn't an everyday occurrence. "These are incredible," she said, examining the bouquet.

"I know you like peonies," Avery said, "but these ranunculi are way too pretty not to share."

And they were. Avery hadn't wasted much space with filler flowers, letting the wild array of peach and white blooms have their moment of glory.

"Those will bloom in a few days," Avery said, pointing to three small red buds deep in the bouquet. "I wanted to make sure you could enjoy this for a while."

"Thank you so much." Nicole shut the door and moved into the kitchen. "Is there anything special I should do?"

"Well, I didn't bring you a *vase*," Avery said with a teasing grin, "because I remember you saying you had too many of them."

Leaving Avery and the flowers in the kitchen, she crouched in front of the cabinets in her living room and pulled out her favorite squat, square vase.

"I'm not showing you the collection," she said as she returned to the kitchen, where Avery was already moving the flowers around. "You'll just have to believe me."

"Do you hoard them?"

"No!" Nicole laughed. "It's just a weird thing that I have too many of." She watched as Avery delicately placed the flowers in the vase, adjusting a few stems as she did. "Beautiful. Thank you."

"You're welcome." Avery looked around. "This place is really cool."

"Here, I'll give you the short tour." Nicole led her through the loft, but considering it was a very open space aside from the bedroom and bathroom, the tour didn't take long at all. They soon settled in the living room in the chairs near the windows. Nicole took her favorite oversized armchair, leaving Avery to enjoy the olive-green velvet club chair that was far more comfortable than it appeared.

"I think I could sit here all day," Avery said as she looked out the windows. "You get great evening light in here."

She was right—the longer spring days blessed the space with golden-hour light that Nicole practically bathed in. Now, just after five p.m., was only the beginning.

"Yeah, I love it. My neighbor across the hall gets all the good morning light, though. I wouldn't mind some of that." Nicole tucked her legs under her. "Shall we get started?"

Avery looked over at her, surprise evident in the abrupt movement. "Cutting right to the chase, huh?"

"No time like the present. Besides," Nicole said, hoping she wasn't being too forward, "it sounds like this is overdue."

Avery half-laughed, half-snorted. "You could say that. Okay. Let's do whatever it is that we're doing."

Nicole grinned, hoping her excitement didn't make her look too eager to rid Avery of a woman who clearly didn't deserve her. "We're going to write a eulogy!"

The expression on Avery's face was priceless, one Nicole couldn't describe despite her talent with words. "You're fucking kidding me."

"I am most certainly not kidding you." She reached over and picked up the pen and pad of paper from the side table, passing them to Avery. "As you know, I believe in the power of eulogies when it comes to highlighting the good in preparation for letting go of something that can't be held on to any longer."

Avery did snort that time, a shameless sound that made Nicole laugh. "Is that what you say to the people you help?"

"Something like that, yes."

"Oh," Avery said, lighting up. "Is this professional Nicole that I'm dealing with?"

Her tone sparked the kindling buried within Nicole. "Yes. Do you like it?"

Avery grinned, mischief lighting up her eyes. "Oh, I do. Please, go on. But before you do, I think you should tell me how the hell you started writing eulogies for people. I mean," she said, sitting back in her chair, "you gotta admit it's not your run-of-the-mill side hustle."

Nicole nodded. She had nothing to hide, and yet she was nervous. "I wrote my wife's eulogy." She cringed. "I mean, I wrote a eulogy and gave it at my wife's funeral."

Avery stared at her. Finally, she said, "You...you wrote a eulogy for your wife. After she died?"

"Yeah." Nicole shrugged, hiding her smile at the whole "after she died" part. "I knew her best, so..."

Avery visibly pulled back, shock shadowing her features. "That's awful."

"Which part?"

"The part where you, just, scribbled out words and just, like, stood there. And talked about someone you'd been married to while they lay there. Dead."

"Well, she was cremated, so..."

"Oh my God." Avery held her hand against her mouth. "Okay. Wow. I feel like I'm missing details here."

"To be clear, we are not here to talk about me," she said, waiting for Avery's nod. "But since I'm about to make you open up in ways you probably don't want to open up, I guess it's the right time to give you more information." Nicole put her elbows on her knees and leaned forward. "Remember when we were axe throwing and you told me to channel my shitty feelings?"

Avery nodded again, her focus intent on Nicole.

"Grief is weird. I spent a lot of time in the sadness and depression, the anxiety and fear. But I didn't spend a lot of time with the anger part of the process, mostly because I don't like feeling angry." She bit the inside of her cheek, wincing when she hit the raw spot she'd bitten earlier that day. "But I let myself feel that anger when you told me to. I probably should feel it more often." Nicole sat up and ran her hands over her hair, a nervous gesture of nothingness since her hair was all neatly tucked into her ponytail. "My wife died by suicide. So, yeah, there's a lot of anger that I don't let myself feel."

"Oh, shit," Avery said quietly, immediately leaning toward Nicole. "I had no idea."

"I know. And honestly, I didn't really want to tell you, because it makes it all...I don't know. Different."

Avery looked around the room. "Did it happen here?"

"No. In our old house. Which is why I moved. And before you ask, no, I didn't find her. The police did." She scratched her cheek. "Ginny had a lot of mental health issues, even before she enlisted in the Army. The PTSD from that experience didn't help. Honestly, in a way, I always knew it was a possibility." She looked down and shook her head. "A probability, if I'm being honest. I just thought our marriage, the love I gave her—I thought it was enough to keep her going. I was wrong, but I also know it's not my fault that it happened."

"Nicole. I don't know what to say."

"Which is why I don't bring it up." She smiled, waving Avery off. "There's nothing to say. I just hope it doesn't make you see me differently."

"No." Avery shook her head. "Well, maybe, but only in a good way. It speaks to your strength," she added.

"Thank you," Nicole said softly. "But seriously, we're not here to talk about my issues. We're here for you."

"Does that...does that mean you don't ever want to talk about it?"

The tender hesitation made Nicole soften. "No. I will definitely talk about it more if we both want that."

That seemed to appease Avery. Her limbs dropped the anxious tension they'd been holding since Nicole uttered the word "suicide." She knew it was a lot to take in, but they had an agenda, and Ginny's death was not part of it.

"I hope you're ready," Nicole said with a smile. "I think this eulogy could be the missing piece to your healing process."

CHAPTER TWENTY-FOUR

Avery could only stare at Nicole as the words crept through her brain and settled in. She still had a bit of whiplash over the suicide disclosure. And she had so many questions. But she didn't want to overwhelm Nicole, nor derail them from the reason they'd gotten together that night.

Which, now that she'd had a little time to warm to the idea, didn't sound terrible. It actually sounded kind of cool. And hopefully useful.

It was the part where she had to admit to Nicole—a woman she perceived as strong, independent, and emotionally intelligent—that she'd clung to the mere idea of a person for seven years that had her nervous.

"Should I just…plunge in?"

Nicole continued to smile at her, and the simple gesture eased some of her anxiety. Avery allowed herself a moment of enjoying the way Nicole's knees were visible through the rips in her jeans, the way that dark-mustard yellow crewneck sweatshirt (all of her black tops must have been in the wash) lit up her blue eyes and gave her face a warm, inviting glow. She couldn't, and wouldn't, deny the fact that she was very, very attracted to Nicole. And it was curious, because Nicole wasn't what Avery perceived as her normal "type," though over the years, she'd felt that shift and shake each time her heart attached to someone else.

But still, this attraction was fascinating. She'd been madly attracted to Shannon, who had a rather boyish frame and slightly androgynous features; now here was Nicole, who couldn't be further opposite when it came to physical appearance. Nicole's body was enticingly feminine, with curves and wide, grabbable hips. And she was beautiful—every feature on her face only served to enhance the others, adding up to an image of aesthetic grace like those Avery had studied back in her art history college courses.

"Whatever you're comfortable with."

Nicole's voice jolted Avery from her reverie. There were quite a few things she'd be more than comfortable with, but none of that could happen until she wrote this damn eulogy and truly, finally let go of Shannon.

She'd promised herself that: not to get in too deep with Nicole until Shannon's door was firmly closed and locked, if not boarded up.

Of course, the way Nicole was looking at her now was making her fucking weak in the knees even though she was sitting, and she worried, not for the first time, that she was already sliding into depths she was emotionally unprepared for.

"Okay," Avery said. "Um. I met Shannon—that's her name, obviously—a little over ten years ago. We were both in relationships then. Well, mine was pretty much over, but hers wasn't." Avery wanted desperately to loosen up, but she couldn't shake the shame. "Do you really want all these timeline details?"

"Stop wondering what I want. Begin again," Nicole commanded, but gently.

Avery stared at her for a moment, then leaned her head back and gazed at the ceiling. The very high ceiling, as it turned out. She let herself sit quietly for a moment before slowly unlocking the chambers of her heart that held nothing but years and years of intensely focused love and busted hope.

"The first time I realized I loved her was the moment I realized she could never love me the way that I loved her." Avery tried to laugh, but nothing came out. "She tried. I really believe she tried. But we got together right after her relationship ended—a different one from the one she was in when we met—and I knew that was a terrible idea, but we'd already admitted we had feelings for each other. She said she felt safe with me. That she hadn't ever felt safe with anyone until me."

"Those are big words," Nicole said softly. Avery was relieved at the lack of judgment in her voice. Not that she'd thought there would be, but it wouldn't have been the first time she'd been wrong about someone.

"Yep. And I fell for them. That's the thing." She looked over at Nicole. "Shannon had the words. She gave them to me, over and over again. But the actions to back up the words were few and far between—just often enough to keep me hooked."

"What did you love about her? Oh, sorry." Nicole winced. "Present tense?"

"Honestly, Nicole, I'll always love her. But the way I love her has changed over time." Avery sat up, tucking one leg under her. "It was passionate in the beginning. And then it became, like, almost frantic. Because I knew I couldn't compete with her ex. Shannon's a cop and her ex is a dispatcher, so they still had this work connection. They couldn't"—Avery moved her hands back and forth like she was stretching dough—"fully get away from each other. So when her ex came back into the picture and Shannon didn't kick her back out, it felt like my love for her blew up to this huge size that I couldn't keep inside of me. But I couldn't go anywhere with it, either." Avery cleared her throat. "You asked what I love about her. I used to say little things, like the way she looked at me or made me feel when we were together. But I'm so far away from that now, and I have been for…a couple years."

"What's kept you hooked?"

"She was my best friend," Avery said quietly. "It's like all the intensity of our early years was forced to be tempered into this, like, loaded friendship that went hand in hand with a mutual attraction and genuine love and care for one another. Which would have been fine if our boundaries were stronger."

"Oh, boundaries." Nicole grinned. "We love to hate them."

"And we love to ignore them. Especially the ones we make for ourselves." Avery shook her head. "I'm not a victim. I know that. I chose to stay connected to her."

"Because you had hope."

She looked at Nicole. "Yes. I did. And she flamed that hope whenever she sensed it was waning."

"So what do you love about her now?"

Avery grinned. "You really want me to answer that, huh?"

"Yeah, I do. It's part of letting go." Nicole looked flustered for a moment. "If you want to let go, that is."

"I do," Avery said, her voice less firm than her conviction. "I've already accepted that if I have a relationship with Shannon, it's just a friendship. There's no chance for anything more because too much damage has been done." She hesitated, hoping she was ready to test out her new knowledge for the first time. "And I've finally realized that I deserve more than what she could give me."

Nicole lit up, then immediately waved a hand in front of her face. "I know my face just did something and I don't want you to think I'm making this about me. I'm honestly really proud of you for coming to that realization."

"Thanks." Avery tapped the pen against the pad. "I think I'm ready to start writing things down."

"Want my company? Or would you rather do it by yourself?"

Avery looked around and smiled. "Where are you gonna go? It's not like you can hide in here."

"There's always the bedroom," Nicole said, grinning. "Sorry, couldn't resist."

"Good," Avery said plainly. "I don't want you to resist."

They sat in the weight of those words until Nicole moved to get up. "To be clear, I'm not walking into the kitchen because of the implied meaning of your words. I think I should give you a little space to start writing. Yell for me when you're ready."

With that, she walked about twenty feet away and sat down at the butcher block counter, putting her back to Avery.

After watching for a moment, making sure she really was giving her space, Avery uncapped the pen and began writing. She didn't pick her head or hand up until nearly forty minutes later, when she called for Nicole.

"Ready?" Nicole asked, lighting another candle.

Avery wrinkled her nose. "Is the mood lighting really necessary?"

"Absolutely. We're faking a death here, so we've got to bring the environment up to speed." Nicole stood back, clearly satisfied with her work. "Perfect. Okay, Avery." She perched on the edge of the armchair. "Let's do this."

Avery shifted from one foot to the other. Okay, fine, the candles were nice, but they were distracting her by bathing Nicole in this hazy glow that only made it harder not to finally, truly kiss her.

Alas, she had one hell of a task to complete before she would allow herself to do that. Now that she was center stage, a battle between anxiety and excitement stirred within her. A deep breath was impossible, so before she began, Avery settled on a medium breath that settled approximately two of her nerves.

"When I think about loving you, I think about your laugh. You know the one—when you find something really, genuinely funny. Whenever I said something that brought that laugh out of you, I felt like I'd won a prize." She glanced at Nicole, who nodded in encouragement.

"The thing was, the prize I really wanted to win was your love. And it turns out that's not something I can ever win.

"When I first met you, Shannon, I knew I wanted to know you. Anything else was off the table, but as the years passed, we discovered we both wanted more than simply knowing each other. Our love came fast and hard, something a romance novel could never compete with. But it also came with earthquakes and tornado warnings. We were the poster relationship for natural disasters."

Avery took a breath, this one deeper than the first. "But the truth is, we never had the kind of relationship I thought we had, or the kind I wanted. We had a friendship that was touched by attraction and more-than-friends love, by a connection that somehow grew stronger through years of lies and hurt. That much I know, and that much I choose to honor.

"Through all the chaos and uncertainty, I still loved you—and I loved the idea of what we could have been. I never knew what our life would truly be like if we could finally, really be together. And I hooked myself on that maybe, on that what-if, for many years. I let it hold me back, thinking it was keeping me afloat." Her voice wavered, but it was with sadness for herself, with angst and hurt over the truth of her words.

"I would like to blame you for every single moment of doubt and uncertainty, for every moment I forgot to love myself more than I loved you." The anger simmering in her gut seethed, sending bubbles of ire up her throat. "I do blame you for lying to me, even when it was lying by omission. And I do blame you for not permanently walking away the first time you tried to. You chose to say things and do things, knowing they would hurt me. You chose to hold me at arm's length, yanking me closer when you needed me, only to dismiss me the moment someone else needed you." Avery closed her eyes briefly. "But I chose to stay. And that one's on me.

"You told me countless times that you would always love me. I let myself believe that to mean something bigger than what it is: the simple truth of the heart. I, too, will always love you. But I don't have to love you in a way that keeps me Velcroed to hope. I can love you from afar, with care and awareness of who you are to me, and who I am to you. But more importantly, I can love you knowing that this is the end of what I thought I wanted. There are no more possibilities between you and me. We love each other, and that's that." Avery looked at Nicole, who was watching her intently. "Nothing more, nothing less."

"You're doing great," Nicole said quietly. "Almost there."

The tears threatening in Avery's eyes weren't borne of sadness, but rather of relief. Nicole was right. She was almost there. Finally.

"And now, because I have dragged my heart over the coals to write this much, I turn to Brandi Carlile to wrap this up and send you off into the sunset." Avery shook the paper with finesse, trying like hell not to let the tears slide down her cheeks. "'There's a road left behind me that I'd rather not speak of, and a hard one ahead of me too. I love you, whatever you do. But I've got a life to live, too.'"

She stood, holding the paper to her stomach. She was afraid to look at Nicole, but when she did, she was rewarded with a wide, buoyant smile.

"Avery," she said, "that was incredible. Absolutely amazing."

She was surprised to find her legs were shaky as she walked to the chair next to Nicole and sat down. "Yeah?"

"Yes! But more importantly, how do you feel?"

She thought for a moment. While she was reading the eulogy (which felt funny to say, considering Shannon wasn't dead—nor did Avery wish her to be; she just wanted any lingering feelings for Shannon to fuck right off and die), she'd only felt that liquid punch of anger. And, similar to what Nicole had said about her own grieving process, maybe that was the feeling Avery needed to spend more time with.

"I'm not sure," she said honestly. "But mostly okay."

"Mostly okay sounds pretty good to me." Nicole reached over and rested her hand on Avery's forearm. "Is there any chance all that metaphorical death and emotional purging made you hungry? Because I'm starving and I could really use some tacos and guacamole in my life right about now."

A rush of relief spun through her. "Tulum?" she suggested, grinning when Nicole's face lit up at the mention of arguably the best Mexican place downtown.

"I have them on speed dial."

Avery tilted her head. "Really? Is speed dial still a thing?"

Nicole squeezed her arm as she stood up to get her phone. "No, but if you sass me one more time, I'm not sharing that guacamole with you."

"Why is this the best, most gorgeous and delectable-looking taco I've ever seen?" Avery gazed lovingly at the soft-shell taco in her hand. She'd gone for the three-pack of carnitas with extra cilantro, hold the onions. She was practically drooling as she ogled it.

"Are we going to skip right over the double taco entendre?"

Avery grinned and looked up to see Nicole watching her with amusement. "I'm pretty sure you're still fully clothed, so yes, we are."

Nicole nearly choked on her chip, which she'd loaded with a toppling spoonful of guacamole. "And just when I think we're falling into a friend zone."

"Hold on," Avery said, setting down her waiting taco. "Is that what you're feeling?" Her stomach twisted uncomfortably as a cold shower of self-blame doused her. Of course Nicole was feeling friends-only vibes between them. Avery was a hot mess who had hung on to a woman for seven fucking years and admitted she still loved that woman even though—

"No," Nicole said, her voice firm. "That was a joke."

Flustered, Avery could only stare at her lap. She wanted to look at Nicole but was too afraid to see what her eyes might be saying—the very things her mouth wasn't, maybe.

"Avery, look at me."

She obliged, though the movement only kicked her nerves into high gear.

Nicole held her gaze with those glowing blue eyes. She was smiling, which eased some anxiety. "I'm an ass for making a joke about the friend zone after you opened up to me about your experience with Shannon. I can assure you that I'm very much interested in being more than friends with you." She picked up a chip, nibbled at the edge.

Avery waited for her to go on, but she appeared to be done.

"I don't want to do to you what Shannon did to me," Avery said. She leaned back on the kitchen stool, shocked that her mouth had betrayed her and spewed out the very thing she worried about every single day.

"Don't worry about that," Nicole said easily. "I won't let you. Now eat your damn tacos."

As Avery agreeably followed her demand, she realized this was possibly the best and worst time for them to have *the talk*. They'd only been on one date; that was hardly enough time together to decide what they were doing moving forward.

But Avery knew, solidly and assuredly, that there was something different about Nicole. There was something significant and special about the way she thought about Nicole, how she felt when she was around her. Not to mention the way Nicole handled her: her empathy, her grace, her compassion and understanding. The mere fact that Avery had allowed herself to be vulnerable by opening up about Shannon spoke louder than anything else she'd said so far.

And yet, making any decisions about their involvement after Avery had, in fact, emotionally vomited all over Nicole's apartment didn't seem like a brilliant idea.

"Listen," Nicole said, "if you have any interest in this guacamole, you better start dipping, because if you don't, I *will* eat it all."

Avery grinned, shutting out that dead-end thought pattern, and reached for the chips.

"Can we move this food festival to the sofa? I feel like we could use some mindless entertainment."

"Say no more," Avery said, loading her hands with tacos.

Later, after the food had disappeared into respective stomachs and two episodes of *The Office* had been laughingly viewed, Avery leaned her head against the back of the sofa while Nicole threw away the leftover debris of dinner.

When she returned, Avery looked over at her. "This sofa is the most comfortable thing I've ever put my ass on."

Nicole laughed, fixing her with an appreciative stare. "I'm a Taurus, Avery. My life is devoted to finding the utmost comfort in all things." She nodded toward the TV. "I don't want to keep you if you have plans, but do you want to watch a movie or something?"

"I don't have plans," Avery said quickly, wanting to ease any potential worry from Nicole's mind. "But I'm very picky about movies."

"I could not be less picky about movies." She passed over the remote. "Your pick."

About an hour into *Dumplin'*, Avery got distracted by Nicole's hand on the cushion between them. She stared at it, missing an entire scene, before taking a breath and inching her hand closer to Nicole's. She didn't touch it, keeping just enough distance to give Nicole a clear out.

"Do you believe that?" Nicole said suddenly, eyes still on the screen.

"What?" Avery had completely missed what was happening. She looked back at the TV. Oh, right. She loved this scene. Nothing like confessing romantic feelings by a dumpster.

"That people can like each other but not work together in the real world." Nicole turned then and settled her gaze on Avery.

"Yes," Avery said quietly. "I think I lived that for seven years."

"Oh shit," Nicole breathed. She laughed then, seemingly more out of embarrassment than humor. "Looks like I'm the one who's going to be apologizing to you all the time now."

Avery waved her off. "I don't know what I believe in anymore. I want to believe there's a 'right' person out there for me, but...I think you can understand why I can't convince myself it's true."

"I can." Nicole continued to watch her carefully. "I think the right people exist for different times in our lives, but I don't think I believe love lasts forever."

"Well," Avery said, trying to sound amused, "aren't we the pair."

With a stealth quickness that Avery had not seen coming, Nicole closed the space between their hands. Avery looked down at their interlocked fingers, feeling a wave of excited contentment.

"We're something, that's for sure." Nicole squeezed.

The touch of Nicole's hand on hers was soothing a part of Avery that she hadn't known needed soothing. With a deep breath, she leaned into the feeling and did her best to focus on the movie. But the truth was, all she could think about was the trickle of conflicting emotions slip-sliding through her.

CHAPTER TWENTY-FIVE

Nicole had to hand it to Avery: she'd really nailed that ranunculus arrangement. Not that Nicole had doubted her ability—she'd seen Avery's talent with flowers. But the addition of the red buds in the otherwise fully-bloomed bouquet had been, in a word, genius. Not only had they slowly opened into a breathtakingly vibrant hue, but every time Nicole so much as caught a glimpse of them out of the corner of her eye, she immediately thought of Avery.

Even without the flowers, she was certain Avery wouldn't have left her mind. A mere thirty-some hours had passed since they'd hugged goodbye. The hug had gone on for an eternity, but an eternity that Nicole would have gladly stayed in for an extra eon. She was fumbling with how *good* Avery felt: her presence, the touch of her hand, her arms looped around Nicole, the side of her head resting gently against Nicole's hair. It didn't make sense, how this person she barely knew could feel like the warmest, safest blanket.

And that was the rub. Avery wasn't safe. She intended to be—she wanted to be, Nicole believed that—but emotionally, there was a piece of her that was off-limits and crackling with electric danger.

Enticing electric danger. Which made it that much more difficult to avoid.

But Nicole kept reminding herself it was not her job to fix Avery. She didn't think Avery needed to be fixed, per se, but she could definitely benefit from some heavy bandaging. The eulogy was as far as Nicole would allow herself to go when it came to helping her let go of Shannon. The rest was resolutely in Avery's hands…

…meaning Nicole had to keep *her* hands to herself.

Even if she was vibrating with her own crackling, electric danger. She wanted more of Avery, and she was finding it increasingly difficult to be patient.

"You're getting in too deep," she told herself as she continued cleaning the kitchen, leaning over the stove and using all her strength to scrub out a stubborn stain. "This was supposed to be casual, an easy way to start dating again." She gritted her teeth. "Easy. No strings. Get back in the saddle."

Well, she was definitely in the saddle. A success, yes, but one that was looking more and more unsteady.

With a sigh, Nicole shook herself out of her thoughts. She didn't want to dissect her connection with Avery, and she didn't want to slat it into the "doomed" category either. She just wanted to be realistic and aware.

Her phone buzzed on the counter. She smiled at the incoming FaceTime.

"Just the person I wanted to see right now," she said when she answered the call.

Hank's face broke into a smile. "There's my baby girl." He peered at her. "You look tired."

She waved him off. "I was just scrubbing the stove. It took some energy out of me." She sat down on a stool at the counter in her kitchen. "How's the weather out there?"

"Moody." Hank turned the phone instead of flipping the camera view (other than that, Nicole had to admit he was pretty skilled with all the phone technology) so she could see out the window of his workshop. Sure enough, the sun was out, but thick gray-blue clouds were moving in quickly. "It's almost sixty degrees so of course it has to rain. Typical Ohio spring."

"It's really nice here," Nicole said. "Somewhere in the sixties and the sun's out. But the temperature is supposed to drop big-time tonight. It'll probably snow before the week is over."

Hank had turned the phone back around so Nicole could see his face. He'd gotten a new pair of glasses, and the thick black frames made him look studious. He was aging gracefully, the wiry white hairs in his thick beard the only indication that he was pushing seventy. She hoped she'd inherited his agelessness. She startled, realizing she had no idea if her mom was aging as well as her dad was. She hadn't seen a picture of her in well over a year.

"So, listen. I know you weren't keen on the idea of a spice rack," Hank said. He continued before she could interrupt. "But I remember you saying you don't have enough shelves in your bathroom. How about I send you some pictures of some ideas I think you might like?"

"I'd love that. Speaking of bathrooms, guess what I did?"

Hank wrinkled his nose. "Is this potty humor, kiddo?"

"No, Dad. Relax." Nicole scooted off the stool and walked to the bathroom attached to her bedroom. "My sink was clogging constantly, so I watched a video on TikTok and unclogged it." She opened the cabinet under the sink and flipped the camera view around. "Turned out, all I had to do was unscrew these… um…water chutes, and use some elbow grease to kinda scrub them out. No more clog!"

When Nicole stood, Hank was shaking his head. She flipped the camera back around so he could see her perplexed face. "What? It worked!"

"I don't doubt that it did." He laughed and shook his head again. "But what in the hell is a water chute?"

Nicole grinned. "I couldn't think of the word 'pipes.' Water chutes seemed appropriate."

After Hank let loose a loud laugh, he looked closely at his daughter. "It was creative, I'll give you that. Now. What else is going on in your world?"

Nicole retreated to the living room and sank into her favorite chair next to the windows. "Not too much." It wasn't quite a lie. She and Avery had texted here and there since Sunday night, but that was it. Nicole was happy to sit back and let Avery take the wheel for the moment. "I'm kind of seeing someone. Or maybe just getting to know someone." She shook her head. "We're taking it slow."

"Is this the gal you went to that party with?"

"Colleen? No. This is…This is Avery."

"Avery." Hank nodded. "I bet she's a redhead."

Nicole gaped at the phone. "How in the world did you know that?"

"Just a hunch. So, what's this Avery like?"

Nicole smiled, letting her thoughts drift. "She's stubborn but kind. Warm beneath a lot of frost, but the frost is just there to protect her. I can scrape it off pretty easily." Nicole bit the inside of her cheek. "But that's the thing, Dad. She needs to scrape her own frost off. I don't want to do it for her."

Hank nodded and stroked the bristly hairs of his beard. "That's smart."

"She's a florist," Nicole went on, aiming her phone at the spray of ranunculus. "She brought this the other night. She's really talented and she owns her own shop."

"So she's motivated."

Nicole knew the comparison he was making: Ginny, though smart and talented, had had little motivation. Granted, Nicole chalked that up to her mental health holding her back—but the truth was, Avery seemed to be the kind of person to go after what she wanted. At least professionally.

"Yes." Nicole leaned her torso against the edge of the counter to put some pressure on the funny feeling in her stomach. "She's just a good person. I can feel it. But she's got baggage. Big baggage."

"Well," Hank said, gesturing with his free hand, "you've got a couple rolly suitcases that follow you around, Nic."

"No shit." She laughed. "I think that's why…I don't know. I feel like I get her, Dad. And she's not just sitting in her misery.

That would be a definite deal-breaker. She's working to get out of it."

Hank was silent for a moment. Nicole could practically hear his wheels spinning.

"I think it's smart that you're taking it slow," he finally said. "I can tell just by watching you talk about her that you like her. And if she really is smart, like you say she is, I bet she likes you, too. Just be careful, kiddo."

"I am," she said. "Very careful." It was as much of an assurance to her father as it was to herself.

Nicole spent most of the afternoon working on a new project for work. The company was just starting out, and its product—a women's formula collagen vitamin—wasn't a trailblazer, but the ingredients used *and* the prebiotic/probiotic capsule that was also launching covered a lot of new ground in the health world. The research didn't bother Nicole; sometimes it helped to force her brain into something new, a place where she couldn't be distracted by her own looping thoughts.

Once she had a good number of ideas and options, she sent them off to her boss, who would go over them before selecting some copy for refinement. Nicole checked the time, then looked outside. She'd had a light lunch on purpose and was planning to take a little walk to her favorite vegan place while the sun was still out.

"Go time," she said, shutting her laptop. Before leaving her apartment, she pulled on the hoodie she'd tossed onto the sofa during a fit of heated writing.

It was still reasonably warm—definitely not *warm* warm, but warm enough to feel like spring was finally setting in. Main Street wasn't crowded, but it was three o'clock on a Tuesday, so that was no surprise. Nicole stuffed her hands in her pockets of her hoodie as she walked. She inhaled deeply, catching the unmistakable scent of daffodils and hyacinth. She much preferred the latter. Daffodils smelled like death. It wasn't a fact—just her nose's interpretation—but she hated daffodils because of that. She also hated lilies for the same reason. She could not be around a lily without smelling death.

Nicole hunched her shoulders. Sometimes she thought about what flowers she'd like at her funeral. Morbid, maybe, but considering her wife's untimely death and the amount of time she spent in funeral homes, it made sense.

She'd always thought she wanted just greens. Nothing but vines and bold green plants. But now that she'd discovered, thanks to Avery, how gorgeous ranunculus were, she thought maybe she'd like some of them intermixed with the greenery.

Definitely not peonies, though. Those were reserved for beauty and happiness—not for death.

Nicole laughed at herself. Of all the things to be thinking about while walking down the street in the middle of a lovely spring afternoon.

"I can only imagine what's going through your head that's making you laugh out loud." Avery's voice jumped out from seemingly nowhere, and when Nicole looked up, there she was.

"Hi," she said, trying to recover from her mild shock. "What are you doing here?"

Avery grinned. She was wearing overalls, leading Nicole to believe she was working, but she had shoes on, thankfully. "Taking a little break. The flowers were getting to me."

"Oh," Nicole said slowly. "Have they started talking to you?"

"Honestly, you wouldn't believe the things they say."

Nicole tilted her head and examined Avery. "You might want to see someone about that."

Avery's grin didn't move, but the sun was causing flickers of gold to flash in her eyes. "I'll think about it. What about you? The dead people getting to you?"

Nicole laughed. "Always. But actually, no. Regular work today. I just spent hours researching vitamins." She looked around, then pointed to the vegan café a few doors down from where they stood. "Thought it was a good time to treat myself with a vegan milkshake."

Avery's nose crinkled adorably, as though the thought of a vegan milkshake had morally offended her. "What? No. That's just wrong."

"Which part? The treating myself?"

"Oh, no. You should absolutely treat yourself." The crinkle increased. "But a *vegan* milkshake? Is that a treat or torture?"

Nicole gawked at her. "Are you telling me you work on this very street and you've never had food from Graze?"

The crinkle intensified into a look of horror. "No! Why would I? I'm a meat-eating woman, Nicole."

"Well, so am I." She threw her hands onto her hips. "But sometimes I like to give love to the plants."

Avery gave her a mock-scathing look. "By eating them?"

"Shut up." Nicole laughed. "Come on. I'll buy you a shake."

As Avery protested mightily, Nicole grabbed her hand and dragged her down the street and into Graze. Avery was mumbling by then, having enough respect for the plants not to desecrate their name in their place of business. Nicole left her by the door, fairly confident she wouldn't bolt in plant-based panic, and ordered two shakes. She peered over her shoulder after she paid, biting back a laugh when she saw Avery standing by the door, arms crossed tightly over her chest. She looked panicked and confused. It was absolutely adorable.

Shakes in hand, Nicole walked back over to her. "Inside or outside?"

Avery looked at the drinks warily. "Why do they look so good?"

"Because they're delicious. Come on," she said, bumping the door open with her butt. "It's too nice to sit inside."

They settled on a bench in front of Graze. Avery sat close, leaving just a sliver of air between them. Nicole smiled to herself, watching Avery square off against the vegan milkshake in her hand. She was pretty sure that if the cup had hands, the two would be fist-fighting.

"Just take a sip," Nicole said, demonstrating the task. "Oh my God," she mumbled around a mouthful of vegan heaven. "Insane."

Avery continued to stare at the offending cup in her hand. "What even *is* this?"

"Avery. Drink it."

With a powerful sigh that could shake the entire foundation of the building in front of them, Avery lifted the cup and tucked the straw into her mouth. She turned to make eye contact as she slowly sucked the milkshake through the straw. Nicole watched as angry bravado slipped away into genuine confusion, which quickly melted into perplexed delight.

"What the fuck," she said, holding the cup out to inspect it. "What is this sorcery?"

"Vegan food," Nicole said before taking a long, deeply satisfying sip.

"But how?" Avery shook her head. "Don't answer that." The straw went back into her mouth and Nicole thought she saw her eyes roll into the back of her head as she got a second mouthful. "Is this supposed to be like dirt pudding?"

"Yes!" Nicole said gleefully. "Did the gummy worms on top of the whipped cream give it away?"

"No." Avery grinned. "The fact that it tastes exactly like the dirt pudding my mom makes gave it away. But hers is definitely not vegan." She held the cup out, again inspecting it as though she suspected a cow holding a "JUST KIDDING!" sign would jump out of it.

"Stop overthinking it," Nicole said, pushing the drink toward Avery's mouth and taking her free hand. "And just enjoy it."

Avery immediately squeezed her fingers around Nicole's, sending a tingling rush through Nicole's nerve endings. They sat like that for a while, as though it was something they did on a weekly basis.

All the while, Nicole was repeating her internal warning: *Don't get too close.* She couldn't focus on that, however, while holding Avery's hand and drinking an incredible vegan milkshake. No, her body was far more focused on the intense happiness those activities were delivering.

"I like you."

Nicole startled, nearly dropping her cup. "You—what? Sorry. Yes. What?"

Avery laughed. "Yeah, that was kinda abrupt." She turned a bit so they were looking at each other. "I like you. I just wanted to tell you that."

Nicole sat quietly, watching Avery look back at her. There was still a missing piece that Nicole felt acutely. She wanted that piece of Avery—badly. But it just wasn't present yet.

"I like you too," Nicole said. It was true, even if she had no idea what to do with it.

"I know I've been kinda quiet since the other night." Avery rubbed her thumb over Nicole's knuckles. "And it's not because I've been talking to Shannon. I haven't, at all. And I don't want to." She looked away then, down the street into a distance Nicole couldn't reach. "But I don't want you to think I'm waiting for her to come back and tell me she wants me. Because I'm not. But," Avery said, looking back at Nicole, "I don't feel completely ready to dive in with you."

"Because you're worried about doing to me what she did to you," Nicole said, repeating Avery's words from Sunday.

Avery nodded as she sipped her shake. "Yes. That's part of it. And the other part is me."

"You," Nicole said.

"Me." Avery's shoulders dropped. "Yeah. Me." She tilted her head back and looked up into the blue sky. "Sorry, I can't really explain that. I want to, but I don't have the words right now." She turned her head and met Nicole's eyes. "But I like you, Nicole."

The unspoken question sat between them. Nicole continued watching Avery enjoy the hell out of her first vegan milkshake, then relaxed a bit when their conversation tumbled into talk of baseball and how the Phillies might do that season.

When they parted ways a bit later, Avery jumping to her feet when she realized how long she'd been away from the shop, Nicole didn't hesitate to pull her into a hug. Avery held her tightly, hands alternately gripping and rubbing Nicole's upper back. Nicole inhaled as much of Avery as she could, uncertain as to when she'd see her again.

She knew she would. It was the timing that she couldn't predict.

For a moment, when their hug ended, Nicole wondered if the moment had finally arrived. They stood and looked at each other, the rest of the world fading into a colorful haze around them. But neither made the move, and with one final smile, Avery turned and walked back toward The Twisted Tulip.

Nicole watched her go, waving when Avery turned around and looked right at her. Her stomach swooped at the over-the-shoulder smile even as she pressed her fingers to her mouth and wondered if she'd ever get to feel Avery's lips there.

With a sigh, Nicole walked back to her apartment. She'd heard Avery's unspoken question loud and clear. Yes, she could be patient. Nicole wouldn't wait, but she could be patient.

CHAPTER TWENTY-SIX

"Remind me why I agreed to take over the Chastain-Weber wedding?" Veronica asked, a groan punctuating the question.

"Because," Avery said calmly, "it was very clear that Liana likes you more than she likes me. Plus, experience."

"Experience my ass," Veronica muttered, swiping a pair of shears from Avery's workspace. "I told you, I don't think I'll ever be able to open my own shop. Especially if I move back to Miami."

Avery jabbed her in the side with a broken stem. "Knock that the fuck off. If you want to open your own store, you will. And if you don't, you'll show up in Miami with loads of wedding experience, including with a really fucking weird version of a bridezilla."

Veronica blew out a breath so hard her choppy dark-brown bangs lifted off her forehead. "She is definitely the weirdest bridezilla. The fact that she won't let go of those single-girl bouquets is freaking me out." She shuddered for extra effect.

"Yeah, well, we'll make them so dazzling that people won't realize the bizarre relationship-status symbolism behind them."

Avery stood up straight and stretched her back. "She'll be here in ten minutes."

Veronica looked up at the large clock on the wall. "Her appointment's not for another half hour."

"Yup. Like I said, ten minutes."

Another groan, this one louder, as Veronica gathered materials and made her way out of the workroom. Avery enjoyed the solo silence as she worked on a rush-order bouquet. She had a feeling this one was for a big, overdue apology; the man placing the order had sounded equal parts exasperated and nervous on the phone.

The clang of the door made her look up. Zuri strode in, carrying a recently delivered bucket of French lavender. It was one of Avery's favorite fillers when she wasn't using heavily scented flowers. She eyed the bucket greedily.

"Nope," Zuri said, turning away and setting the bucket on the floor at her workspace. "This is mine."

Avery sighed. "It wouldn't work in this one, anyway. Can you just wave a couple stems in front of my face?"

Zuri rolled her eyes. "Stressed?"

"No," Avery said quietly. "Not really." She stepped back to study the arrangement. "I really don't want to fuck up Maya and J.C.'s wedding."

Zuri laughed, surprising her. "You expect me to buy that?"

"What? I'm serious. It's my first lesbian wedding and I want it to be amazing."

"Avery, please." Zuri leaned against the counter and turned her full attention to Avery. "You couldn't fuck up that wedding if you tried."

"It's not the flowers I'm worried about. It's the other stuff." Zuri didn't say anything, so Avery fumbled along. "The, like, building a relationship with the clients stuff. What if they think I'm boring? Or what if I don't get their angle, their vision?"

"Do you do this with your straight brides?"

Avery recoiled. "No, never. Cut and dry."

"And because these two are lesbians…"

"I'm overthinking it." For a moment, Avery swore she could taste that ridiculously good vegan milkshake she'd had with

Nicole on Tuesday. She'd almost overthought herself out of that, which would have been a gustatorial sin.

"No," Zuri said. "That's not the issue."

Avery grumbled. "Okay, then what is? I want them to like me because they're gay and I'm gay, and I don't care as much about that with my other brides? Or that I'm worried this is my one big chance to nail a lesbian wedding, and if I screw it up, I'll never have another one?"

"No."

"Christ, Zuri. Just fucking say it!"

Zuri smiled, the picture of calm. "Whatever's bothering you has nothing to do with the lesbian wedding."

It took a minute, but the words found their way into Avery's ears, and once they sat down and kicked up their feet, her shoulders slumped. The fight went out of her, replaced with a deep pool of worry.

"I don't know if I can do this." Her voice was barely above a whisper, but she knew Zuri heard her. "I feel like a failure."

"Because you couldn't make Shannon love you the way you deserve to be loved?"

It was truly eerie, how Zuri snuck right into her brain and tugged out the very thoughts she tried to hide from everyone, including herself. It was also a relief, since Avery could just nod instead of saying that painful statement aloud.

Zuri made a scoffing noise. "Come on. You know that's not your fault. You can't make someone be someone they're not."

"Because they don't want to be, or because they're not capable of being?"

"Oh, hell no. I thought we were done with this."

Avery nodded. "Old habits die hard. I know it's because she's not capable."

"Kill that habit."

"I'd like to." Avery picked up a fallen leaf and began ripping it into tiny pieces. "I think I've finally realized that Shannon and I...We're just not meant to be."

"About damn time."

"It's a weird thing to let go of, though."

"Only because you held on for so long, thinking she was the only woman out there for you."

Avery cracked a half-smile, hearing some of her own thoughts from the eulogy. Then she sighed heavily. "And now that I've found another woman, all this shit is coming up. I don't know how to be in a relationship anymore. What if I'm terrible at it? I might be too damaged. Fuck, I don't even know if I *can* be in a relationship."

"Do you want to be?"

"No," Avery said. Then she paused. "Maybe. But not right now."

Zuri leaned her elbows on the table and eyed her. "I don't think that's true."

"It is."

"Nah, it's not. You see, you deprived yourself for years. You set yourself off on this little-ass raft, hoping that shiny cruise ship would scoop you right out of the ocean. But she didn't, because she can't. Sometimes the ship would throw you a rope and you grabbed on to it every damn time, probably so hard your hands bled. But the rope always got yanked back, leaving you on your raft."

"I don't like this story," Avery said.

"Too bad. So now you've got rope burn on your hands, and the salt water is stinging it every time you touch the water. But you have to touch the water because you lost your damn oar the moment your raft set sail. Finally, the ropes stopped coming and you paddled like crazy. For the first time, you got close to the ship, and you saw it was hella rusted and beaten down. It wasn't as perfect as you thought it would be. And that's a big blow. It's a big hurt." Zuri shook her head, braids swinging. "Your raft got dinged as fuck in that ocean, but you're still floating. And then winds came in."

"Oh my God," Avery said, half-amused, half-intrigued.

"Yeah, you know the winds. Crazy as fuck." Zuri grinned, evidently very pleased with herself. "And they're blowing you toward this cute island with big trees and lots of coconuts."

"Coconuts? Seriously?"

"You know damn well your fancy-ass vegan milkshake was made with coconut milk. Let me have my moment." Zuri raised her brows. "That little island is beautiful. It's peaceful and warm and you feel amazing every time the wind blows you closer to it. But your bitch ass keeps paddling back out to sea because you got used to the restless waters."

"I hate you," Avery murmured.

"Because you know I'm right. Now, that island's name starts with an N, but you already know that. Your raft is trying like hell to move your ass onto the island. But the rest of you is being a damn fool." Zuri shook her head. "Listen to the raft, Avery."

She tapped her fingers against the counter, restless and frustrated. "Okay, but am I rebounding?"

"Are you serious? You've been single for seven damn years."

"Technically," Avery said, and regretted it immediately.

"I should capsize your raft," Zuri huffed.

"Wait. I'm serious." She waited till Zuri stopped rolling her eyes. "I know Shannon and I haven't been in a relationship—"

"You've just been emotionally attached."

Avery sighed. "Yeah. Even after the physical stuff stopped."

"Avery, you're gonna love Shannon forever. But you gotta let that love change and get quieter as you change and live louder."

She cleared her throat, dreading her next question. But Zuri was the only person she felt comfortable having this conversation with. "Do you, uh, think I need to tell Shannon?"

"Tell her what?" Zuri's eyes bulged.

"That I'm dating someone."

"Are you…No, clearly you're not kidding." Zuri looked like she wanted to toss Avery into the ocean. "You don't owe her shit."

"I know."

"Do you? It doesn't seem like it right now."

The words chilled her. She still hadn't had any communication with Shannon, but she couldn't shake the feeling that Shannon was going to try to reach out at some point. Avery didn't think she'd closed the door hard enough; space wasn't goodbye, after all. And while she didn't relish the idea of telling Shannon she was dating someone (talking to someone…with the intention of dating them…whatever—the point was, Avery had someone new in her life), she didn't feel like doing so would be impossible.

"Maybe this will just be a fling," she said, dropping the Shannon element.

Zuri, ever able to keep up with her bouncing chatter, laughed heartily. "Please. Stop lying. It's not cute."

"But you—there's nothing—I don't—" Avery stumbled, trying to land on the perfect retort.

"Listen, and listen carefully 'cause I'm only gonna say this once." Zuri leveled her with a stare. "You like this girl, and she likes you. Stop selling yourself short, Avery. Stop pretending you don't want a relationship when that's the only thing you've wanted for the last seven years. You deserve to be happy. But more than that, you deserve to be with someone who wants you to be happy. Get off your dumb fucking raft and wade onto that island."

Avery grunted in response, turning back to her bouquet as a sign that she was now finished with another lesson from Zuri's School of Hard Knocks. Zuri, too, began working, and they went on in companionable silence for some time, until Avery just could not keep her mouth shut any longer.

"Why'd I have to be on a raft? Why not a canoe, or a kayak?"

"No. It was a raft. Trust the process."

Avery smiled, even though she'd continue to bother Zuri about the raft for weeks to come. "I'm surprised you didn't throw in a mythological siren or two."

Zuri cursed and dropped her first onto the table. "I knew I forgot something."

Avery's meeting with Maya and J.C. went a thousand times better than she'd imagined it would, allaying some of her fears. They were a chill couple—they knew what they wanted, but were entirely open to suggestions and other ideas. Their plan for a simple wedding, they'd told her, shrank every time they sat down to plan something. Avery, while she was certainly *not* a wedding planner, assured them that it would balance out at some point. Her job as a florist was simply to give the couple the flowers of their dreams. She worked with many wedding planners, and when the couple told her who they were working with, Avery was relieved, and assured them they were in the best of hands.

The day, mostly because of her conversation with Zuri, had been unusually stressful. When Avery got home, she ate a quiet dinner by herself. Gavin had taken Thea to swim class and left a note telling her to enjoy leftovers from earlier in the week. After she cleaned up, she grabbed her phone and went onto the back deck, Houston trotting at her side.

Houston made a beeline into the yard, barking happily as she enjoyed her post-dinner zoomies. Avery sat on the steps of the deck, shivering. The temperature had dropped significantly over the past two days. She was tired of the back and forth. She hated the intense summer heat and humidity, but some consistency with real spring temperatures would be nice.

She'd replayed her conversation with Zuri multiple times, coming to the same conclusion each time. It was a small town: Avery was bound to run into Shannon at some point, or points. She would likely never be completely unattached from her, simply because of that and the silent love for her that would rest, untouched, in some corner of her heart.

But what she could do was block her number. Avery looked down at her phone. Old habits really did die hard: she whirled back and forth between wanting to hit the block button and wanting to call Shannon to tell her she was blocking her number. She didn't owe her that notification, nor did she owe her any explanation about Nicole. But the pull was there, the need to communicate and explain, even if Avery had been the only one communicating and explaining for a long time.

Houston bounded up the steps and sprawled down next to her, tongue lolling as she panted. One paw landed heavily on Avery's thigh.

"You here to give me moral support?" Houston blinked. "Yeah, you never liked Shannon." A tail wag. Avery laughed.

"Okay," she whispered into the night air. "I'm doing it."

And she did. Quickly, surely, silently. She put her phone in her pocket and looked at Houston.

"That's it, pal. I finally—"

She cut herself off, jumping a bit at the feeling of something cold and wet hitting the top of her head. For a flash, she wondered if a bird had just shit on her. Wouldn't be the first time. But no, it was snowing. In April. Because, Pennsylvania.

Houston had her tongue fully out, lapping up the gentle snowflakes like they were made of chicken (her poultry of choice). Avery spun her body so she could lie down and rest her head on Houston's side.

Content but cold, she stared up at the sky, blinking as snow drifted into her eyes. It wouldn't amount to anything, and she was sure it would end within minutes. But while it lasted, Avery let it float down onto her, numbing parts of her she desperately wished had been numbed years ago.

Eventually, she was no longer certain if it was snow or tears on her cheeks. Either way, it was the cleansing she needed.

CHAPTER TWENTY-SEVEN

"So, about today…"

"Oh no you don't." Nicole shook her head even though she knew Brynn couldn't see her. "You are not canceling on me. I won't allow it."

"I think you will when I tell you why."

Nicole sighed heavily, mostly as a guilt trip but also because she was genuinely disappointed Brynn was canceling their plans. "I shall be the determiner of that."

"Is that a word?"

"What? Determiner? Yes, of course it is."

"Huh. Never heard it before."

"Determiner," Nicole said grandly. "One who determines things. Now stop avoiding your explanation as to why you're breaking my heart and ditching me today."

"Speaking of your heart breaking…Have you heard from Avery?"

Nicole sighed again, this one peppered with disappointment and confusion. But also never-ending understanding for someone who was going through a grieving process. "No. Not since Thursday morning. But it's fine, Brynn."

"Is it, though?"

Yes and no, Nicole thought. As much as she wanted to push her way into Avery's life and thoughts and feelings and emotional processes, she also wanted to respect whatever Avery was dealing with. She'd seen the effect the eulogy had had on her, and she'd also seen the way Avery looked at her over their vegan milkshakes earlier in the week. The woman was conflicted in ways Nicole could not begin to understand, but she could empathize and respect Avery's position…even if that meant their communication was a bit…unpredictable.

"Stop avoiding telling me why you're abandoning me today."

"Wow, you're really ratcheting up the verbs there, Nic."

"I'm hanging up."

Brynn laughed. "Okay, okay. So, I have a date."

Nicole gawked at her phone. "Shut up."

"And that's all I'm telling you right now. I think you should text Avery and ask her to go to the festival with you."

She accepted the quick change in conversation, knowing that Brynn preferred to keep her cards close to her chest. "I don't know, Brynn. I don't want it to seem like I'm pressuring her, or pushing her."

"She's a grown woman. She can say no."

"Yeah, well, maybe her saying no is worse than not knowing if she'd say yes."

Brynn was quiet for a moment. "You really like her."

Nicole pulled her knees to her chest and rested her forehead against them. "Let's not say 'really.' But, yeah. I like her. And I'm also very aware that she is not in a position to give me what I want."

"That emotional attachment."

"Yes. But," Nicole said, shutting her eyes, "let's appreciate the fact that I know that's what I want."

"And," Brynn continued, "that you even *want* that. That's huge, Nic."

"Huge and scary. Terrifying," she amended. "So I'm not pinning any hopes on Avery, but I'd like to keep seeing her and getting to know her."

"Well, and I say this with kindness: I'll be here when your flimsy little plan to not get attached falls through."

Nicole grinned. "You're the best." She lifted her head and looked out her windows. Bright sunlight streamed into her apartment, beckoning her closer. "I can't believe it was snowing two days ago."

"You're still gonna go to the festival, right? It's too nice outside not to."

"And it's literally outside my windows," Nicole added. "Yeah, I probably will. I'm pretty much a professional at doing things alone."

"I have a feeling you won't be doing so much by yourself for much longer," Brynn said.

"Says the person who just told me my precious little plan not to get attached will fall through." Nicole stood up. "Go get ready for your date. And don't think for a second I'm not going to ask for a recap."

In the time since her wife's death, Nicole had become accustomed to doing things by herself. Seeing as her dad was in Ohio and she didn't have many friends in Balsam Lake, it was a reality that came hand in hand with losing the one person she'd done everything with. Ginny had preferred a quiet life with closed doors, and Nicole, content spending her free time with her wife, never felt the need to bring friends into their world. When she lost Ginny, however, that choice suddenly seemed like a mistake. Though she'd been a loner for her entire life and had never been bothered by that, in the wake of intense grief and learning how to be a widow, Nicole had often found herself wishing she had close friends who could support her.

Brynn had been her rock—and Nicole was only just realizing how much she'd leaned on her over the last nearly three years. She knew Brynn didn't resent her for it, but Nicole was acutely aware of the fact that she could benefit from a couple friends who weren't deeply entrenched with her past.

As she strolled Main Street, Nicole wondered if that's what Avery was meant to be in her life: just a friend. It wasn't a horrible concept, but if she were being honest with herself, Nicole wanted much, much more than just friendship. But because Nicole was who she was, if it came down to Avery not being able to give her anything more than that, she would be okay with it.

She smirked as she walked around a couple who had crouched down to tend to their crying toddler in a stroller. She and Avery hadn't even kissed, so landing in the friend zone should be plenty easy. No problem at all.

Right. Simple. Because you don't think about grabbing her and kissing her till you can't breathe. Nope, that thought doesn't cross your mind at least six times a day.

Nicole shook her head as she walked, turning her attention to the booths and the clusters of people lining the street. The spring festival was always a risky move, considering April's temperament. But the organizers had lucked out this year. The sun was blazing and it was warm enough for T-shirts, but Nicole couldn't help but judge the teenage boy wearing shorts and a tank top. It definitely wasn't summer weather.

She moved from booth to booth, looking over handmade jewelry, sniffing handmade soaps, and gazing at abstract art. One booth had nothing but popcorn. Nicole gaped at the flavors, wondering if cookies and cream popcorn could taste good. She declined a sample of it, but did accept a small cup of the Dark Turtle popcorn. The dark chocolate covering the salty popcorn melted as soon as it hit her tongue, and the thin strip of caramel popped with a burst of sweetness. Nicole wasted no time in buying a bag of that.

A familiar voice slunk into her ears as she was debating between the Ocean Dream soap and the Spring Fever. She angled her head, trying to see if she was having an aural hallucination, or if Avery really was nearby. Her insides squeezed pleasantly when she caught sight of that messy bun, lazy curls falling from it and lifting in the light breeze.

Nicole's insides squeezed in a different way when she saw that Avery was talking, quite animatedly, to a uniformed police officer. Avery hadn't said much about who Shannon was, but she had let it slip that Shannon was a cop.

Clenching her jaw, Nicole turned away from the soap and tried to assess her best escape route. To her horror, she realized that Avery and the ridiculously hot cop were now walking, and heading in her direction. Fortunately (or not), Avery's attention was focused entirely on the unnervingly attractive police officer. Nicole took a moment to look her up and down. It wasn't how she'd pictured Shannon in her head, but she could certainly see how literally anyone with a pulse would find that woman attractive.

She'd looked too long. Nicole felt her face heat as she locked eyes with Avery, who was now just five feet away. She tried to smile, certain it looked more like a crooked grimace, and stepped to the side. She was shaken by how happy Avery looked. That wasn't the look of someone who was tormented by her emotional attachment to the person she was standing so close to. No, that was the look of someone who truly enjoyed being around the person they were talking to, even if that person had led on and gaslit Avery for years.

Nicole was pretty certain she was going to throw up. Her sidestep had unfortunately been the exact wrong move, as it had locked her into the perimeter of a group of elderly women, all wearing oversized sun hats. She tried to step back where she'd come from, but her soap-sniffing spot had been taken by a woman pushing a double stroller. One side held a sleeping child, and the other held a small, fluffy dog wearing bright pink sunglasses.

Nicole spun in a slow circle of disbelief. She was trapped. She would die here, in the soap booth, just feet away from Avery and her hot cop non-girlfriend. Cool, cool.

Just as the double stroller pulled away, the space was filled by a new person, prompting Nicole to curse under her breath.

"Who are we hiding from?" Avery whispered.

Nicole startled, then looked up. She was utterly confused by the expression on Avery's face, and how at odds it was with the fact that she'd just been with Shannon. Nicole's emotional response to being this close was so intense that it took her a moment to remember the day she'd whispered the very same thing to Avery.

No. Not the same thing. Nicole had said "who are *you* hiding from," and Avery had gone ahead and turned them into a "we." Nicole's stomach flipped incessantly, performing an entire gymnastics floor routine in a matter of seconds.

"You," Nicole blurted. Then she straightened her shoulders. If nothing else, she would keep the promise she made to herself: she would not allow Avery to do to her what Shannon had done to Avery.

A blur of emotions passed over Avery's face: shock, sadness, confusion. Then, with a rush, relieved understanding. "Come on," she said, taking Nicole's hand and tugging her out of the soap booth of doom.

So much for your promises, Nicole thought as she allowed Avery to pull her across the street where, somehow, a bench sat unoccupied. It was in the direct line of the unforgiving sun, however, so when Nicole sat down and jumped right back up, scorched from the burn of iron on her butt through her jeans, she understood the vacancy.

"Jesus!" Avery said, also jumping up. "Okay, maybe we don't sit."

Nicole stood a foot or so away from her. She was willing to listen, but she needed to hold up her end of the bargain, too.

Avery eyed her, then nodded, still wearing that look of understanding. "I'll cut to the chase, because I think I know what's happening in your head. That wasn't Shannon."

"No? You just happen to know a whole variety of hot Balsam Lake cops?"

Avery laughed, then shook her head. "I'm sorry. But yes? Well, two, anyway."

Nicole narrowed her eyes. Her defenses were starting to melt a bit. She felt like she knew Avery well enough to believe that she was being honest, and whoever this other sexy cop was, she wasn't a threat.

Not that she could be a threat, because—*oh, fuck off. You want her. Stop talking yourself out of it.* "Okay..." she said. "I'm listening."

"That's Fallon," Avery said, looking over her shoulder, then pointing to the blond cop who was now kneeling on the street, adjusting a young girl's pigtails. "And Fallon is my sister. Well, technically my stepsister."

Nicole took a moment with that. "You realize this wouldn't have had to be a thing at all if we'd spent a little time talking about our families, right?"

Avery looked like she wanted to laugh but caught herself. "Nicole, there's a lot we haven't talked about. But you're right," she conceded. She threw her shoulders back as though preparing to address her royal subjects. "My mom married Fallon's dad when I was five. Fallon's a month older than I am, and yes, she loves holding that over me. She's a sergeant in BLPD and is also freakishly strong, so be careful around her. No, I don't know my biological dad. Do I have deep-rooted trauma from that?" Avery shrugged. "Maybe, but my stepdad is amazing and I don't really know life with anyone but him, so I think I'm good. Oh, and my mom is very nice. She loves to garden, which is probably where I get my love of flowers. She can't make a nice flower arrangement for shit, though."

"Okay—"

Avery held up a finger, cutting her off. "We always had dogs when I was growing up. Mostly mutts we rescued from shelters. My stepdad gave me shit when I adopted Houston, since she's a purebred, but he secretly loves her. Yes, my parents live locally, and yes, I see them pretty often." She smiled, pleased with herself. "How's that?"

Nicole gazed at Avery, wondering how she could so quickly erase those anxious bubbles that twisted in Nicole's gut. "It's a start."

Avery looked around. "Are you by yourself?"

Nicole nodded. "Brynn was going to come with me, but she apparently has a date, which is a big deal for her."

"Good. Hang out with me."

Nicole looked to where Fallon had been, but she was gone. She was clearly working, hence the uniform, so Avery must not have been there with her. "Are you by yourself?"

Avery hesitated, then shook her head. "Come on."

An hour later, Nicole felt like she had never known life without Gavin and Thea. Gavin had made her feel instantly welcome, holding out a paper cone filled with candied almonds. He asked questions but didn't pry, taking serious cues from Avery occasionally shooting eye-daggers at him. And Thea was too cute for words. Nicole had instantly recognized her as the little girl Fallon had been helping with her pigtails. She had a big personality and was more than happy to have a new adult to entertain with explanations of every little thing she saw as they walked the street.

As for Avery, Nicole caught her staring several times. The look on her face wasn't easy to decipher, but it warmed her to the core.

"Nicole," Avery said suddenly, grabbing her arm. "Look."

She followed the direction of Avery's extended finger and gasped when she read the sign. "No. We have to."

Behind them, Thea was beginning what sounded like a tantrum. She was very upset about the lack of blue cotton candy. Nicole couldn't blame her, as blue was the superior color.

"I think we're going to head out," Gavin said as he picked up Thea and spun her around effortlessly until she landed on his shoulders. She let loose a half-hearted wail, then patted her dad on the head several times. Her pigtails were so askew that one was practically on top of her head, the other dangling below her ear. "It was great to meet you, Nicole." He nodded at Avery. "Let me know if you'll be home for dinner."

"Sketti!" Thea exclaimed, then remembered her current concern. "Daddy! Con candy!"

With an exaggerated grin and a wave, Gavin walked off, Thea repeatedly calling out for her cotton candy.

"Before you say anything, yes," Avery said, turning to Nicole, "Gavin makes dinner. We're a very evolved household."

Nicole bumped her elbow against Avery's arm. "The only thing I was going to say is that we need to go get one of those fried pickle hot dogs. *Immediately*."

Avery leaned against her, and Nicole breathed into the feeling of the skin-on-skin contact of their arms. "Immediately it is."

They walked over to the vendor, not bothering to look at any other items on the menu. Several minutes later, they beamed at their thick corn dogs, then grinned at each other.

"You first," Avery said.

"Oh, no. This is a one, two, three, we bite—hey!" She laughed as Avery took an enormous bite of the hot dog. Nicole watched her overjoyed reaction.

"Oh my God," Avery said, but it sounded more like "ommagah," considering the amount of food in her mouth. She pointed at Nicole's hot dog, then at Nicole's mouth.

She got the hint. The first bite was an explosion of salty, fried goodness: the hot dog was encased in a pickle, which was encased in whatever made up a corn dog. Nicole could care less about the specifics. Her mouth was in heaven.

"Cheese!" Avery said excitedly.

Sure enough, Nicole's second bite included a delicious, if lava-hot, squirt of cheese. She mumbled something incoherent as she chewed.

The two women lapsed into reverent silence as they ate. Only when the sticks were empty, Avery's licked impossibly clean, did they speak again.

"That was unreal," Nicole said, holding her stomach. "I'd probably explode if I did, but I want to eat another one."

"We could split one," Avery said, her eyes sparkling. She wiggled her eyebrows.

Nicole laughed and shook her head. "Let's walk a bit and see if there's anything else we need to try."

They walked aimlessly and contentedly, circling families and groups of teenagers. When they were side by side, Nicole was acutely aware of the tiny space that remained between them. She liked that it allowed them to sometimes bump into each other as they walked, each touch a little burst of curious excitement.

"I'm glad Brynn canceled on you," Avery said as they walked back toward The Twisted Tulip.

Nicole elbowed her, enjoying the increasing physical touches between them. "That's not nice."

"Maybe not, but I'm still glad we got to spend time together today. Even if it was only because your friend dipped out on you."

Nicole laughed. "We've had this conversation before, you know. The whole, let's stop just running into each other and make some damn plans to see each other."

"Oh, yeah," Avery said, drawing out the words. "Wow, we're really terrible at this dating thing."

"Well," Nicole said, glancing over, "I think we're both being careful."

Avery was quiet as they walked. Her hands were tucked into the pockets of her loose-fitting jeans, and her dark green T-shirt hung just so over her hips. She seemed to be deep in thought, so Nicole turned her attention back to the sidewalk as they approached the shop.

At the door, Avery turned to her. "Come in for a minute?"

Nicole nodded, following her in. Zuri was at the front desk, helping a couple pick out flowers for a bouquet. She nodded at Avery and smiled at Nicole as they passed. A moment later, Avery held open a door for Nicole and she walked in, looking around the space.

"This is nice—" Nicole's words halted in the heat of feeling Avery's hands on her arms, slowly spinning her around.

"I think I'm ready to be a little less careful." Avery hadn't let go of Nicole's arms, and she was leaning against the closed door of her office. Her eyes darkened, the golden flecks melting into dark-brown swirls.

Nicole nodded, swallowing as Avery pulled her closer, erasing that tiny protective space they'd so carefully held between them. She put her hands on Avery's hips, unable to stop herself from pushing her thumbs up to touch the skin beneath her T-shirt.

Avery's mouth dropped open, and her hands moved to Nicole's face, cupping her jaw and pulling her close until their mouths met in the middle. The first touch of Avery's lips sent a rush of warmth and tenderness through Nicole's body. The kiss was so gentle, so searching—it was at complete odds with Avery's assertive movements leading up to their mouths meeting.

Avery's hands moved so they were around her shoulders. One hand grazed the hairs at the base of her neck, and she shivered into their kiss. The way their lips moved together— Nicole knew instantly that *this* was what kisses were supposed to feel like.

She bit her lower lip when Avery pulled away. Avery's eyes were luminescent as she held Nicole's stare.

"Why—how does that feel so good?" Avery shook her head slightly. "It just feels insanely *good*."

Nicole reached up and ran the back of her fingers down the side of Avery's flushed cheek. "I think it's supposed to feel that good."

Avery's eyes fluttered shut, then opened. "But it's not, like— electric. I don't feel like I'm on fire, or that I need to rip your clothes off." She tugged on Nicole's ponytail. "I *want* to rip your clothes off, so don't think otherwise." She shook her head, seeming to struggle for an explanation.

"I know what you mean," Nicole said, and she did. Truly. But defining the sensation of their kiss didn't seem imperative in that moment. "Maybe we should try it again to see if that—"

Avery didn't need encouragement; her mouth was back on Nicole's before she could finish her sentence. Nicole pulled her closer, focusing on every inch of their bodies and all the places they connected. When Avery deepened the kiss, Nicole moved her hands to the back of Avery's neck, gently running her fingers through the loose, short curls.

"Friday," Avery said, her mouth still slowly moving against Nicole's.

"What?" Nicole tried to pull back but Avery held her tight.

"You and me, Friday." Avery did pull back then. "No more leaving this up to fate, okay?"

Nicole nodded, leaning in for more kissing. "Okay."

CHAPTER TWENTY-EIGHT

At least once every hour since roughly four thirty p.m. on Saturday, Avery had regretted making plans for Friday. More specifically: she regretted making herself (and Nicole, presumably) wait that long. There were far too many days between Saturday and Friday, and by Wednesday morning, Avery was restless and agitated.

But the timing was what it needed to be. She had a busy week, and she wanted to be relaxed and energetic when she saw Nicole again, not moody and tired, overthinking every stem she'd twisted over the course of the day. Plus, over the course of their texts and phone calls, Nicole had informed Avery that she had three eulogy clients she was working with that week, in addition to her actual full-time job. So despite the fact that neither woman *wanted* to go an entire week without seeing each other, it seemed that fate was yet again interceding.

Avery brushed the back of her hand over her sketchbook. She didn't often sketch her ideas anymore; she preferred the trial and error of hands-on experimentation. But she was fully stuck on making Maya and J.C.'s wedding beyond perfect, so she'd turned to her old, trusty sketchbook.

The couple wanted classic but simple. After some debating, J.C. had won the color war, and they'd decided on navy and cream. They were pretty clueless when it came to preferred flowers, giving Avery a carte blanche that both excited and scared her. She was used to brides having specific requests, which she happily worked with while making suggestions. Having free rein was rubbing the edge of overwhelm.

Avery scratched the side of her face as she looked at her sketch of the bridal bouquet. "Huh," she said, leaning closer. Looked like dahlias and strawflowers. Okay. She could work with that.

She resumed sketching, trying to focus on ideas for the reception and table arrangements. As she drew, her mind drifted back to Nicole. Since that long-awaited kiss had finally happened, she'd had a hard time thinking of anything but Nicole's mouth and the way it had felt against hers.

She'd meant what she'd said—she really had thought their kiss would feel different somehow. Avery was used to intense, pent-up passion that flooded out the moment her lips met someone else's (okay, let's be real: Shannon's). She loved that explosion of lust, the thick shimmy of electricity running through her entire body, rooting itself in her most tender spots. Kissing Shannon had always felt good, even when things between them weren't; it was as though that physical connection was *the* thing that prevented them from being just friends. As long as they were kissing, or having sex, Avery was in the haze of believing Shannon was the only woman for her.

But when it went away, when they were left with distance and sporadic communication, the passion leveled out, faded into friendship. The hook, of course, was that Avery knew the intensity of their physical connection. Just because it wasn't happening didn't mean she forgot about it.

She drew her lips in and dropped her pencil on the table. Kissing Nicole was nothing like kissing Shannon. And for the first couple of seconds, Avery had been silently freaking out. She was so used to all-consuming passion that she had no idea what real, quiet intensity felt like. When she'd said that it just felt *good*, she'd meant it. It was the only word she could think of. Kissing Nicole felt good. Solid. Inviting. Alluring. Incredible. But in a word: *good*.

And in other words, it was and wasn't at all what Avery had been expecting.

Explaining that to herself was something she'd been working on since Saturday night. She hadn't gotten very far, so she wasn't yet ready to talk about it with Nicole. She worried, though, that even though they'd continued kissing and it felt like Nicole liked it as much as she did, it wasn't enough.

Avery blinked, then looked across the workroom. No, that wasn't it. She was worried that *she* wasn't enough.

"Fucking shit," she muttered, dropping down onto a stool.

Yet another reason why she knew she shouldn't be messing around with Nicole. Avery needed reassurance. She needed to be told she was a good kisser, that Nicole had loved every moment of their short make-out session as much as she had. She wanted to know that Nicole wanted more, that she—

Avery sighed. That wasn't Nicole's job. And the fact was, Nicole was giving her more reassurance than Avery could see or hear. Having existed in an intense back-and-forth situation where it felt like feelings were often held hostage, Avery had a difficult time understanding and believing that Nicole's consistency was exactly the kind of reassurance she needed. It wasn't that she was consciously waiting for the other shoe to drop. She was at a point where she trusted Nicole (for the most part).

No, the problem was that Avery didn't quite trust herself enough.

"Hey," Zuri said as she walked into the room. "Maya's here with some fabric samples for you."

"Oh, great." Just the distraction she needed. She brushed off her overalls and walked into the front of the shop where Maya was waiting with a big smile.

"Hi! I hope it's okay that I just stopped by like this."

"Yeah, of course. Zuri said you have fabric samples?"

She pulled out the samples with a flourish. "Yup, here's my dress, and this one is J.C.'s suit."

Avery leaned over the counter, inspecting the samples. "Perfect," she murmured. "So I have some ideas I've been working on."

As she went over some of the things she'd come up with, the shop bustled around them. At some point, Avery went back to the workroom to grab her sketchbook. When she returned, Zuri was standing with Maya, showing her a few different dahlias.

"This one is what I'm thinking," Avery said, touching the petals of a lavender flower. "You'll want a little pop of color in your bouquet, and this shade of lavender looks great with the navy of J.C.'s suit."

"I love it," Maya said with a big smile. "Can I see the bouquet sketch?"

Avery showed it to her, pointing out places she'd like to add greenery. She was so wrapped up in the conversation that she barely registered the sound of the bell over the door twinkling repeatedly.

"I think we're definitely on the right path," Maya said several minutes later. "I have to get to work. Should I leave the fabric with you?"

"Yeah, that'd be great." Avery slid the two samples into her sketchbook. "I'll keep working on ideas so when you and J.C. come in for your next meeting, we should be able to settle on specifics."

"Sounds perfect. Thanks so much, Avery. See you in a few weeks." Maya waved as she left the shop.

Avery waved back, then bent her head back over her sketchbook. An idea had come to her, and she wanted to get it down before it flew out of her brain.

Less than a minute passed before she put her pencil down. She stood up, arched her back, and raised her hands to undo her bun because it was pulling too tight somewhere on the top of her head. She looked around the shop as she did so, making sure she wasn't missing any quiet customers.

She froze with her fingers pulling her hair tie.

"What are you doing here?" she managed to say, arms still uncomfortably frozen.

Shannon smiled in the way that only she could: the smile of a woman who refused to respect boundaries, and knew she was attractive and manipulative enough to usually get away with it. "Hello."

"Shannon," Avery said. "What are you doing?"

"Working," she replied. And indeed, she was in full uniform. But that still wasn't an explanation for her being in the shop.

"Did someone call 911 from the shop?" Avery said, biting each word as it came out.

"No." She was still smiling, though Avery thought maybe it wavered. Just a bit. "I was in the area and thought I'd stop by and say hi."

Avery felt her mouth move, but no noise came out. She wasn't surprised. This was exactly what Shannon did, and had done for seven years. Avery had stuck to her no-communication rule, as had Shannon, but now Shannon was tired of it. Three weeks had passed, and that was more than enough "space" according to Shannon. Avery didn't even need to ask; she knew that was precisely the case. What she didn't know was whether Shannon had figured out that Avery had blocked her number. But she wasn't feeling inclined to ask.

"Avery," Shannon said, her smile reflecting some sadness. "Can you honestly say you're happier not talking to me?"

She hated that question. It wasn't the first time Shannon had posed it to her, and the truth was a real bitch. Was Avery happier? In some ways, yes—but that sense of *happy* was more a feeling of being *free*. She missed Shannon. She genuinely liked talking to her. They were friends, after all, and had a closeness that Avery did sometimes rely on. But that closeness was too often blurry and gray, not at all clear and understandable with firm boundaries. And that's where Avery constantly got tripped up.

"You know I'm not," she heard herself say, then winced. "I don't like not talking to you."

"Me either."

"But," Avery continued, "what we've been doing isn't healthy."

"*But*," Shannon said, taking a step toward her, "we both want our friendship, right?"

Avery squirmed. That was the piece she hadn't yet figured out. The eulogy had done its work in helping her let go of the hope she'd been clinging to for dear life, but she still hadn't decided if she actually could be friends with Shannon. Or, really, if she wanted to.

"Shannon, I—"

They were interrupted by the delicate ring of the bell over the shop's door. Both Shannon and Avery turned to the door, but only Avery reacted to Nicole walking in and stopping dead when she saw that Avery wasn't alone.

Avery watched in silence as Nicole looked back and forth between her and Shannon, her face showing a mixture of confusion and surprise. Avery was pretty certain her own face showed absolute shock when Nicole said, "Hi, I'm just here for some flowers," walked past the thick confrontation, and parked herself in front of the cooler.

When she pulled her eyes off Nicole, Avery found Shannon studying her. She nodded, seemingly to herself, and pulled her keys out of her pocket.

"I'll let you get back to work." As Shannon approached the door, she turned to Avery and said, her voice low enough that it would have been very hard for Nicole to hear, "I'll call you later."

The moment she left, Avery felt her shoulders drop from her ears. She wanted to scream and she wanted to flee. But she could do neither.

Nicole stayed at the cooler, and Avery watched as she carefully examined the flowers. Avery wanted to break the silence but found she didn't have the words to do so.

Finally, with her back still to Avery, Nicole said, "So, you weren't kidding about knowing a lot of hot cops."

A flame of regret lit up Avery's insides, then, as her irritation with Shannon made its way to her gut, the flame was doused with gasoline and raged into a full-blown fire of agitation. She was going to kill Shannon. No, Avery wouldn't do well in jail. Fine. She'd settle for severely maiming her and bribing Gavin to hold up her alibi.

She refused to lie to Nicole, though, and wanted to set a precedent of being upfront with her. "That was Shannon," Avery said carefully, making sure her anger stayed tucked inside and didn't spark out on the tail end of her words. "She came by unannounced."

Nicole turned but stayed near the cooler. "Is that a thing that she does?"

Avery shrugged, then nodded. "In a way, yes. Every time I decide I'm done with her, she waits until the exact right amount of time passes, and then she shows up in some way. Sometimes it's in person, sometimes it's a phone call."

"Are you?"

She shook her head, trying to keep up. "Am I what?"

"Are you done with her?" Nicole asked. "Really done?"

Avery's defenses soared up, kicking her calm, rational mind to the side. "You heard my eulogy," she said, tone bordering on cold.

"Words are one thing," Nicole said. "Emotions are another."

The fire was easing its way up Avery's throat. She swallowed hard, trying to keep it calm. "I know that. I have never lied to you about how I feel about her. I want to be done with her, Nicole. I do. I blocked her number. I had no idea she was going to show up today." Avery swallowed again. Her throat felt scratchy, like the fire had cloaked it with crunchy ash. "That part of my life is over."

"And when she calls you later?"

Avery stared at her. "You heard that?"

Nicole half-smiled. "I was blessed with impeccable hearing."

"Apparently." Avery gave herself a shake, reminding herself that Nicole was not the enemy here and she did not deserve to be splashed by the anger that was boiling Avery from the inside out. "I blocked her number," she repeated, then shook her head. "But I'm going to unblock her so we can finalize this. When she calls me later, I will remind her that I cut off communication because I do not want to communicate with her." Either the anger was too intense, or Avery really didn't have a feeling connected to that idea any longer. She wasn't sure, but she was hoping it was the latter. "I will set a firm boundary that works for me and ask that she respect it, even if she doesn't like it. And then I will block her again. For good."

Several tense moments of silence passed between them. Avery hugged her arms to her chest, waiting.

"Okay," Nicole said simply. She stepped away from the cooler, and without looking at Avery, walked to the door and left the store.

Avery watched her go, feeling as though something incredibly important was moving further and further away from her. And all she could do was stand there and watch.

CHAPTER TWENTY-NINE

Nicole held her hand to her nose, trying to ward off the sneeze that was threatening to explode. She recoiled as soon as she inhaled, jerking her bleach-scented hand away. In defiance, the sneeze blasted from her, spraying itself across the freshly Windex-ed mirror. She stomped her bare foot in frustrated fury, then felt her body puddle to the floor. She sat there, knees drawn to her chest, head pressed against her knees. She wrapped her arms around her legs as tightly as possible and rode the swelling waves of her feelings.

It wasn't Avery—or, more accurately, it wasn't *just* Avery. Nicole was having a hell of a hard time trying to erase the image of Shannon and Avery from her mind. And they'd only been talking; there was only a flicker of intimacy between them, one Nicole had felt as soon as she'd walked into The Twisted Tulip. It hadn't felt like unbridled passionate intimacy. No, it was more the kind of intimacy that hovered between two people who'd had an intimate relationship at one point but no longer did. An invisible string that linked them, but only when they were in the same space.

She could have done without walking right up into that string and feeling its tenacity cut a thin but gaping line right into her torso.

But maybe, she thought as she rubbed her eyes, she had needed to see that, and feel that. For all Avery had said about Shannon, Nicole knew there was just as much—probably more, no, definitely more—that was buried beneath Avery's layers of memories. It was a strange place to be in: Nicole wanted to understand the pull between the two women, but she also wished she'd never had to know that such a pull even existed.

Now she understood Avery's hesitation to completely remove Shannon from her life. There was history there. History and unresolved feelings.

She also understood Avery's reaction to their kiss.

Nicole grumbled, sounds not adding up to words. That kiss. It felt like coming home, like standing at the ocean's edge and watching the sunrise. It was the kind of kiss that made sense, that brought long lost dreams and abandoned hopes back to life.

Avery was right, after all: it had simply felt *good*. But Avery, Nicole assumed, wasn't familiar with how *good* good can be. How *good* is meaningful and promising and the best kind of kiss there is.

Nicole pushed herself to her feet. She had a sinking feeling she was going to spend the day lost in her thoughts. The least she could do was continue her intense, anxiety-fueled deep cleaning of the bathroom while she overthought everything that lingered in her mind, unresolved.

She picked up the sponge and attacked the counter. With dismay, she realized the cleaning spray had mostly evaporated and she had to spritz again to get things moving. Nicole scrubbed with vigor, wishing she was a dirtier person so that this venture was more satisfying.

The sink proved a better project. It amazed her how toothpaste gunk collected around the drain. The intensity of her scrubbing started a low burn in her biceps. A single bead of sweat trickled from her hairline, passing over her lips before dropping into the sink. She scrubbed that away, too.

After cleaning the mirror a second time, thanks to that exuberant sneeze, Nicole turned her attention to the shower. She was convinced no one enjoyed cleaning showers. It was an annoying process: remove all the shampoos and soaps and razors, wet the walls, spray, scrub, rinse, scrub the tub, rinse. She hated it.

But what she hated more was knowing she'd blown it and ended up liking Avery way more than she'd intended to. More than she presumed she was ready for, too.

Nicole paused, shampoo and conditioner bottles in hand. That part she wasn't sure about. Maybe she was ready to like someone as much as she was beginning to like Avery. Maybe the problem was that she'd gone and selected someone who wasn't in a position to reciprocate those feelings.

"Great," Nicole muttered. "So now I'm Avery, and Avery's Shannon."

Not liking the sound of that one bit, Nicole dropped the shampoo and conditioner onto the tile floor and threw all her negative energy into cleaning every single centimeter of the shower. It was going to sparkle by the time she finished.

Ten minutes later, she was soaking wet and unsure how that had come to be. She could only stare at her T-shirt and sweatpants, perplexed with the amount of water that was staining them shades darker. Yet another joy of cleaning the shower.

After replacing her variety of shampoos and soaps, Nicole turned to the mirror. She half-expected to need to clean it yet again (surely the shower cleaning adventure had somehow splattered the mirror), but instead, all she saw was herself. And she didn't love what she saw.

Her eyes were dull, her skin pale. She looked lifeless, empty. She turned her head a bit. In an unsettling way, her reflection reminded her of the days when she'd leave Brynn's bed and stare at herself in the mirror, searching for a change or a shift. She'd been so lost then. She thought she'd come so far, and now, looking at herself, she feared she'd slid right back to the very place she'd fought to get out of.

To Nicole's surprise, it wasn't sadness that she felt. Far from it. She continued gazing at herself, feeling all the heat drain from her body. She stood, chilled to her very bones, until the formidable warmth returned with a volcanic vengeance, lighting her limbs aflame. Yes, she was angry. Finally.

She gripped the cold, wet sponge, not knowing what to do with this wild, virulent sensation. Nicole wasn't sure how much time passed as she stood, frozen only in motion as her blood boiled and bubbled with liquid that felt like it was covered in spikes.

As the turbulent feelings tossed within her, she thought about little other than the fact that she still needed to clean the floor, so it was a complete surprise when some time later, she was opening her apartment door and looking at Brynn.

"I don't understand," Nicole said for the tenth time. "When did I call you?"

Brynn held out her phone yet again. "Forty minutes ago. Drink."

She obediently took a sip of the water Brynn had gotten for her. "Did I black out?"

"I don't know, Nic," Brynn said patiently. "Maybe the cleaning chemicals got to you?"

She shook her head. "That's never happened before."

"Doesn't mean it couldn't happen." Brynn shifted on the sofa, never taking her eyes off Nicole. "How are you feeling now?"

She took a slow, deep breath, and considered the question. There was numbness in some areas, but the anger that had overtaken her was still simmering, splashing around recklessly. "Messy," she settled on.

"Looks like that whole not getting attached thing didn't work out so well?"

Nicole tensed. "No," she said quickly. "That's not what this is about. I mean, maybe it started with that. But...Brynn, it's Ginny."

Brynn was quiet. When Nicole looked at her, Brynn was nodding, almost rocking. Then she looked up and met Nicole's eyes.

"Okay. What happened?"

"I got mad." Nicole half-laughed, half-sobbed. "Like, really, really angry. I thought I was going to put my fist through the mirror." She set down her water and looked at Brynn again. "She left me, Brynn. She made a decision and went through with it, and she left me. She did it knowing it would destroy me. How could she have ever loved me and done what she did?"

"We've gone over this," Brynn said.

"I know. Ad nauseam. But I've never felt *this* before. I never let myself be angry. And you know why? Brace yourself, because it's fucked-up." Nicole gripped the edge of the sofa, feeling another callous wave of rage. "Because I don't want to be mad at a dead person."

Brynn started to laugh, but caught herself. "That's…"

"Ridiculous," Nicole finished. "What does it matter? She's dead, she doesn't know how I feel. She could not care less if I'm mad at her."

"So be mad, Nic. Just don't get lost in it."

Nicole nodded. She hated being mad at someone who wasn't around to work through the anger with her—and work together to solve it. She dropped her head as a slow-moving train of thought steamed its way into her already cluttered mind.

"I don't want to go back there. I don't want to love someone only to lose them again."

"Avery doesn't strike me as someone who would take her own life."

"Me either, but you never really know, do you?" Nicole shook her head. "But that's not what I'm worried about."

Brynn held on to her response for a few moments, seeming to teeter between wanting to say it and wishing to avoid it. "It's her ex."

Nicole released the breath she'd been holding, even though letting it go washed her with emptiness. "Yes. I believe Avery.

I do," she said, holding up a hand to stop whatever Brynn was thinking about saying. "But after seeing them together, it's clear to me that her ex hasn't let go of her. And knowing what I know…I feel like it's only a matter of time before she tries to get Avery back."

"I'm sorry for this comparison. Really, I am. But, Nic, you had no control over Ginny's choices. And you have no control over what Avery's ex does. Or what Avery does, for that matter." Brynn rubbed her hands against her jeans. "I think she just needs time. And *you* need to stop taking on her problems."

A dangerous chord struck deep inside Nicole, its sonorous reverberations pounding over and over again. When, exactly, had she stopped paying attention to her own grieving process and turned all her energy over to Avery's?

Nicole clutched her throat, mortified. She thought she'd done grieving right (aside from that troublesome anger part, of course), and here she was, dipping out on her own emotions to focus on unpacking someone else's baggage.

"Do you really think Avery is ready to let go of her ex?" Brynn's voice was as gentle as Nicole had ever heard it, and she was thankful for the way it moved her right out of her little mental tailspin.

"Yeah," Nicole said. "I do."

Brynn nodded. "Then trust your gut. And trust her."

"I'm trying."

Brynn's hand landed comfortably on Nicole's shoulder, giving a single squeeze before returning to her lap. "I know. That's all you need to do right now." She reconsidered. "Well, that, and keep moving through your own grief. Don't put yourself aside again."

"Can you stay for a while?" Nicole twisted her hands in her lap. "I don't want to be alone right now."

"Only if you let me beat you in Mario Kart."

Nicole smiled as she got up to get the controllers. "Never."

CHAPTER THIRTY

The phone call hadn't gone well, not that Avery had expected it to. Shannon never seemed to like it when Avery put one or both feet down, standing her ground and speaking firmly. It probably wasn't Avery's determination that bothered Shannon; more than likely, it was the fact that the determination came with boundaries and brick walls built in the sand.

Avery paced her foyer. It had taken cajoling and persuasion, but Shannon had finally agreed to come over so they could talk face-to-face. Her little drop-by in the store yesterday had rattled Avery in ways she couldn't explain, but she knew this conversation—the final one, she hoped—deserved an in-person interaction.

She looked over at her phone lying on the half-wall that separated the foyer from the living room. It was silent and still. Nicole hadn't reached out, and they were going on twenty-four hours with no contact. Avery wanted to text or call her, but she understood the purpose of the silence. It was an unspoken move, a push of the ball firmly into Avery's court. *Your move.*

Avery jumped when a knock sounded on the front door. She paused in front of the mirror, giving herself an encouraging nod. Houston, who had been pacing along with her, sniffed the air before trotting into the kitchen.

Some of her confidence fizzled when she opened the door and came face-to-face with Shannon. That godforsaken attraction was still there. Shannon's body language, however, dampened the excited surge. She was not happy. Not one bit.

"Hello," Shannon said, her mouth barely moving.

"Hey." Avery waved her in. "Come on in."

Wordlessly, the two women walked into the living room and sat down. Avery wasn't surprised when Shannon chose the chair directly across from the sofa she'd chosen. She was grateful for it. Every little bit of distance between them could only help this conversation, and what came after it.

"Thanks for coming over." Avery stopped herself, reconsidered. "I wanted to do this in person."

"Do what?"

She hadn't expected that Shannon would make this easy. But she also hadn't been prepared for the purposeful ignorance.

"End this," she said, the words slipping out of their own volition. "I can't—we can't do this anymore."

"What? Be friends?"

"Right. We can't be friends. Because us being friends isn't like me being friends with Gavin, or with Zuri. And it never will be."

Shannon shifted her posture, not enough to give away her emotions but enough to signify she was feeling something. "But we both know our friendship will always be different. Because of our connection." She leaned forward, resting her elbows on her knees, steepling her fingers and pointing them toward the ground. "I want you in my life, Avery. That has never changed."

"I feel the same way. But it's too complicated now."

Shannon raised her eyebrows. "What does that mean?"

Avery tucked her hands under her thighs. Snippets of her conversation with Zuri fluttered in her brain like autumn leaves freshly shaken from a tree. As much as she wanted to avoid the topic of Nicole, there was a small, perverse side of her that wanted to see if Shannon would even care if she was involved with someone else.

"Everything that's happened lately," Avery settled on.

Before she could elaborate, Shannon spoke. "Is this still about the wedding?"

Well, Avery thought. *The guilty conscience speaks.* "No, it's not. It's about me. It's about you, it's about the idea of *us* that I've held on to for all this time. But more than that, it's about me. Just me," she said, trying not to cry out of frustration. She cleared her throat, hoping that was enough to wipe away the emotion. "I wanted us to have a relationship." She looked Shannon straight in the eye. "I wanted to be the only woman in your life."

Shannon smiled in a way that told Avery she was going to diffuse the tension. It was one of her tells, a clear sign she wanted to avoid any and all emotion. "What about my mom?"

"You know what I mean."

"Avery," Shannon said, exasperated. "It's not about her."

Her. Shannon so rarely used Marie's name. "But it is—"

"No," Shannon interrupted. "It's me. It's my issues."

Avery took a breath that tripped as it came through her lungs. "And what are you doing about your issues?"

The silence in the room provided the answer Avery knew all too well. They both knew Shannon chose to remain paralyzed in her fear of making a decision. And for a long time, Avery had willingly stayed there with her, buffering her from an additional loss (Avery) that would add to her existing losses (too many to count). She'd taken on the role of protecting a woman who could only give bits and pieces of herself, a love made of words hanging, clipped to a clothesline, over a barren field.

All this time, Avery had been waiting for the one solid gust of air that would set their shaky promise of a relationship flying far into the distance. She had only just realized she, in fact, was the wind.

"We don't want the same things," Avery said. She thought Shannon would interrupt her, but she stayed quiet. "I want a relationship. You want a friendship."

"I never asked you to wait around."

That would have stung weeks ago, but there was new armor over Avery's heart. Shannon was right—she had never outright asked (except for the few times she'd said, "please be patient with me," which could easily be turned around to mean whatever Shannon wanted it to mean). It had been Avery's choice to stay.

And now it was her choice to leave.

"I want a relationship," Avery repeated. "And I understand that I can't have that with you." Her fingers were going numb, so she pulled them out from under her legs and rested them on her lap. "But I need to move on."

"Without me," Shannon said.

Avery nodded. "You can't show up at the shop. You can't stop by here. We can't talk anymore, Shannon. I need to move on. And I need you to let me move on."

The words stung as they left her mouth, but as soon as they were out in the air, she felt a new lightness within herself. She had never wanted life without Shannon. But there was no other option anymore. Yes, she was losing a person who held a piece of her heart. But Avery had already learned to live without that piece.

"You and I," Shannon began, her dark-brown eyes holding steady on Avery, "will always be connected. Even if we're not in each other's lives. But I need you to know that this isn't what I want, Avery. It breaks my heart to think of not having you in my life."

Avery had said the same so many times, and yet she couldn't bring herself to say it again. Instead, she stayed quiet, watching Shannon.

"I love you, Aves. I truly do."

Avery pushed her thumbs into her thighs, just to feel something real. "I love you, too. But I also need you to respect my decision. I think it will be good for both of us."

"I will. You know how to find me if you change your mind."

Another line she'd heard the countless times she'd tried to cut the string that kept them connected. Avery wanted to say she wasn't going to change her mind. She wanted to say a lot of things, some hurtful, some draped in anger. But there was no point in dragging this out. She'd already said so much over the years, and nothing had ever changed.

Shannon stood, seeming to take her silence as a sign, then hesitated. "Not a day will go by that I won't think about you."

The temptation to toss out the idea that maybe someday they could be friends kept shoving against Avery's tongue, but she kept her mouth shut. If that would be their fate, then so be it. Time would tell.

"I'll miss you, Shannon."

At the front door, they both paused, unsure of what to do. Finally, Avery stepped forward and wrapped her arms around Shannon. She shut her eyes against the familiar onslaught of emotion. Maybe time would give them the space to let their connection wither so that one day, they could be just friends. Friends without an emotional entanglement. Friends without a pile of destroyed hopes. Friends without "maybe someday."

When Shannon left, she didn't turn back, and Avery shut the door quickly. At the sound of the bolt sliding shut, Houston came back into the foyer and immediately wrapped herself around Avery's legs.

"You never did like her, huh?" Avery laughed a little, petting her dog. "I should listen to you more often."

In a flash, she remembered the way Houston had found Nicole in the dog park and wasted no time in giving her affection. Avery smiled through the desolate sadness creeping through her bones. She really should listen to her dog more often.

As she scratched Houston behind her ears, Avery looked up at the closed front door. She imagined Shannon driving away, stuffing down her emotions as she always did. For so long, she'd wanted to know that Shannon *would* miss her, that there would be an Avery-shaped hole in her life that she would regret creating every time she caught sight of it.

But Shannon's feelings were no longer Avery's priority. She'd had her chance, and she'd lost it—or, rather, she'd repeatedly chosen not to do anything with it, taking for granted the idea that Avery would simply always be there at her beck and call.

As the minutes ticked by and the cool breeze of her final decision swept in, Avery found herself grabbing hold of the feeling of being free, of releasing herself from the confines she'd held herself in for so long.

Avery was lying on the sofa, enjoying a rare moment of peace in a quiet house, when the front door opened and the foyer filled with commotion. She didn't move from her cozy spot, but Houston darted to the door, only pausing to give Avery a look that said something like, "Sorry, Mom."

"Pizza's home!" Gavin called out.

Avery sat up like a snapped rubber band. "Pizza? Seriously?"

"Would I joke about something like that?"

"Honestly? Yes, you would." Avery twisted on the sofa and watched Gavin walk into the kitchen. Sure enough, his arms were loaded with three pizza boxes. "I'm sorry, did I miss the memo about a party?"

"Hi, Avey!" Thea yelled, skip-stomping into the room with Houston hot on her trail. "Daddy got us pizza!" She jumped up and down, Penelope the platypus flailing helplessly in her hand.

"No party," Gavin said. "Just us and Fallon. And you know how much pizza she can cram into that body."

Avery shuddered. "The eeriest thing about her."

"Oh, because you're Miss Prim and Proper?" Fallon said as she strode into the room. She picked up a pillow and whacked Avery with it.

"Stop it, I'm sensitive." She saw the look that passed between Gavin and Fallon. "What? What do you two know?"

"I drove by earlier and saw a familiar car parked out front," Fallon said. Avery could tell she was trying to keep her tone on the kinder side of interrogating. It was a nice effort.

"That will be the last time you see that car parked out front."

Gavin kept quiet as he moved around the kitchen getting out plates and glasses. Fallon stared Avery down.

"Is that so?"

"It is." Avery stood up and walked past Fallon, giving her a little push. "I'm done with her. Moving on to better things."

Fallon raised her eyebrows. "Like a certain black-haired woman who looks at you with the kind of adoration you've been trying to get from Shannon for seven years?"

Avery shot Gavin a look, and he held up his hands in surrender. "She saw you talking to her at the festival. I didn't say a word."

She turned her glare to Fallon, who was grinning. "Maybe," Avery said. "If I didn't screw up my chance with her."

Fallon clapped Avery's back as she walked past her and headed directly for one of the pizza boxes. "Just be real with her, Aves. You deserve someone who gives and loves as much as you do. And I saw the way she looks at you. That's something you don't want to screw up."

Avery blinked back the sudden spring of tears. She was used to Fallon's brand of Tough Love, so it was a little disconcerting to hear actual heartfelt words come from her sister's mouth.

"Come on," Gavin said as he set the other two pizza boxes on the table. "Eat with us."

After pouring herself a glass of soda because she absolutely could not eat pizza without Coke, Avery looked around the table, feeling a new kind of peace. Gavin was leaning over Thea's plate, cutting her pizza into bite-size pieces. Each time he sliced off a new piece, Thea moved it to a pile and clapped. Avery knew Houston was lying next to Thea's chair, hoping against all hope that she'd drop her most treasured food (other than spaghetti, of course). Fallon had been given babysitting duties for Penelope, and was taking her job seriously: she'd propped Penelope against her pizza box and at Thea's direction, offered Penelope a bite every so often.

Her makeshift family was the most solid, stable thing in her life. While she was happy with what she had and the love that came along with banter and good-natured bullying, Avery couldn't help but wonder if having Nicole at the table with them would complete the picture.

She paused with a slice of pizza centimeters from her mouth. She couldn't remember the last time she'd tried to picture Shannon here.

Relief and a lingering sigh of sadness intermingled as she chewed her pizza. She'd made the right decision. As for what came next—well, Avery was finally ready to open herself up to the possibility of *what next*.

CHAPTER THIRTY-ONE

Nicole was doing everything she could to avoid looking at her phone. She'd been tempted to leave it in her apartment when she left to take what she hoped would be a long, brain-clearing walk. The morning had started off foggy—both internally for Nicole and externally for the city—but the sun had burned it off, leaving warm air and crisp blue skies. It was the kind of weather dreams were made of.

Her brain was still a little foggy, but nothing she couldn't handle. It never ceased to amaze her how easily and possessively grief could saunter in any time it wanted and cloak her entire being in a shroud that was heavy and smothering. Since the bathroom cleaning breakdown, Nicole had been going through the motions of keeping herself upright and moving. She'd given herself time last night, after Brynn finally left, to ugly-cry and rage at the world. After tossing and turning most of the night, she'd woken up that morning feeling like, while the grief was still making its presence known, at least the shroud had shifted to the ground. She could still see it in her peripheral vision, a benign lump of fabric holding whispers of tears, but it was silent and still, allowing her to move freely.

As Nicole walked away from the lake (tempted as she was to sit there all day, soaking in the sun, she did have work to do), she thought again about her new fixation on the leaving piece. For so much of her grieving process, she'd been muddling through the sadness and loss; it was almost too much to think about the fact that her wife had left her. Granted, she had left the entire world, but Nicole couldn't shake the feeling that Ginny had purposely decided to leave *her*. Her wife. The very person she'd claimed to love so, so much.

And it wasn't like a divorce, which Nicole had never experienced but imagined felt like a very different kind of leaving. A divorce meant an end of love on one or both ends. A spouse's suicide meant they didn't love the other person enough to stick around and work through—

Nicole stopped and put her hands on her hips. She knew her thoughts were doing that thing where they were lying to her in order to hurt her. Or, okay fine, she was thinking something to deliberately hurt herself. And what she was thinking had the potential to not be true.

"You've hurt enough," she said softly, gazing up toward the cerulean skies.

After a few deep breaths, Nicole continued walking. She thought about her phone, silent in the pocket of her leggings. She wondered when she would hear from Avery—and the bitter, worried voice prancing around at the front of her brain, stomping on the newly budding flowers of attraction and excitement, wondered *if* she would ever hear from Avery again.

Nicole didn't think she'd imagined the connection growing between them, but she was having a hell of a time erasing the image of Shannon and Avery standing across from each other as though they were facing off in a debate that wanted to be heated but was dulled by the nearly enviable heart connection still drawing them together.

But it was Friday. Avery had said they would see each other that night. She'd said so as recently as Wednesday morning, which felt like a lifetime ago but by timestamp was just about forty-eight hours ago. Nicole could absolutely text her and check in, make sure they still had plans...but she didn't. She wanted, maybe needed, Avery to make that move.

After stopping in Graze to pick up some lunch to go, she continued on toward home. She did have a pile of real-job work to do that would keep her busy for the rest of the day. Surely at some point she'd hear from Avery.

And if not—fine. Nicole knew she was becoming emotionally attached to Avery, right along with the possibility of what she thought they could become. But she wasn't willing to attach to someone who couldn't attach back. So if she had to cut it off, she would, and Avery's lack of communication would only make that hollow-feeling decision easier.

Just as Nicole was telling herself to shut up for the sixtieth time that morning, she saw a familiar flash of red hair across the street.

Of their own volition, her eyes traveled until they settled on Avery, who was standing in the doorway of the boutique hotel that had opened a month ago. It was swanky and hip, but rumored to have an absolutely gorgeous courtyard in the back with a bar that served outrageously good drinks. Nicole had been meaning to check it out, and was hoping Avery would join her.

She smiled despite her body's rumble of confusion. It looked like Avery was having an animated conversation with someone who was hidden in the darkness of the door's shadow. For a split second, Nicole imagined it was Shannon, but the thought bounced out of her head with the same speed it had arrived. It simply didn't make any sense, but besides that, everything about Avery was different than it had been when she'd been face-to-face with Shannon.

Then, Avery had been stiff. Her shoulders were clenched tightly, like strings crossing the bridge of a violin. One overzealous strike of the bow and something would have snapped, Nicole was sure of it. And Avery hadn't been smiling. Her expression had mirrored the one she'd had the first night they met—an injured combination of lost and hurt, untrusting and disbelieving. It had pained Nicole that first night, and it pained her again in the flower shop, but differently the second time.

Now, Avery was loose, laughing. Free. It was the version of her that Nicole felt most pulled to, when her energy was most magnetic and inviting. As Nicole watched, Avery turned from the doorway, sending one last wave to the person Nicole now saw was a short, extremely well-dressed bald man.

She was so caught up in watching that she didn't realize she was still halted on the sidewalk, clutching her takeout bag as she stared. She continued watching as Avery looked right at her. It was only when Avery smiled—tentatively, but it was a smile nonetheless—and stepped toward the curb as though to cross the street that Nicole mentally kicked herself and whipped around, intending to sprint back to her apartment.

However, she wasn't a runner. She'd taken just two steps when Avery called her name. Nicole thought about ignoring her, but didn't really want to. No sense in prolonging whatever was happening next, she told herself, and cemented her feet to the sidewalk as Avery jogged over to her.

Her usual work overalls had been replaced by tan cargo pants that were just baggy enough. Her basic black T-shirt was rolled at the sleeves and matched the black slip-on Vans on her feet. It was a simple look, but everything simple that Avery did was touched with the slightest bit of grace and beauty, and Nicole was far from immune to it.

She glanced down at her own black leggings and oversized pale-green T-shirt, which she'd knotted at her lower back. Fingers crossed Avery liked simple-athleisure on her.

"Got a milkshake in there?"

Nicole held up her bag from Graze and shook her head. "Not today. Just lunch."

The smile on Avery's face slid just enough to be noticeable, but Nicole held her ground. She had no intention of making any of this harder for Avery, but she wasn't going to throw herself at her, either.

Avery scuffed one foot back and forth. "I'd still like to go out with you tonight. If you want to."

Nicole batted down the piece of her heart that took flight at the sound of those words. *Not yet*, she commanded. "I'd like that, but I think we should talk first."

Nodding, Avery said, "Yes. Now?"

"Now is great." Nicole held up her free hand. "Wanna walk and talk? Or sit and talk? Or eat and talk?"

Avery poked the bag. "Are you offering to share?"

Nicole yanked the bag up to her chest. "Absolutely not. You'd need to get your own."

"Then let's sit and talk," Avery said with a grin. "Bench?" She eyed the closest one warily. "Unless it's going to burn the skin off my ass again."

Nicole plopped down first, the most chivalrous maneuver she'd ever done. "Just warm enough."

She expected to sit in hesitant silence, but to her surprise, Avery started talking right away, as though she'd been holding it all in and couldn't wait a second longer before it spewed out.

"I hate that you saw what you saw the other day," she began, rubbing her hand over the back of her neck. "But I need you to know that what you saw was…Well, it was nothing." Avery shook her head, working her jaw back and forth. "I mean, it wasn't anything that meant anything. She just showed up."

"Avery," Nicole said softly. Avery looked up and Nicole felt a surge of protection at the distress painted over her features. "Just tell me what happened after I left."

She nodded, seeming more confident now that she had a direction to take. "We did talk Wednesday night, but I felt like she wasn't hearing me. Or I wasn't saying what I needed to say. So I asked her to talk face-to-face, and she came over yesterday afternoon." Avery's hand went back to her neck. "I closed the door. It's done." She glanced over at Nicole. "I can't guarantee that she won't pop up at some time or try to contact me, but I feel good about handling that if it happens. And she's blocked again in my phone. I'm not undoing that."

Avery leaned forward, turning her stare to the street. "I'm not going to lie and tell you I suddenly feel amazing, that that was the best fucking moment of my life. But I do feel…better. Relieved, maybe." She rubbed her palms on her thighs and sat up, turning toward Nicole. "I know what it feels like to be in the dark with someone who won't communicate with you. Someone who won't be honest and say the shit that needs to be said, even if it doesn't feel awesome to hear it. But I promise you I've been nothing but honest about everything related to Shannon, and that's not going to change. And," she continued, "not for one second do I want to do what she did, so that's why when I saw you over here, I had to talk to you right away. I don't want you to spend one more minute thinking that stupid-ass conversation in my shop made me fall back in love with her." Avery shook her head once. "I can't fall back in love with her."

The sincerity of Avery's voice struck all the right sentiments inside Nicole, and she felt her guard loosen. "It scared me to see you two together," Nicole said. "It brought up a lot of what-ifs for me." She smiled, trying to hide her embarrassment. "I know this is really jumping the gun, but what happens if we're together and Shannon comes back, promising you all the things you wanted for so many years?"

Avery was quiet for a moment. "It wouldn't matter, Nicole. I'm not saying it would never happen, that she would never try, but I am saying it wouldn't matter if she did."

"Do you want to elaborate on that?"

Avery gave her a lopsided grin. "Not right now. But someday."

Nicole nodded. "I respect that. Just remember that I know how hard it is to love someone who can't be who you need and want them to be." She angled her body, tucking her right leg under her, so she was facing Avery. "It's like, you can't let go of the hope that if you love them enough, then they'll meet you where you are."

The grin shifted into a half-smile. "But they can't."

"No," Nicole said, "and that's so hard to accept. I still struggle with that sometimes, with Ginny. I know she loved me, maybe more than I loved her, but she couldn't do what she needed to do to be happy and healthy. It had nothing to do with me. Doesn't mean it doesn't still hurt, but it's less...I don't know..."

"Ownership." Avery shook her head. "Blame. Self-blame?"

"That's it."

Avery laughed a little. "It's kind of a sick thing for us to have in common. Loving people who can't love us back the way we deserve to be loved." That unmistakable darkness skittered over her face but disappeared in the space between Nicole's heartbeats.

"Yeah, but let's flip it around." Nicole brushed a flyaway hair off her cheek, not missing the way Avery's eyes followed her movement, causing a swoop in her stomach. "We've been through it, and we know how much it sucks. So we know what not to do, right? We're smarter now." She held Avery's stare. "And it's different with us than it was with us and them."

"Very different," Avery said, her voice low but rippling with warmth.

Relieved, Nicole smiled. The words had been a risk, but a necessary one. She waited for her heart to catch up with the reassurance of Avery's reply.

"Are we having a cheesy-ass Hallmark moment?" Avery whispered.

"It's only cheesy if we profess our love or one of us proposes despite having known each other for, what, two months?"

"Wow, nope, not there yet." Avery gave her body a good shake.

Nicole laughed at her discomfort. "Not even close."

A silence swaying with words that couldn't yet work their way into meaningful sentences wrapped around them, holding space for all that was to come. Nicole, comforted and relieved by the honest conversation, leaned in closer, brushing her fingertips over Avery's hand.

"Take me out tonight?" she said, smiling coyly.

Avery blinked, then a grin cracked over her face, lighting up her eyes. "Nothing would make me happier."

CHAPTER THIRTY-TWO

A gentle breeze, one holding the promise of a pleasantly cool spring morning, whispered through the window, snaking its way around the bedroom. The scent of earth and freshly blooming flowers snuck in with it. The air was just cool enough to soothe sleeping bodies, but when the birds started up their morning harmony, the calmness was disrupted, one irritating chirp at a time.

Avery blinked. Then she blinked again. She never slept with the window open. And birds were the exact reason why. Those loud-mouthed feathered fuckers woke up way too early, especially on a weekend, and had way too much to say.

As her sleepy vision cleared, Avery realized she hadn't made the inexplicable error of leaving her bedroom window open overnight. Or maybe she had, but she couldn't tell from her current location, since she absolutely was not in her own bed.

Slowly, with caution and a rousing curiosity, she turned her head to the side. As soon as she focused on the tousled mess of black hair spread over the light-gray pillowcase, her breathing evened...before kicking right back up again, but in a far more pleasant way.

She didn't even have to see Nicole's face to watch the movie trailer highlights of the previous evening.

When Avery had met Nicole at her apartment, she'd stared for a solid twenty seconds until Nicole swatted her and told her to stop acting like a prepubescent boy who'd just seen his first nudie mag. But Avery couldn't stop staring. The faded jeans accentuated every curve of Nicole's lower body, and her loose, lightweight black Henley sweater hit her hips in such a way that Avery couldn't stop staring at her butt every time she moved.

And it wasn't just her body—it was also her eyes, and the way she took Avery in, those strikingly bright blue eyes dancing over her body. Avery stood taller, prouder, more confident as Nicole eyed her appreciatively. And when Nicole leaned in to press her lips against the corner of Avery's lips—a move that was deadly sexy, somehow—Avery inhaled her scent, closing her eyes. Suddenly, she couldn't get close enough.

She'd found Nicole attractive from the moment she'd stepped up to the table at Looper's. But now that she'd flipped the latch of the door that had been hiding and suffocating parts of her (apparently her libido, most notably), she could fully realize how utterly gorgeous and irresistible Nicole was.

And she, *Avery*, got to take this beautiful, kind, incredible woman out.

At Nicole's behest, they'd gone across the street to The Maxwell, the boutique hotel Avery had just begun supplying flowers for. As they walked through the hotel to get to the outdoor courtyard and bar, Avery chattered excitedly about the new business deal. She only realized that she couldn't *stop* talking when Nicole turned and pressed her finger against Avery's lips.

"You just told me the same thing three times," she said with a mischievous smile. "Honestly, I think it's hot that you're nervous, but let's get drinks and relax before you recite the Averypedia entry on spider lilies for the fourth time."

Avery did relax over drinks, a Southside for her, and a French 75 for Nicole. (Nicole earned bonus points for being a fellow gin fan.) They talked animatedly and openly, continuing the pattern and expectation that they'd already set in their interactions. Nicole opened up about her family, and the way she spoke about her father had Avery hanging on every word.

And while everything between them had felt comfortable, there was a persistent flicker of changing, charging energy that flared up over brief but loaded silences and prolonged eye contact. Avery had known it was there, but now that she was feeling it for the first time—really allowing herself to feel it and lean into it—she couldn't imagine anything more promising.

When Nicole's stomach rumbled so loudly they were certain the group next to them heard it, the two retreated back to Nicole's apartment. There, they made dinner together, something Avery hadn't ever done with someone she was dating. After Nicole teased her about that, they set about making flatbreads. Nicole loaded hers with pepperoni and pesto, while Avery opted for Italian sausage, extra cheese, and red sauce.

Later, when they were sitting closely on the sofa, watching a movie, Avery looked over at Nicole and just before kissing her, could only think that everything felt so easy, so *good*.

Yes, it was early days, but the peace Avery felt when she was with Nicole was nothing she'd ever experienced before. She hadn't believed it could exist, but there it was, surrounding her in the most comforting, reassuring way possible.

As an added bonus, that peace came with an intense attraction that was growing by the minute.

What she'd intended to be a mostly innocent kiss quickly heated into their most passionate kiss yet. That wasn't saying much, given it was only their second kiss (which seemed both crazy and criminal to Avery, but she knew she was largely responsible for how slowly things had been moving between them). When Nicole asked if Avery would let her hair down, she immediately obliged, and just as quickly, Nicole's hands were in her hair. She remembered a lot more kissing, but soon, Avery submitted to the magic Nicole's hands were working in her hair and on her scalp. She'd ended up lying with her head on Nicole's lap, eyes half-shut, melting as Nicole played with her hair.

From there, Avery's mental highlights reel faded. Back in the reality of the new morning, she looked over at Nicole, who was still asleep. Avery reached over and ran her fingers through Nicole's hair, returning the gift she'd so thoroughly given Avery the previous night. She didn't *want* to wake Nicole, but she wouldn't be upset if she *accidentally* did.

"Morning," Nicole said softly. She squirmed backwards until her back was against Avery's stomach. Nicole reached around for Avery's hand and pulled it around her torso, tucking both their hands between her breasts.

"Good morning," Avery said. She adjusted her head so she could stop inhaling Nicole's hair into her nostrils. "So much for taking this slow."

Nicole's body shook with laughter. "Avery. We're fully clothed."

"But a sleepover? On, what, our third date?"

Nicole rolled over and gave her a sleepy smile. Avery traced the smile with her finger, brushing her thumb against Nicole's lower lip.

"Considering all we did was sleep, I think we're still in Taking it Slow mode."

Avery ran her fingertips up and down Nicole's jawline. "Can I borrow a toothbrush so we can take it a little less slow?"

Nicole raised her eyebrows. "Why yes, that can be arranged." She gave Avery one last look before getting out of bed and padding into the bathroom.

Alone, Avery sighed and rolled onto her back. She didn't want to get ahead of herself. She didn't want to throw herself in, or rush anything, or plow ahead without paying careful attention. But the way Nicole looked at her sent constant shivers down her spine, then warmed her through and through. It was calming and exhilarating, the contrasting feelings melding together into a yearning that sparkled with newness.

To think that she could have held herself back from Nicole... It was a thorny, spiraling thought that Avery didn't want to focus on, but she gave herself a moment of self-gratitude for finally letting go of Shannon, for giving herself a chance to move forward with someone who could maybe be everything she'd ever wanted.

CHAPTER THIRTY-THREE

While Avery was in the bathroom, Nicole set to work making tea. She paused at the microwave, remembering that Avery was a coffee drinker. A ribbon of panic wound through her as she glanced around her kitchen. Definitely no coffee maker in sight, nor did she have any kind of coffee beans.

She threw her hands against her hips and gave the kitchen a firm nod. "I can fix this," she said aloud, then walked to the door and tugged on her shoes.

When Nicole's hand hit the doorknob, Avery's voice echoed through the room.

"Are you seriously running away from me by leaving your own apartment?"

Nicole grinned as she turned around. "I don't have any coffee for you. I panicked."

Avery crossed the room and pulled Nicole into her arms. They stood there, holding each other. Nicole breathed deeply, giving herself the go ahead to enjoy this feeling with *this* woman.

As soon as she'd opened her door last night, she'd seen the difference in Avery. If she really thought about it, she'd probably noticed it when they spoke earlier in the day, but it was far more evident in the evening.

In a word: free. Avery looked unburdened. Sure, there was a weight she still carried, and Nicole imagined it would be there in fragments for some time to come, but the difference—the newly visible lightness—was impossible not to see.

Part of it was the way that Avery looked at her. There was little guessing room left, and Nicole felt a dizzy rush of attraction that she tried to keep in check. Now that Avery had removed her mask, she, too, felt free.

And when *that kiss* had tumbled and twisted between them last night, it was then that Nicole finally admitted to herself just how into Avery she was.

The truth was, it was a lot. And while those feelings still scared her a little, the physical admission of attraction and desire had dissolved the last piece of flimsy protection Nicole held over her heart. She was letting Avery in, for better or worse, for beauty or pain.

"How about we go get coffee together?" Avery said, running her hands up and down Nicole's back.

"At your beverage station in the shop?"

Avery laughed and gripped her shoulders, pulling her back so they could see each other. "No. Never again, either."

"Oh come on," Nicole said. "That was adorable."

Avery groaned and shook her lightly. "You have a weird sense of what's adorable."

"I think it works to your benefit that I find your awkwardness adorable."

Avery gasped loudly. "Me? Awkward? Never."

"Maybe not awkward," Nicole conceded. She tightened her grip on Avery's hips. "More like confused."

"I wasn't confused," Avery said, the joking gone from her tone. "I just didn't know what the hell to do with you. I was freaking out."

"Are you done freaking out?"

Avery answered first with a kiss, her lips gentle against Nicole's. Then she looked her in the eye and nodded. "I am. Are you?"

It was a valid question, one Nicole continued to navigate. She was terrified of being left again, but she was more afraid to ignore her connection with Avery and not give their blooming relationship her all, to not see this through and explore what it could be.

"Yes. No more freaking out."

Avery nodded. "Great. Good. Glad we got that settled. Can we get coffee now?"

As they walked slowly down Main Street, preferred iced caffeinated drinks in hand, Avery caught Nicole's free hand and held it tightly. Nicole smiled as she sipped her iced London Fog. She'd missed the simplest things the most, like holding hands on a Saturday morning, or throwing pieces of pepperoni at each other while making dinner and arguing about which member of *The Babysitter's Club* was the coolest. (Avery made a strong argument for Kristy, but Nicole would never give up her vote for Dawn.)

Nicole didn't expect nothing but easy roads ahead. She knew well the way relationships could slip and slide even when both people were happy. And she knew this one would be a work in progress for both of them. Avery still had work to do—she had admitted as much last night—and she needed compassion and grace, understanding and kindness. Nicole could give all of that, and more, as long as they were moving forward together.

She gave willingly now, knowing Avery was ready to give back as much as she received.

Avery stopped walking and pulled Nicole closer to her. The look of sincerity in her dark-green eyes did funny, fizzy things to Nicole's insides.

"Are we doing this?" Avery asked.

Nicole squeezed Avery's hand. "Yes. We're doing this."

There would be time for more words, longer sentences, and cascading explanations. For now, that was all they needed to know: just as the world was in bloom around them, so, too, were their hearts.

Bella Books, Inc.
Women. Books. Even Better Together.
P.O. Box 10543
Tallahassee, FL 32302
Phone: (800) 729-4992
www.BellaBooks.com

More Titles from Bella Books

Mabel and Everything After – Hannah Safren
978-1-64247-390-2 | 274 pgs | paperback: $17.95 | eBook: $9.99
A law student and a wannabe brewery owner find that the path to a fairy tale happily-ever-after is often the long and scenic route.

To Be With You – TJ O'Shea
978-1-64247-419-0 | 348 pgs | paperback: $19.95 | eBook: $9.99
Sometimes the choice is between loving safely or loving bravely.

I Dare You to Love Me – Lori G. Matthews
978-1-64247-389-6 | 292 pgs | paperback: $18.95 | eBook: $9.99
An enemy-to-lovers romance about daring to follow your heart, even when it's the hardest thing to do.

The Lady Adventurers Club - Karen Frost
978-1-64247-414-5 | 300 pgs | paperback: $18.95 | eBook: $9.99
Four women. One undiscovered Egyptian tomb. One (maybe) angry Egyptian goddess. What could possibly go wrong?

Golden Hour - Kat Jackson
978-1-64247-397-1 | 250 pgs | paperback: $17.95 | eBook: $9.99
Life would be so much easier if Lina were afraid of something basic—like spiders—instead of something significant. Something like real, true, healthy love.

Schuss – E. J. Noyes
978-1-64247-430-5 | 276 pgs | paperback: $17.95 | eBook: $9.99
They're best friends who both want something more, but what if admitting it ruins the best friendship either of them have had?

Printed in the USA
CPSIA information can be obtained
at www.ICGtesting.com
JSHW020326230923
48990JS00001B/1